Cupcakes
&
Condoms

Naheed Elyasi

TO PETER

Dearest Carrie,

Be in your own flow

Love,
Naheed

ACKNOWLEDGMENTS

To all the colorful and flavorful characters of NYC.

CHAPTER 1

Every girl has a list of "never" rules, and I certainly was no exception. You know, "never date a married man," "never date a guy with an ex-wife," or "never date a guy with a kid." Right from the beginning Peter had two strikes against him. Thank God, he wasn't married. That's something I could never see myself doing. Peter was divorced and had a child from his first marriage. But after years of dating all sorts of freaky guys with mommy issues and weird sexual hang-ups, I was ready to bend a little. I mean one guy I dated literally cried out for his mommy as he had an orgasm. I didn't want to stick around to see if he sucked his thumb also. And then Peter came along. He was smart and good looking, and had the right balance of depth and silliness. Peter also had a level of emotional maturity that I wasn't used to seeing in the men I dated, or at least he didn't cry out for his mommy. Yes, he was divorced and had a kid, but his divorce happened five years ago, and his only child, his teenage daughter, Zuni, lived in Los Angeles with her mom.

So, after much deliberation, and many nights of being lonely and horny, I decided that Peter was "rule-bend" worthy. I rationalized to myself that he was a good and present father, and that I could deal with the divorce and kid factor. I decided to not necessarily break my never list, just do a simple test, and temporarily cross some things out with a pencil…a highly erasable pencil. Or so I thought.

Fast forward to the present and we just celebrated our one-year anniversary two months ago. Peter is a private chef and one of his wealthy clients let him borrow his yacht and crew to take a romantic cruise around the City. Peter planned the menu with great care and had a gourmet chef prepare a succulent meal of fig salad, lobster risotto, and toffee cake bread pudding for us. A separate wine to enhance the flavor of the food accompanied every course.

That night over dinner, he asked me to move in with him by giving me a Tiffany's jewelry box with his apartment key tucked neatly inside. How can a girl say no to that? Isn't every girl's dream to find a guy like Peter? So I gave up my small, four hundred square foot studio in the West Village, which was located on a quiet and dark street (dark being the important word) that was regularly visited by transsexual prostitutes, and moved in with him into his two bedroom rent-controlled Tribeca apartment.

***

When you're hot, you're hot. First, I get a boyfriend, and now a career. A year ago, I would have never imagined things would work out so well in my life. I came to the Center fourteen months ago as a temp making $10 an hour, and searching for some purpose in my life. In the past, I kept looking for meaning in whatever job I had and was never satisfied or happy. I had tried a gig as a marketing assistant only to find myself feeling like a waste of a human being just pushing a high interest credit card targeted to the elderly. Then there was my stint working as an assistant at a fashion company. What a waste of time that was. Those people thought they were curing cancer, and would flip out if a button was black and not navy blue. It was all so pointless and I felt so hopeless and useless.

If I had seen all the jumping around in my own resume, I would not have hired me. Somehow in me, the temp sitting in the corner, Chester McMadden, the CEO of the Center for Ethical Business, saw a diamond in the rough. He took me on as his assistant, mentored me, and recently gave me more responsibility and promoted me to be the Director of

Communications. And while I was a bit hesitant to accept the new responsibilities, Chester assured me that, "he would continue to mentor and support me." Despite my insecurities, Chester has helped me believe in myself, and I consider myself lucky and grateful to have found a good boss, a good job, and a purpose and mission. I made a commitment to myself to stay at The Center for a few years so I can grow professionally.

One of the other reasons I am excited about my new position is that it comes with a new office. Before my promotion, I sat in a cubicle, one of the seven cubicles packed together like Legos. Each cubicle has a 24x12 glass window that connects it to one of the other cubicles on each side. There is absolutely no privacy, and not only can everyone smell each other's food, but we can even hear each other chew and swallow.

My new office overlooks Bryant Park, on 42nd and Sixth Avenue. It is a sweet deal that comes with a door I can close and a nice big window I can gaze out of and contemplate my new responsibilities. I can see myself playing an important role in one of the best causes, Ethical Business, and even have ideas of some big things I want to accomplish. I have the power to wield the pen, use my prose, and craft messages. Every CEO in the country will be parading through my office and that ensures a bit of exclusive cache for me. It is both nerve-wracking and exciting, but I decide that I am up for the challenge. How can I grow professionally if I don't step out of my comfort zone?

***

CHAPTER 2

My new position demands more participation, and Chester specifically wants me to become more engaged. One of my first tests is the upcoming meeting Chester is having with some hotshot CEO, Wish Michaels, founder of Wish Foundation. This is my first big meeting, and I am excited to prove myself.

As I walk down the long hallway towards the reception area, I see him standing tall and upright in front of me looking at the shelf full of important and oh-so-timely materials of The Center for Ethical Business. I catch a reflection of myself in the mirrored wall and quickly brush my hair out of my face, smooth out my dress, and suck in my gut. The man before me is exquisite, impeccably dressed and radiating power. I, along with the office, suddenly feel so unimpressive. Everything from the walls to the chairs surrounding him is completely monochromatic, only a few variations of a weird light gray. The reception area seems so tacky with him standing there.

When the time came to re-decorate the office, Chester put Matilda Hinny, the office manager, in charge. Matilda works in a cubicle at the far end of the office, far away from other staff members and clearly out of sight to visitors. She shows up at the office with her hair either dripping wet from just being washed, or wild and frizzy from not being washed at all – it seems a happy medium escapes her. Her pants are usually some variation of a khaki color and always wrinkled; her shirts are usually old cotton t-shirts with faded colors and fabric balls that need shaving. Her pink nail polish is always chipped.

Matilda is socially awkward, and the people in the office are not very nice to her most of the time, but I feel sorry for her more than anything else, and try to occasionally strike up a conversation with her about her five cats. This, ladies and gentlemen, was our designated interior designer.

Matilda decided to put her creative genius to work by choosing some very fancy sounding colors and even had a whole office staff meeting to present the colors to us. The walls were cast iron gray. The carpet was drowning in stone gray. The window shades were wild lynx gray. The chairs were shiny gray, and the bookshelves were just plain old gray. But despite the schmancy names, it all added up to dull, dead, and depressing. The light from the large floor to ceiling windows in the office only magnified the humdrum surroundings and made Wish stand out even more.

He looks regal, in a dark navy suit and lavender shirt that is surely tailor-made for his six foot and at least three-inch masculine frame, a purple tie, discreet gold and amethyst cufflinks, a Cartier watch, and carrying a Prada briefcase.

I take a gulp of air. "Hello. Are you Wish Michaels?"

He turns around, smiles, revealing full symmetrical lips, perfect white teeth that look even whiter against his glistening sienna colored skin. He blankly stares at me. I stare back. Getting my bearings, I extend my hand.

"Hi…. are you… ok?"

"Oh…aahh…yes…I'm sorry. You caught me off guard. I'm Wish Michaels."

I shake his hand. His large hand completely envelopes mine. It feels soft and tender, like the bottom of a baby's feet.

"I'm Nikki Johnson, Chester's assistant and the Director of Communications here at the Center. It's nice to meet you. I've heard a lot of great things about you."

I am actually lying, having only heard the office gossip troll, Bren, tarnish him even before the senior staff has had a chance to meet him. Bren Dabraccio, aka Gutter Bully, aka she-devil, or any other variation of battle-ax, is a Vice President here at the Center. She hates everyone, man or woman, and ever since Chester promoted me to Communications Director, and took away those responsibilities away from her, I've been on her shit list.

"I'm so happy to finally meet the great Wish Michaels. I'll let everyone know you are here," I say as I lead him into the conference room. My knees feel strangely shaky as I think of the email Bren sent earlier in the day.

I don't know why we are even wasting our time with such a degenerate of a man as Wish Michaels. I personally cannot stand him. I have heard rumors that he is into the oil business, and that he is going around promoting ethical work and business to promote his own interests. He is one of these men who thinks he can get away with anything. I don't think we should trust him. --- Bren

After a few minutes, key members of the senior management team, which consists of Chester; Henry Gross, the COO and next in line vying for the CEO throne; Bren Dabraccio; and myself, assemble in the conference room to meet with Wish. After the usual round of introductions and blah blah boring pleasantries, the meeting commences.

Chester begins the meeting, "I've asked Wish to come meet with us to share his expertise, and for us to begin discussing a way we can work together to further the mission of The Center for Ethical Business. Wish is the leading advocate for ethical business. He has won numerous awards, and has been an advisor to the past three U.S. Presidents. Can you believe that his bio is longer than mine?" He lets out a jovial laugh.

Chester continues without giving anyone time to react, "Wish, let me tell you a little bit about our work here. The Center's mission is twofold to promote ethical business through advocacy of best ethical practices by engaging leaders in ethical dialogue, and to support ethical activities."

I look intently at Chester and then to Wish to see if he understands

Chester, and make a mental note to myself that as the Communications Director, I need to know what the Center's mission really means.

"I am happy to help in any way I can," says Wish. "I believe in this wo--"

"I've taken a look through your website and have done some asking around about you," Bren slams her pen down, leans forward and crosses her arms on the conference table.

All eyes shoot to Bren, "and I am not sure, how we can work with you." Her nostrils are flaring, thin lips pursed so hard together that there are jagged wrinkle lines above them, her hazel eyes are scrunched up into two beady angular slits, and she is glowing magenta with anger.

I cringe and sink down in my seat as an awkward silence fills the room. This is typical Bren behavior, always angry and needing to take the spotlight with her rants. I call it fabricated outrage – a false dishonest anger, accomplished by speaking in a loud aggressive voice to intimidate people into thinking she is right. The problem is that most people usually fall for her act, including Chester and Henry. My assessment is that they are both terrified of her since she has more balls than both of them combined.

Bren continues, "I don't understand how we can work together, considering you are our competition. The Center and your organization, Wish Foundation, are competing for the same funds that are out there from the same funders. There's just no way I see this working." She slams herself back into her chair with her legs spread open to show off her cojones.

Chester's eyes are bulging out as his brain works quickly to remedy the situation and lessen the embarrassment. Even though he wants to say something, the poor guy looks shell-shocked. I guess nothing seems to come to mind.

"Well Bren that is a good point you bring up." Wish says. He is as calm as snow falling in a forest, completely unshaken by the she-wolf's rage.

"I don't see your organization and mine as competition. There is something bigger here, than you and I. Than The Center for Ethical Business and Wish Foundation, and that thing is hope and empowerment. To give the poor and the hungry of the world, hope. To give them a hand up and not a hand out…to teach them how to fish. We essentially have the same purpose."

Bren maintains her same spread leg posture and simply shoots Wish a glaring dirty look. I am so ecstatic to finally see someone who can stand up to Bren.

"Well, as I was saying, I am committed to this work. And I don't let anything get in my way. I believe we can fix humanity's biggest problems. We can empower the poor. We can eradicate poverty."

I try not to let my internal smile show on my face.

"We can make a difference in the world, by working with and through business," says Wish, not missing a beat. "And sometimes, I get so focused on my vision and mission, that it upsets some people who have their own agendas." He challenges Bren by directly looking at her. "Don't worry Bren. There is enough suffering and poverty to go around." His perfect pink lips part to reveal his white teeth. "But, I am sure we can somehow work together. In fact, I would love for us to work together." He flashes his pearlies at me.

Ahhhh…be still my beating heart. I could learn a thing or two from this guy.

"Well said, Wish," chimes in Chester. He probably feels emboldened by Wish. "I am thinking of the Center convening a big Summit and I would like to partner with you and have you be one of our keynote speakers," announces Chester as Henry and Bren shoot a quick glance at each other. "I'd like us to work together."

"What? Excuse me?" Asks Bren. "What are you planning? And why was this not discussed with Henry and I, as the senior management group?"

Bren, you are not that important. Don't let the senior management thingy get to your head.

"Discussion?" I think not." Chester sits as upright as his belly will allow him and protrudes his chest. "Last time I checked, I am the CEO!" He quietly slams both of his palms down on the conference table. "I am making an executive decision." I have never seen Chester challenge Bren.

"Well….ummm…you know, Chester…ummm," says Henry as he stares at his blank notepad and pulls at his collar.

I wish he would just spit it out for God's sake.

"Ummm…I kind of think we should…you know, maybe discuss this….ummm…. before we make a decision and ummm...invite speakers," says Henry, staring at Bren for affirmation.

Since this is my first big meeting, I feel like I should say something…anything. I sit tall, push my notepad away, and clear my throat, "Well, I think it is a great idea." I look at Chester. "The Summit….I mean." I finish off.

Bren leers towards me, her eyelids narrow. "Nikki, I'm sure you think it's a great idea." She points her finger at me. "But since you're only a Director and not a Vice President, like me, what you think doesn't count for much at this point. You're a newbie."

"Everyone calm down, please," says Chester with a smile, holding his hands up like he is being robbed at gunpoint. "We will discuss the matter as a group later. I am sure Wish does not need to be a part of this little brouhaha."

I feel Wish watching me and try my best to not turn red out of embarrassment.

"Well, whatever you decide, I will be happy to help in any way I can. The Summit is a fantastic idea. I would love to discuss it further and even think about how our two organizations can partner together on this," says Wish.

Wish handles the awkward moment with grace, and as the meeting progresses, I periodically feel his eyes on me, even though I am now quiet. I feel so humiliated by Bren, that I can't even make eye contact with him. I pretend to be busy taking notes about the meeting when I am simply writing my grocery list and doodling, drawing pictures of flowers and stars.

So, while on the inside I am not feeling so empowered in my new position, I feel confident in how I look on the outside. Well, sort of confident. For the past few weeks, I've been working out in an attempt to shed a few winter pounds, and this morning I mustered up the courage to wear my royal blue vintage Diane Von Furstenberg wrap dress that hugged my curves in all the right places. But throughout the meeting I feel oddly self-conscious. Wish has a way of looking at me that makes me feel insecure and uncomfortable. I have a sinking feeling in my gut, and now that I feel two inches tall, I begin to wonder if I look pudgy. God, I hope he can't see my belly fat roll.

After the meeting ends, as everyone else is saying their goodbyes, I duck out of the conference room, and run to my office. I slam the door shut and flop myself into my chair. With a loud thud, I let my head drop on my desk. I feel like a total loser. And why did I have to run out like that? Why couldn't I just hold it together, be professional and say goodbye to Wish Michaels?

Suddenly someone is knocking on my door. Damn, go away, whoever it is. I'm in no mood to talk to anybody right now.

"Come in," I yell as I rest my chin on my desk and roll my eyes. Wish pushes the door open. I pop up, pushing my chair against the wall with a bang. The generic office motivation poster about going after success, with the image of a rocky coastline and a lighthouse falls to the ground. Luckily the frame is plastic and doesn't break. It's too late though, Wish has already seen me slumped on my desk.

I throw my hair back and give him my nicest smile, pretending that nothing has happened. "Oh, hello. Can I help you?"

He returns my smile. "Are you ok?"

"Sure! Of course." I run my hand through my hair. "Why wouldn't I be?" I shift my weight to one side as I cross my arms.

He closes the door and proceeds towards the chair. "Can I sit down?" He sits down before I can answer.

I catch his eye looking at my notepad with my grocery list and my doodles of flowers and trees. I hastily grab the notepad and flip the page. He has a smirk on his face and catches my eye.

In my most adult voice I say, "So, is there something I can do for you?"

"Well, Chester suggested I speak with you about scheduling a private meeting with him regarding the Summit. He thinks there's a good possibility of it happening."

"Sure, my pleasure. I would be happy to do that for you."
As, I review Chester's calendar, I can feel his eyeballs burning a hole right through me. I pretend to not be bothered and remind myself to breath. "Ok, how about next week at 3 pm?"

As he pulls out his phone and takes his eyes off me, I notice his thick wavy dark brown hair, his long black eyelashes, his defined face, his full lips...his very full lips.

"Is there something on my lips?" He asks.
I meet his eyes and feel my face getting hot. "Oh...just a little spot on the corner." I lie and gesture to my lips. He wipes the corner of his mouth.

"You got it," I say, still feeling hot in the face. "So, is that time ok?"

"Sure, but let's make it a phone call. I'm traveling and can call in."

"Great. I'll schedule you in."

He stands up to leave and reaches out his hand to shake mine. "It was nice to meet you." I look up at him from my seated position and notice that he looks like a giant over my five-foot three-inch frame. I quickly jump up.

"The next time I'm in town, can I call you for a lunch or dinner meeting? I want to know more about your work here." He says as he grabs my outstretched hand.

"Definitely, that would be great."

***

CHAPTER 3

That evening, I leave work partially high from meeting Wish and partially rooted in reality due to the Bren encounter. I gear myself up for my talk with Peter.

Earlier in the day Peter had called me at work. "What time are you coming home?" he asked.

"I'm not sure. I have a busy day and a big meeting."

"I just have something I want to talk to you about."

Despite the fact that Peter is perfect in so many ways, sometimes his penchant for drama unnerves me. This is one such time. I never like it when Peter says those words, 'I want to talk to you.' It feels so parental and it means that he's been thinking, which most often than not, is problematic. Peter has a tendency to get a thought in his head, run away with it and reach a conclusion without involving me in the discussion. When he reaches the point of talking, the tiny issue turns into some serious baby mama drama. So, when he said those words to me on the phone, I stopped myself from even asking him any further questions.

"Ok. I'll try to get there by 7ish." I appease him, already dreading the talk.

"7ish? Can you be more exact?"

"I'll be home at 7, ok?"

I can't possibly imagine what he wants to talk to me about as I run down the subway stairs at Times Square huddled in my winter coat and hat, in a rush to get out of the chilly New York City weather. I review a possible list of things he may want to talk about. It could be that there's something about our living situation that's not working out or maybe he wants to take a trip together. What if he wants to get married? God, I hope he doesn't ask me to marry him. I'm not ready for all that.

I jump onto the waiting number two train and wiggle my way into the packed rush hour train. I love most things about New York City, most everything, except rush hour. I always feel like cattle being herded towards the slaughterhouse. The doors close behind me, and all of a sudden my nose is assaulted by one of the foulest smells in the City. Ok, another thing I don't like about the City, the smell of a homeless guy in tattered and urine and number two infested clothes. Homeless guy looks like he hasn't washed in a year. The wild hairs on his full gray beard are flying in every direction, reaching all the way down to the top of his chest. He has pubic like hair coming out of his nose and ears and my man has a few missing teeth. He looks quite gnarly.

He shouts, "Ladieeessss and gentlemeeen." His words are highlighted by the sound of a hollow whistle due to his missing front teeth. "Welcome to the P train."

There is no P train. This guy is obviously insane. Of course, this being New York City, everybody ignores him, and casually shuffle away from the stench radiating off his body. Since there is nowhere to go, people are practically climbing on top of each other and stepping on each other's feet to get some distance. I look around desperately to see where I can escape. But, as hard as I try, I am stuck just a foot away from him. Nowhere to go. As I turn around towards Homeless guy, I see him unzipping his pants with his spotted brown hands. He pulls out his ashy penis and pees in every direction, like a sprinkler watering the yard.

"Ha...ha...ha...ha... Welcome to the P train. Ha...ha...ha..." He shows off the gaps in his teeth.

"Shit." I scream as I jump back, squashing someone's toes under my heel. "Oh my God. I'm so sorry." I snap my head back to see the face of a poor pregnant woman twisted in pain.

It seems like I'm too late. Homeless guy has gotten me. There is a line of fluorescent yellow piss going across my vintage, wool cream jacket and black suede boots. People begin to yell.

"Come on man." From a tall white lanky guy who looks like he's a delivery messenger.

"That's disgusting." From a Caribbean nanny pushing a stroller.

"This is unbelievable." From a middle-aged granola looking yogi woman.

"Gross. What the fuck is you doing?" From a scruffy teenager with fuchsia hair.

The sprinkler has gotten a few other people, and everybody has the same twisted look of disgust on their face. God only knows what's in that urine.

A pee-stained balding man looks at me, then down to his suit. "Now I have to burn this suit," he says.

"I know," I respond, as I lift the bottom flap of my coat to show him the stain, debating if I should take off my jacket. "I have to take a bath in Clorox when I get home."

Homeless guy continues his maniacal laugh, "ha...ha...ha..," and jumps out of the car at the next stop.

Only in New York City do these kinds of crazy incidents become the norm. I've seen so many bizarre people. There is one older Black man who's blind and rides the #3 train. During rush hour, he walks through the train with his long cane usually singing a song that completely tugs at your heartstrings. In the past, I've heard him sing, 'What a Wonderful World,' by Louis Armstrong, 'Stand by Me,' by Ben E. King, and 'When A Man Loves A Woman,' by Percy Sledge. The guy actually has a decent voice, and almost always, after his mushy, over the top emotional song is over, you can observe people pulling out dollar bills from their purses, wallets, and pockets, usually with a tear drop or two in their eyes. At his rate, I'm sure he makes a few hundred dollars a day.

One weekend while waiting for a friend at a restaurant in Carroll Gardens, a loud group of older men at a nearby table caught my eye. They were having a good old time drinking beer and laughing it up. It was an innocent guy's night out. One of the men looked familiar and it took me a few seconds to realize that this same guy before my eyes was the singing blind man on the train. I was flabbergasted and shocked that someone would go to such lengths to bamboozle people out of a dollar. Then my shock quickly turned into embarrassment since I, too, fell for his trick. Yup, I've got to admit it, I was one of those saps with a tear or two in my eye that gave him a few dollars over the years. I vowed, never again.

Luckily I now live in Tribeca and my commute is short, only about twenty minutes. As the train pulls into the Chambers Street Station, I jump out onto the platform and take the steps two at a time and basically gallop home. I don't want to stay in my clothes any longer than I have to.

"Peter?" I shout as I unlock our apartment door. I stand outside waiting. No answer. "Peter?"

Panicked, he comes running out of the kitchen wearing a white apron that reads, 'Kiss Me. I'm The Chef.' "What's wrong?" He is perplexed with a heavy frown on his face.

"Some dirty old homeless guy peed all over me."

"What?"

"I got peed on."

"What do you mean, you got peed on?" He waves around some fancy looking cooking utensil that I don't know the proper name for.

"I got peed on!" I wave my arms at him. "You know, piss...urine?" I throw my hands up in the air.

He stares at me with his big blue eyes, as if in a trance, and still slow to catch on.

"Can you bring me a plastic bag for me to put my clothes into? I don't want to walk around the house infested."

"Uhh…ok." He runs back into the kitchen and reappears with a black hefty garbage bag.

After I remove my contaminated jacket and boots, I hand it off to Peter as I jump in the shower.

"Sweetie, hurry up. I have dinner ready," he yells after me. He's made a very fancy dinner - calamari with hearts of palm, banana, cashews, chicory and radicchio, sesame orange dressing and Cuban barbecue chicken with Thai coconut sticky rice and broccoli rabe. Yum. I love Peter's cooking. His cooking skills were another reason I broke my never list, but it does make me wonder what he is up to.

"Whoa. This is very nice sweetie. You went into a lot of trouble to make dinner." I say as I go sit on his lap and plant a kiss on his lips. "Yes I did." He smiles at me, showing his dimples. I know you are trying to lose a few pounds, but today is a special occasion, and while I made all this great food, you can just eat a small portion of everything."

Peter has a lean and healthy body, and his five foot eight frame can appear skinny, while I, on the other hand am not fat, but do occasionally like a slice of chocolate cake or a cupcake from one of the many New York City famous bakeries. Sweet Revenge in the West Village, Magnolia, and Buttercup Bake Shop on the Upper East Side, being my favorites. It's safe to say that no matter where I am in the City, I always know where the good bakeries are. A few weeks ago, Peter nonchalantly suggested that the cupcakes were catching up with me and that I should try to lose some weight. Although I took offense to his suggestion, I didn't say anything because, besides Peter, I always feel a little chubby. I decided to give it a try and work on losing ten pounds.

I wince at his comment and walk over to my chair. "What's the special occasion?" I eyeball the food. I sure am starving.

"We'll get to that in a minute. How was your day?" He continues to smile at me.

"It was ok. I had an important meeting and didn't do so hot. Bren completely humiliated me in front of everyone." I stuff a calamari into my mouth. "I don't know why she's so angry."

"Don't let her get to you. She sounds like a miserable person."

"Everybody is afraid of her." I take in another calamari. "I don't know how to handle her. Ever since I got promoted, she has been like a heat seeking missile and I am the heat. You know?" I reach for a piece of the chicken and shove it into my mouth. "I can't shake her. At every turn, she tries her best to make it hell for me, and…. "

"Let's not talk about negative things. I don't really want to hear it." Peter's smile is gone. "Did anything good happen today?" he asks.

"Well, yea. I guess," I say, wanting to complain a little more about Bren. I mean, isn't part of being positive, expressing and getting rid of your negative feelings? I decide to go along with Peter's modus operandi. "I met someone today, Wish Michaels," I say as I take a forkful of rice.

"Sweetie, stop picking at the food."

I put down my fork and sit down. "Have you heard of him?" I ask.

"Yea. He's pretty well known in the business world." Peter scoops out a tablespoon of the chicken and two tablespoons of the broccoli rabe into my plate, and heaps his plate full of rice, chicken, and broccoli rabe.

"Really?" The calamari is so good. I feed myself another piece. "I have never heard of him, until Chester told me about the meeting and I did some research," I say talking with a mouthful of food. "But, he's pretty interesting. Very committed and focused, and he's written several bestselling books."

"I once heard him speak at a conference. He held the whole room in the palm of his hand." He says, as he watches me reaching for another calamari. "Babe, slow down, the calamari isn't going anywhere."

I shoot him a mischievous smile and take one last piece.

"Sounds like you were really impressed by him?"

"Oh, well, a little bit. You know, I admire driven people," I say.

"Hey, I need to talk to you about something that I've been thinking about for a while," Peter says to me. He is furrowing his eyebrows as he pushes his plate away.

I wish that he would let me eat this amazing dinner before he has his 'talk' with me.

"I am thinking of having Zuni come live with me," he blurts out.

I nearly choke on the calamari, and take a sip of water to wash it all down. I stare at him.

"Look. I got a call from Janice, about a couple of months ago. She has to take in her mother, who is in the early stages of Alzheimer's, and she can't take care of Zuni and her mother at the same time." Peter reaches over to put his hand on mine. "Besides, she's a teenager now and at this age I want to be more present in her life. Janice is concerned that Zuni is getting involved with the wrong crowd."

I push my plate away.

"A couple of months ago? Before we moved in together or after?" I ask.

"As we were moving in," he responds.

I pull my hand away. "And you never thought you should tell me? Considering I gave up my apartment and all of my furnishings to move in with you?"

"I wasn't sure what to do myself and I didn't want to get you involved."

"Excuse me? Well, now I'm involved, but I appreciate you talking to me about it now before making a decision."

He stares at me in silence.

"What?" I ask.

"It's done," he says.

"What's done?"

"Zuni."

"I don't understand what you mean," I respond.

"I've talked to Janice and Zuni, and we have agreed to have her move in with me." He runs his hand through his wispy blond hair, and lets out a deep sigh.

"What?" I murmur.

"Look, I know this is hard for you. But I love you and I want us to work out. At the same time, Zuni is starting her teen years and she needs a strong male role model in her life."

I push my plate further away, "isn't there another solution?" I hate arguments and don't want this to turn into a full-blown confrontation, and besides, I've got nowhere to live. I can't just run off to my own apartment.

"I mean, can't you just give her more child support to hire some extra help?" I feel myself getting hot.

"I want us to be a family." His voice is pleading.

"When is she supposed to move in?"

"At the end of the month."

I feel my stomach boiling, but do my best to act calm.

"Wow." I shake my head. I blankly stare out the window for what feels like slow achingly painful hours.

"Say something……….are you ok?" He finally asks.

I answer in a low whisper, "I lost my childhood because I had to raise my siblings. The last thing I ever want to do is raise another kid. It's my turn to live my life for myself." I begin to cry.

"I'm sorry." Peter comes over and attempts to hug me. I pull back.

"I know you had a difficult childhood, but this is different. You are a grown woman. You are not that little kid who has to raise herself and two other kids."

I can barely swallow. It feels like there is a lump of coal in my throat, "Do you want me to help pay for Zuni too – food, clothes, and all of the costs that go with raising a teenager?" I manage to croak out.

"I can't do this without you." His big blue eyes are pleading. "Look, this is life. It's messy. It's unexpected. Everything can't be defined and planned."

I don't respond. I hate him for doing this to me.

"I wish you wouldn't be so uptight." He says to me in an exasperated tone.

"I don't want to talk about this anymore." I stoically walk out of the room leaving all that yummy food. "You don't have to worry about me getting fat tonight. You made me lose my appetite." I slam the bedroom door behind me.

Uptight? I never thought of myself as uptight. I simply like a certain order and plan to my life. If I promise somebody that I will do something or be somewhere, even if I change my mind later, I keep my promise. At the beginning of our relationship, Peter and I talked about kids. I didn't want kids anytime soon, and because he already had a child, he was not interested in having another one. Having his daughter living with him was also not in his life plan since his ex-wife had custody. And now, through some sort of agreement between the three of them, he wanted to drastically change our life together.

***

CHAPTER 4

The week after the infamous Wish meeting, there are a lot of closed door, hustling, bustling meetings between Chester, Bren and Henry. I can only assume that it has to do with Wish. But most of the time their meetings are a total waste of time. I've seen better decisions come out of rock paper scissors. On one of these mornings, I run into Bren in the kitchen as she is about to go into Chester's office for yet another closed door meeting.

"What a dreary morning. This is my third cup of coffee already," Bren says as she slams the cup down under the coffee machine and stabs the button to fill her cup. She shoots me a sideways glance that burns a hole right through me.

I remain silent and simply give her a closed lip half smile. One of those smiles that say "I really don't care and don't want to talk to you," and return to cutting up my grapefruit.

"Nikki." She takes a step towards me.

Crap. Does this mean I have to engage in a conversation with her? I quickly give her outfit a quick glance over. She is wearing an asexual gray jacket with gray pants with a loose black scoop neck t-shirt underneath, and what looks like men's black oxford shoes. I think Bren really wants to be a man.

"What's up?" I pick up my fruit plate and turn around to face her doing my best impersonation of 'you don't bother me.'

"At the meeting with Wish, no one asked for your opinion about the Summit." Her voice is low, almost like a growl. Her lips are narrow and I can see the jagged little lines above her lips. Her face has turned amaranth pink, but not quite magenta yet.

"What?" I curl my lip. I'm completely dumbfounded by her comment, and I have to admit, scared.

She takes a step closer to me. Bren is taller than me by a few inches, and her mouth is close to my forehead. She is looking down towards me. The only thing between us is my small paper plate. My eyes meet her nose and I can see the large clogged pores and blackheads on it. I can feel her hot breath on my face, and inhale her old coffee breath as she speaks. The stench of it goes all the way to my gut. I try to take a step back, or sideways, but there is nowhere to go. Behind me is the generic white Formica kitchen counter and stainless steel sink, and to my right is the common old white refrigerator (remember, I said Matilda was our decorator). I am trapped.

"No one cares about your opinion." The she-wolf growls, as she points at me. I see her finger coming towards me in slow motion.

"You." She jabs my right shoulder and pushes me back. My plate falls from my hand and bursts of red ruby grapefruit scatter all over the floor like coagulated blood.

"Were." Jabs me in the same spot. "Out." Jab. "Of." Jab. "Line." Jab. She stares at me, and chomps down on her sparse bottom lip.

I stare back not knowing what to say or do.

"Don't you ever do something like that agaaaiiiin," she hisses in a low tone, then proceeds to take her pointy finger and jab me in my forehead in between my eyes.

She gives me a large smile, and with that, turns around, picks up her third cup of black coffee, and walks out of the kitchen as I am left there paralyzed. At some point, I think I must have stopped breathing, because all of a sudden I take in a big gulp of air. I look down and see my hands shaking. I can feel the place on my shoulder that she jabbed. It's sore and throbbing. Everything is still moving in slow motion. I look down and see the grapefruit on the floor and on my shoes. My feet feel like they are planted in cement and I can barely move them. I somehow manage to slowly step over everything and walk out of the kitchen. I think I'd rather have the homeless guy pee on me than go through this.

"Nikki, are you ok?" asks Matilda as she passes me on her way into the kitchen.

Her strong perfume jolts me out of my stupor. "Yea." I continue walking.

"Is this your fruit on the floor?" She yells after me. I don't respond and walk out of the office and to one of the restrooms on our floor. I lock myself in the stall, sit on the toilet, and bury my face in my hands. I start sobbing.

How did I get myself into this situation? Growing up with an aggressive and unpredictable mother, I swore that I would never let anyone bully me again. Yet here I was with Bren. Bren's behavior was all too familiar to me. Maybe that is why I tolerate her and not defend myself? The truth is that as irrational as it is, Bren scares me. She makes me feel like an incompetent, dumb child by pushing all those emotional buttons that my mother placed in me. Logically I know all this, but when the moment comes to feel or behave differently, I completely shut down and go to the place I know best – a weak and scared little girl. I sometimes feel like someone else is living my life. I know that inside of me I am stronger than what my outward actions show, but something gets lost in translation, and I am left feeling afraid and not in control of anything.

After about thirty minutes of sitting in the bathroom stall, I clean myself up and manage to get back to my desk. I make up an excuse that I'm not feeling well and need to go home. The weather completely matches my mood on the inside -- cold, windy, and rainy. Luckily, it's during the day and the trains are not that busy. On the whole subway ride and walk home, I replay the scene with Bren over and over again in my head. It's like a broken video that is running on a loop. Could I have done something differently? What if I pushed her back, or yelled at her to not touch me, or even better, taken the coffee mug and hit her on the side of her head. The least I could have done is to jab her back. *"Bitch! Back. Jab. The. Jab. Fuck. Jab. Off. Jab."*

If only I had the courage. I pray that Peter is not home. The last thing I feel like doing right now is engaging Mr. Positivity. I have been distant ever since his Zuni announcement to me.

As I get out of the subway in a mad dash to get home and out of the cold steely rain, a man in a business suit approaches me.

"Excuse me Miss. Are you from this area?"

Before me stands a man in a blue pinstripe business suit, and a black jacket, and a black umbrella. If you ever see New York during a rainstorm, it looks like an ocean of black umbrellas floating and dodging one another, moving to their own currents.

"What? I'm sorry?" I am caught off guard.

"I asked if you are from this area?

"Why do you ask?"

"I need directions."

While I want to be nice, I don't want to stop in the rain and be bothered. He better make this quick. "Yes, what are you looking for?"

"I'm looking for the club."

"The club?"

"Yes. The club. You know? "

"I don't know what you are talking about."

"You know…the gentlemen's club for single men. For no couples."

With a roll of my eyes, I take a quick sidestep and run home without answering him.

When I finally walk into my empty apartment, I let out a deep sigh of relief. I tear off my work clothes, dump them on the ground, change into my black sweatshirt and PJ bottoms, and crawl into bed. I cover my head with the comforter, and hide there the rest of the day. When Peter gets home that evening, I tell him that I'm not feeling well and ask him to let me sleep.

The next day, back at my desk, I send an email to both Chester and Henry about the pushing incident, and a copy to Matilda, who handles the personnel files. Almost as soon as I hit the send button, Henry walks into my office. Henry is the CFO of the Center for Ethical Business, a bean counter who has no creativity or vision. The guy must weigh a good 350-400 pounds. He has thick black hair growing out of his ears that he sometimes remembers to shave, and other times not. His face is bloated and red from what the office gossipers say is too much alcohol. Henry waddles around the office like a bulldog, looking gruff and angry, and leaves the top two buttons of his shirt unbuttoned so his black and gray curly chest hairs stick out. It can be spine chilling.

"I…ummm…just read your email," Henry says.

I shake my head in the affirmative, "yup."

"Ummm….are you sure she pushed you?" He asks as he rubs his big nose.

"You don't believe me?"

"Well…ummm….you know…Bren can be sometimes very straightforward…ummm….and that can be misinterpreted by …ummm….some people--."

"Excuse me Henry, but I know the difference between straightforward and someone putting their hands on me." I'm surprised at my own force.

"Nikki…Nikki…calm down." He reaches across my desk and touches my arm. "I'm not…ummm…you know… implying that you are

28

lying."

"Well she pushed me." I pull back from him. He looks at me silently.

"Would you like me to reenact the incident?" I ask.

"Sure."

"Ok. Stand up." I get up from behind my desk and even though he is taller than me, I walk over to face him. I make an attempt to focus and not be distracted by his ear fuzz.

"No one cares about your opinion." I do my best Bren impersonation, scrunching my face, narrowing my eyes, gritting my teeth, and puffing out my chest. I point at him. "You." I jab his shoulder so hard that he takes a step back. I can feel his mushy flesh under my finger. "Were." Jab. "Out." Jab. "Of." Jab. "Line." Jab. I step back, and put my hands on my hips, "Is that clear now?"

He shakes his head, "I'm sorry about that. I know that she…ummm…can be hard…ummm…you know…to work with."

"That's an understatement. And yes, it's ok, you can say that she is a horrible person."

Henry is not sure how to handle my aggression since he's never seen me so upset.

"Ok." He shakes his head as if he's thinking of how to handle the situation. "Hmmm. Ok. Thanks Nikki and I'm sorry that you…umm, experienced that."

He leaves me standing there wondering what will happen next. Next, Chester calls me into his office. He is clearly upset by my email.

"Nikki, I don't know what to say to you. I know Bren can be very aggressive and angry, but I never thought she would put her hands on anybody," Chester says to me with a deep frown on his face.

"She's beyond aggressive. She's a gutter-bully. She's abusive," I respond with a sharp tone.

"She's been here at the Center for six years and in those six years, she's had seven assistants come and go from under her." He looks down at his hands resting on top of his desk, and begins to tap his fingers. "I don't want you to worry about this anymore. I will have a talk with Bren."

"Ok. Thanks." I calm down.

"Now, I want to talk to you about something else." He pauses and smiles at me. "The Summit." His eyes light up.

Over the course of our working together, Chester has come to trust me and confide in me. One of his favorite lines to me is, "Nikki, you know all my secrets." And I have to admit that unfortunately, I do.

"You were the one that actually planted the idea in my head, when you talked about reaching out to more corporations."

That was one of my ideas in my initial excitement for my new position.

Chester continues, "Nikki, this event can be a very big deal and will position the Center for Ethical Business as the leader and the expert in this area," he says excitedly. "We can really be the catalyst for change."

Chester's passion is contagious and I can't help but admire him for his ideas and vision. In some ways, he can be absolutely brilliant.

He continues, "Bren and Henry are against planning something so powerful and big. Besides, you know how Henry is. He can move a bit slow sometimes."

Chester is right. It takes Henry months to make a decision about even the simplest of things, like which brand of coffee to order for the office. My nickname for him is Turtle. In fact, even his daughter had jokingly given him a turtle to symbolize how painfully slow he makes decisions and moves to accomplish anything. He has it proudly sitting on his desk.

Everything and anything has to be approved by him, but the problem is that he completely constipates the organization, and everyone at the Center resents him for being such a micro-manager. I think of him as more of a limp wet noodle and one of the most passive aggressive, emasculated men I have ever met. Bren completely rules him.

"I want us to bring together Fortune 100 companies along with major global nonprofits." Chester sits upright with a glee in his blue eyes. "To discuss best corporate practices and how we can encourage corporate social responsibility."

In corporate social responsibility, businesses embrace responsibility for the impact of their activities, and would eliminate practices that harm the public. It is honoring people, planet, and profit.

"Now that you are handling all of the Communications for The Center, I want you to be in charge of making this happen. I've given you incrementally more responsibility and you've done well, and I think this could lead to another big step in your career." He continues. "I am lucky to have you as my confidant. I trust you."

Yes, I know. Sometimes, I wish you wouldn't trust me sooo much. As Chester's assistant I work very closely with him, from answering his emails and correspondences to handling some of his personal and private business. In the course of my time here, I've found out that his thirty year-old son suffers from a drug problem. Chester is always trying to help him pay either his rent or various bills. He even bailed his son out of jail when he was arrested for starting a fight at a bar. I've seen email exchanges between him and his ex-fiancé discussing the intimate details of their failed relationship and the possibility of reconciliation. She apparently was never happy with anything he did or didn't do. I've seen email exchanges between Chester and some of the women he dates, and surprisingly enough, there are quite a few. Four to be exact, and all of them are significantly younger than him. This last bit of information has been a bit too much for me to bear. Chester is seventy years old, no taller than five feet eight inches, with a pudgy belly and barely any hair on his head. Yet according to the emails I've had the unfortunate experience of seeing, Chester appears to be quite the lady's man. The Casanova about town, who lavishes his women with gifts and makes them feel like a princess.

"And I hope you don't take this the wrong way, but I feel like a father figure to you. You are smart and a fast learner." He lets out a sigh and runs his hands over his face, "Nikki, I'm getting old," he says as he sinks in his chair. "I don't have the energy of my younger days to run all over the world giving speeches."

He knows how to endear himself to me, "please don't say that," I respond, feeling sorry for him.

"No. It's true. I'm not young and energetic anymore. My enthusiasm is waning."

"What do you mean?"

"If all goes well with this Summit, as the new Director of Communications, I want you to be the new spokesperson for the Center. I think people would prefer to look and listen to a young, attractive, and smart woman, versus me – an aging, balding, old white man." He lets out a laugh.

Ok, now I feel protective of him.

"Wow. I'm very flattered that you see me as someone who can do this job. I would love to manage this project."

"I believe in you and I will be right behind you the whole way. You're not on your own on this."

"Thank you, I really appreciate you saying that."

"Oh, and there's another thing. We've found a funder. The CEO of InCare has agreed to sponsor the Summit."

"InCare? Isn't that the company that was fined and sued for millions of dollars for dumping toxic waste into the community?"

"Yes. But they have paid those fines and have changed the name of the organization and are working to change their image. They're rebranding."

"Are you sure about having them sponsor this event?"

"Who else will give us $1 million in such short notice for an event of this caliber?"

I'm not sure if that's a rhetorical question or if he actually wants me to answer. I decide not to answer. I guess it was a rhetorical question, since Chester continues speaking, "the time is right for them to partner with us. They want to change their image and we can help do that for them. Besides, I feel their intentions are genuine."

"Ok, well, as long as you say so. "I decide not to push the subject since I'm the novice here. "You are right. If... no...when we pull it off, it will put us in a great position. And I am grateful for the vote of confidence. What date are you thinking?"

The light reflects off of his gold cufflinks as he throws his perfectly manicured hands in the air, "in five months. So you better get to work." He chuckles.

Oh my God, Henry is going to crap his pants over this. I hope Chester has talked it out with him already.

"But an event like this takes a year to plan," I say. He can't possibly be serious. "Are you joking?" I ask with a glint of worry in my eyes.

"Yes I am serious."

This is one of my many conundrums of working for Chester. He comes up with an idea and expects me to be his designated magician in charge of making things happen. And I usually do, but it means there are times that I do everything, from taking out the garbage to securing the speakers to making sure we have an audience, to getting press coverage. I am responsible for it all. And on some level, I guess I don't mind, since he is helping advance my career. It's nice to have someone believe in me.

***

CHAPTER 5

Back at my office, I think about calling Peter to tell him the good
news, but we've been on a little bit of distant terms since his big
announcement about Zuni. Or rather, I've been on an I-hate-your-guts-
and-don't-want-to-look-at-you-or-hear- your-positivity crap" mode.
Instead, I call Weston, my good old reliable gay work husband and make
lunch plans. Weston is tall and lean, a bit on the lanky side. Sort of looks
like Jim Carey with a moustache and beard. He's into hiking and riding a
motorcycle. Just enough man to give me a guy's perspective and safe
enough where I don't have to worry about him trying to get into my pants,
yet not so effeminate and bitchy to compete with me.

"Are you free for lunch?" I ask.

"I brought my lunch today, but I'll save it for tomorrow. Let's go
Mexican. I could use a drink."

"Having a rough day?" I ask.

"Not really. Well, sort of."

"Meet me by the elevators at noon. We'll chat over lunch."

We head over to our favorite Mexican restaurant, Tacocina, in the
Theater district a few blocks away. I love the rich amber colored walls that
are adorned with Mexican art and lots of images of Frida Kahlo. Weston
orders a margarita, which is totally a no-no during work hours, but between
the two of us, Weston is the rule breaker. I tell him the good news.

"I hope you plan on asking for a lot of money after you pull off this
event," is his only response to me. "But let's talk about more juicy things."

"There's nothing juicy in my life." I reply. "Your life is more juicy.
What's going on with you and Omar?"

"What do you mean what's going on with me and Omar?" He asks.

34

He is clearly upset with me for bringing up the topic.

He takes a big gulp of his margarita, "we're having sex. He's totally in the closet. I'm his secret. There's nothing to talk about."

Weston has been having a six-month long secret love affair with his boss, Omar Tariq, one of the managers here at the Center. Omar has been married for over ten years and has four kids, but according to Weston, has recently discovered and has admitted to himself that he might possibly be gay. According to Weston, Omar admitted that he has always been attracted to men, but because of his strict Muslim upbringing and his conservative and traditional family, denied his feelings, and condemned himself as a sinner. Up until he became involved with Weston, he had never had a sexual encounter with a man. I guess you could say he was a gay virgin.

"Ok. Sorry I brought it up, but there's nothing juicy in my life either."

"Helllooo. Peter," he throws his hands up and rolls his eyes with an exasperated look. "What are you going to do? What's the kids name again?"

"Zuni," I roll my eyes. "I don't know. I'm so confused. I am so angry at him," I whine.

"What a weird name," he mutters in between a mouthful of tortilla chips and guacamole.

"I know. They wanted to give her a unique name, so they named her after a Native American tribe, the Zuni."

Weston doesn't care. He seems to be more focused on picking up the right amount of salsa and guacamole so that his tortilla chip doesn't break.

"What should I do? I can't just up and leave. This is New York City. You know how hard it is to find an apartment. And, I feel bad for not wanting to take his kid in."

"Let's order our food before we get into this heavy duty

conversation."

We order some fried calamari with sweet sauce and steak fajitas to share.

"I shake my head. "Weston, I'm not sure I can or want to do this," I say as I push my chair away from the table to make room to cross my arms, "I don't think I want to raise a kid."

"This has nothing to do with you Nikki," he says.

"Yes it does. Part of the reason why I agreed to date Peter and move in with him is because his daughter doesn't live with him. And it was never an option."

"Well, welcome to life. It's throwing you an unexpected curve ball."

"Don't be so flippant. I am serious. As the oldest child, I took care of my three siblings. I've raised enough kids in my life. I'm done." I slice my hand across in a karate like gesture for dramatic effect. "How can he make a decision like that and not involve me? It's my home too. How can he not talk to me about this?"

"Have you talked to Peter about how you feel?" Weston asks.

"Nope. I feel guilty telling him how I feel. Apparently the kid has gotten into some kind of trouble."

"No way, are you serious?" In his excitement, Weston sprays me with some of his guacamole. "Oops, sorry."

"Anyway, yes. She's gotten in with the wrong crowd and her grandmother is old and sick. I mean how can I say no to that? I want to help, but just not in that way, and it makes me feel guilty."

"Well maybe Peter knew that if he talked to you about it, you would react this way."

I shake my head. "What say do I have on the matter since the three of them have discussed it as a little family unit already, and the decision is made?"

"And how have things been between you since he told you?"

"Funny that you ask, cause I've been using the excuse that I'm busy at work and preoccupied, just to avoid spending a lot of time with him. Luckily, his job is keeping him busy. I'm afraid that I don't know what to say to him."

"Well, I think you would make a great stepmom. Why don't you give it a try?"

I stare at him flabbergasted, with my jaw open.

"Close your mouth. I can see your chewed up food. And don't look at me like that! Besides, you can always change your mind."

"I don't understand why you're trying to convince me to go through with this?"

"You guys seem like a nice couple." He pauses for effect, "and Peter is a good guy. He cooks. He cleans. He's got a nice body, and those blue eyes. He's perfect."

"Then why don't you date him?" I roll my eyes in defiance. "Besides, is that all you care about, that he's hot? You're supposed to be on my side Wes." I stuff a chip into my mouth. "Besides, Peter's perfection is over-rated."

"Don't have a hissy fit. I am on your side." He lifts his almost empty glass to signal the waiter for another round.

"You shouldn't be drinking so much during work hours."

"Everybody is not Miss purrrfect like you. Ok? I want another drink. Is that ok with you?"

"Fine. But you're just drowning your sorrows."

"Nothing like a good watermelon margarita." He lifts his glass in my direction. "You're right. I'm upset, so, leave me alone." He takes a swig to finish off his drink.

"Sorry. You want to talk about it?"

"Nope. I just want to enjoy this perfect margarita."

Secretly, I feel that Weston shouldn't be having an affair with a married man with kids, but I keep that to myself. I wonder sometimes if he feels my judgment and that's why he never wants my advice about his situation.

"Ok, back to me then," I say, feeling bad for him. "You know what? I've worked really hard at my relationship with Peter. I've fought my own fears and challenges."

"Yeah, and this is just another hurdle. Who knows? You may actually like it." "I don't know about that. But I guess you're right, maybe I should give it a try. Besides, we've been together for a year."

Being in a relationship with Peter has been serious work for me. Even though we've had great times, Peter demands a lot from me, or at least what I perceive as a lot. Peter is an over talker and sharer. He likes to delve into my psyche, wanting to know every little thought and feeling, and at times tries to tell me what I'm thinking or feeling, even before I usually know. So over this past year, I've worked hard at learning to communicate with him and setting boundaries. It's still a work in progress, and some days are worse than others.

"I don't want to just give up and run out because of this," I say.

***

CHAPTER 6

The next afternoon in the office, excited about my first big project, I begin my work on the Summit by making a list of possible speakers, CEO's of major corporations and nonprofits, when I am interrupted by a phone call.

"Hello. Nikki Johnson speaking"

"Hi," says the Barry Whiteish voice on the other end of the line.

"Hi," I respond, slightly turned on by the man's deep voice.

"It's Wish Michaels."

I find myself embarrassed even though there is no one in my office to see me.

"I had a few minutes in between meetings, and just called to say hello."

"Hello, then." I smile.

"I've been thinking of you. "

"You have? Dare I ask what you've been thinking?" My heart starts to beat faster for some reason, and I feel awkward. I look at my reflection in my office mirror to make sure I look ok, still feeling a bit heavy from my Mexican lunch from yesterday, which probably added back on the few pounds I had lost. Eye makeup a little bit smeared, A little bit of a hat head, a possible pimple popping up on my chin, but other than that, not too shabby looking, I guess.

He lets out a laugh. "I can tell you're smiling….umm…."

I immediately stop smiling. He sounds incredibly sexy, and I imagine him lying in bed in a sexy pose.

He continues, "I've been thinking about you since we met. There's something very special about you."

"Thanks…I guess. But, I'm not really sure what you mean."

"Well, to state the obvious, you are beautiful. And to get to where you are, I'm sure you are smart."

Being just five foot, three inches, with big brown eyes and thick wavy dark brown hair, I've never seen myself as a head turner. I have a full round moon face and a big head, with a too pointy nose and lips that look like God had an accident with the collagen injections. I decided early on to develop my personality and brains, by reading art and philosophy books, since my looks weren't going to get me far. And I'm not sure how to describe my body, definitely not Playboy material. I have a broad back that tapers down to a small waist. Well, not so small anymore since I've become a cupcake addict. I have full round childbearing hips, and solid muscular legs. Some of the compliments I received in the past were that I was solid or thick. That's right, T.H.I.C.K. I mean what girl wants to hear that? While I am no ugly duckling and certainly no dummy either, I've never thought of myself as beautiful or smart. I suppose out of insecurity, sometimes I wonder why Peter is with me. But I will take Wish's beautiful and smart over T.H.I.C.K. any day.

"Well that's sweet of you to say. Thank you." I blush into my mirror, working hard to contain my smile.

He keeps the charm oozing, "you seem to have passion and purpose. You know how hard it is to find people who actually believe in something?"

"Well I do believe that we can make a difference through business. Nowadays corporations rule the world," I declare, feeling boosted by Wish's astute observations of me.

"Most people want a nine-to-five job that just pays the bills, and to take a two hour lunch. You are different."

"Well I don't think there's anything wrong with that. Everyone's priorities are different I suppose."

We talk for a few minutes then he puts me on hold. "I just cancelled my next meeting."

"Why?"

"To spend more time with you, of course."

I catch a glimpse of myself in the mirror again, and see myself smiling like the joker. Well, a few minutes turns into an hour. "I want to know about you," he said. We talk about my love of photography and nature pictures, Peter Lik and Steve McCurry being my favorite photographers, Ansel Adams his. We both love cycling – his favorite places for biking are the French Pyrenees and the South Island in New Zealand. Since that's a little out of my budget, I tell him I stick to the west side highway, and the gritty streets of New York City, dodging cars, taxis, pedestrians, and avoiding inhaling exhaust fumes. We both love books on philosophy and self-development. He's currently reading *The Power of Intention* by Wayne Dyer. On my morning commute today, I caught up on all the happenings between Brad Pitt and Angelina Jolie from my current issue of Us Magazine, but decide to tell Wish that *The Power of Intention* was next on my reading list, which is sort of true. He asks why I'm at the Center. "Same reason why you are in this work," is my reply, "to work towards the greater good."

I can see his smile in my mind. I smile back.

"I have to leave for the airport soon. I am speaking at a conference in South Africa, but I will be in New York City soon. Would you like to get together for a lunch meeting to plan the Summit?"

"That would be lovely." As I hang up the phone, I notice a funny tingling feeling in my whole body. My hands feel like they are vibrating. Peering into my mirror, I wonder what just happened. I am still awkwardly smiling, but smoosh my cheeks back into place.

***

CHAPTER 7

I can't avoid the whole Zuni situation anymore. Two weeks has already gone by since Peter told me of his decision to have her move in with us, but despite my screaming inner voice and out of pure unadulterated guilt, I approach Peter one night after work.

"I will become a member of Zuni nation," I say knowing that I don't really have an option.

"This will be great. Just watch. I will have my family all in one place." He practically bulldozes me over to give me a hug and a kiss.

Despite that fact that he made a major life decision without me, I can feel his sincerity and earnestness. I uncross my arms and let him hug me. I hug back. Peter is right, I am not a child anymore and I have to remind myself that I can still live my life the way I want with Zuni here. I just hope that he's learned his lesson and doesn't ever make such serious decisions without including me in the discussion.

Peter plants a kiss on my lips and smiles, showing his perfectly aligned and glistening white teeth, "I'm so happy right now."

I pull back, "I'll assume we will give my room to Zuni," I say. I sometimes use the smaller second room as a place where I can meditate, and occasionally when the creative spirit hits me, do some watercolor painting.

Over the next few weeks, I rush off after work to meet Peter at the paint store to choose wall colors. Unlike me, Peter is a meticulous shopper. At the paint store, after two agonizing long hours of looking at paint swatches, long discussions with the salesman, and me sweating profusely and constantly checking the time, Peter chooses ten different color palettes, everything ranging from subtle shades of pink to different shades of yellow to different shades of white. I never knew one had so many options. While I can't see much of a difference between some of the colors, Peter is adamant that he can tell the difference. I conclude that he must have taken the same design course as Matilda.

We bring the swatches home and Peter discusses with the appropriateness of the colors for a teenage girl are, and whether the color palette will fit into the rest of our apartment's scheme. I try to tune him out as he thinks out loud to himself. We finally narrow it down to three colors in the pink family -- cherry blossom pink, carnation pink, and pretty in pink. Peter buys paint samples and paints large two by two squares of each color on the bedroom wall. He then proceeds to observe the painted squares during different times of the day, until he finally decides to have one wall painted cherry blossom pink and the remaining three walls pretty in pink, which to me, look more like a white outfit that was accidently washed with something red.

Since it's my first time painting, the decorating process takes longer than expected. Peter shows me how to tape the edges around the molding and on the floor, and take the covers off the sockets and outlets. In his words, "It's good for a woman to know how to do this stuff for herself."

In some ways, Peter and I are total opposites. One of my initial attractions to him was his positive outlook on the world, especially since I thought of myself as a bit of a melancholic, who was prone to bouts of long empty stares into nothingness. Peter made me happy by helping change my perspective and pointed the upside to every downside that I saw. But lately, I find myself doubting his glass half full approach to life, and often feel shut down when I express something that he defines as negative or complaining, to the point that I've completely stopped expressing my feelings and just put on a happy face for him.

During this past year with Peter, there have been many times I let myself get caught up in his constant quest for self-empowerment and constant positivity. I wanted to prove myself to him, that I was adequate, capable, happy, cool, and funny. Anything but insecure, melancholy, or uncertain.

Next, we take on the task of decorating Zuni's new pink chambers. Peter takes his time to research and read product and consumer reviews for what feels like every type of bed, mattress, desk, chair, and bed sheets that have ever been manufactured. I can't believe he actually cares about the thread count for Zuni's sheets. He finally decides on a loft bed since we need to take advantage of all the space we have in the small bedroom.

Peter decides to put a small desk, computer station, and bookshelves under the loft so Zuni can have a place to do her homework. We throw in a couple of deep pink beanbags, and buy new sheets and a comforter with cherry blossom designs for her bed. Zuni's bed faces the window, which has great views of the west side and the Hudson River. Peter and I are quite proud of ourselves, and agree that this décor is as worthy as any fancy New York City hotel room…a very pink hotel room.

Over the course of decorating Zuni's room, I really did forgive Peter for his decision. I mean how can I stay mad at a father who wants to raise his child, and make sure that she is safe, happy, and comfortable. To my own surprise, I had a little bit of fun in the process of choosing colors, sheets, and even began to bask a little bit in the domesticated bliss. I need an attitude change. Maybe it wouldn't be so bad to have a family of my own without actually going through the pains of pregnancy and childbirth.

Sure I have some doubts, but I did not want to share them with Peter. I finally rationalized to myself that since I raised my siblings, that raising a teenager couldn't really be that difficult, especially now, that I was older, smarter, and wiser. Zuni and I could spend time bonding over girl things. I can help her buy her first bra. I can teach her how to use make up. I'm sure she will need someone to speak with about boys and sex. I can help her deal with her first crush or the first time her heart gets broken. And maybe this has a good chance of working out if I can treat her like a friend and not a child. She will probably be busy with her own friends and activities most of the time anyways.

***

CHAPTER 8

"I've been in an accident," says the barely audible voice on my voice mail. "This is Wish. I'm in the City and have been in the hospital tied to a gurney all day. I'm finally in my hotel room. I have a bad concussion. It would mean a lot to me if you can come by to check on me…please….oh…I'm at the Four Seasons."

Why is Wish calling me? I'm sure he knows tons people here. I listen to the message again, not out of worry, but because of how insanely sexy he sounds, even with a concussion and tied to a gurney. It is one of those throw me against the wall and rip my clothes off kind of voices that turn you on, even if he's cursing you out. I get chills just thinking about it. Over the past few weeks, despite the fact that I've been swamped with the beginning plans for the summit, and in spite of accepting the Zuni situation, for some reason, I have not stopped thinking about Wish. I'm not sure exactly what it is about him that makes me feel jittery.

I'm in agony as to what I should do. Should I just call Wish back and check up on him? Should I ignore him? Should I go visit him? Arrggh – all this is giving me a stress headache. Ok, so we've talked on the phone a few times and had a few meetings about the Summit, but that is no reason why I should feel this responsibility. I think about asking Weston what I should do, but decide against it. I don't feel like hearing a lecture from him. Besides, I'm with Peter. Wish is a married man. I can go make sure he is ok. I would do that for anyone in his situation, I make up my mind. After work I rush over to the Four Seasons to find Wish laid out in bed, the top of his head wrapped up like a mummy and his left hand in a brace.

"Oh my god," I rush over to him. "What happened?"

"I was on my way to a meeting," he says. Damn, he still looks sexy. "I usually take a car service, but this time, I took a cab. The driver was driving like a lunatic. Taking off. Breaking suddenly. Next thing I know, my head hit the back partition. Luckily, I have a thick head," he smiles, but is lethargic and mumbles his words out with his eyes half open.

"I can't believe you have a sense of humor about this."

"I'm alive. It could have been a lot worse. I was in the hospital, left tied to a gurney for four hours, and nobody would pay attention to me until I finally pulled some rank and told them who I was."

"You waited four hours to pull rank?"

"My head felt like it was going to explode."

"Yea. That's something I really don't like to do, but it was necessary."

"Well with a concussion, all you can do is rest. I hope you're planning on not working or traveling over the next few days."

"I am resting. Sit down?" He pats the king sized bed, and sits up on the bed.

The executive suite at the Four Seasons is quite posh with incredibly lush views of Central Park. The room is decorated in rich neutral earth tones of beiges and browns with contemporary furniture. The living room includes an oval partner-style desk, a marble-top bar, an armoire, two leather armchairs, and an entertainment center, all of which tastefully fit together.

I face him as I sit down on the edge of the bed, pretending to not be phased by the executive suite at the Four Seasons, "Why are you getting up? You should lie down," I say.

"I've been in and out of sleep all day. I could use some conversation." He looks at me with eyes that pierce right through me.

I don't know why Wish has this effect on me. Peter is definitely better looking, but there is something about Wish that makes melts me like butter on a hot potato. He's not good looking in the pretty boy, Brad Pitt type kind-of-way, but in a more rugged, manly, lumberjack kind-of-way, sort of like Daniel Craig or the Brawny paper towel guy. Wish's deep brown eyes, full face, and a slight five o'clock shadow are nothing to get excited about. He's physically fit from the cycling and has a body that is solid but not cut or muscular. I think that in his case, the whole is definitely greater than the sum of his parts.

He catches me off guard with what he says next, "What is it about you, Ms. Nikki Johnson?" He looks at me for a few seconds in silence as I stare back, "there's something." He smiles.

"There's not particularly anything interesting about me."

"Let me be the judge of that. You told me that you raised your siblings. That's interesting. What about school?"

"Well, I basically put myself through school. I worked almost full time and went to school full time. I've waited tables and cleaned houses, whatever it took to pay for school. I didn't really have time to party or do the normal things that kids do in college."

"Really? That's quite an experience. I'm sure it had to be difficult."

As he says this to me, I am flooded by memories of that time. That was a difficult time in my life. I knew that getting a college education was important to my family, but more importantly to my future. I didn't want to be burdened by massive amounts of student loans, so while I borrowed a little bit of money, I worked my butt off to pay for school. There was no wild partying, drinking binges, or hooking up with drunk boys for me.

Wish's compassion makes me feel safe. I continue, "I went to Wake Forest University in Winston Salem, North Carolina. It was a very small town, and jobs were difficult to find. I was grateful to find a job as a house cleaner for a woman that owned her own cleaning company. It was one of the lowest periods in my life. I set up my schedule to have my classes in the morning, and I cleaned houses in the afternoon and into the evening, six days a week for two years, and then did my studying at night. It was the most difficult thing I have ever done. There were evenings, I would come home, yank my shoes off, and literally drag myself into bed without taking off my work clothes or washing my face."

"You know my mom was a maid."

"Really?" I am surprised by his admission.

He shakes his head, "Yup. She worked very hard and instilled in me an incredible work ethic."

"I would have never guessed."

"What? That I was poor as a kid? Why not?"

"I don't know." I twirl my hair and fidget on the bed. "You just seem so sophisticated like a blue blood and I don't know...just so sure of yourself, that's all."

He cocks his head to the side and let out a loud laugh. "I'm not that sophisticated."

I wonder if I've said something wrong.

"You're sweet. Well, I think my secret is that my mom let me know that I was loved every single day of my life. Maybe, it's as simple as that."

"That's really important."

"Tell me, how did you feel cleaning houses?"

I let out a deep sigh, and lean back on my hands. "Well, often times, the houses we cleaned were luxury homes that were at least over 3,000 square feet. There were many times that I was treated as the 'help' and felt invisible."

"Really?" Wish's eyes are furrowed in concern.

"Yea, but don't feel bad for me," I say suddenly feeling self-conscious.

"That experience helped me develop a respect and appreciation for janitors, hotel maids, and any person who has a service job. It helped me know who I was, no matter what my job title. Even now, I always remind myself to recognize everyone's humanity and treat another human being with the same dignity regardless of the position in life they have."

"That's an incredible experience and lesson you carried away with you," he says.

"Thanks." I give him a smile and quickly look away. I feel exposed for some reason. "I've never really shared that story with anyone. I have mixed feelings about that part in my life. Even though I learned a great lesson, there's a part of me that's a bit embarrassed also."

"No, you shouldn't be." With his one good hand, he reaches over, turns my head toward his, and brushes my hair from my face. "You should really be proud of what you did. Do you know how many people would be angry or bitter? You've come out a winner...really amazing."

"Thanks." It feels nice to be validated. I'm a little surprised that I've shared this much with Wish in such a short time.

He moves lower on the bed to lie down again. "I want you to lay with me for a bit." He scoots over to make room for me.

I'm a bit rattled by his request, and stare blankly at him, feeling that awkward tingly feeling all over my body again.

"Please..." He looks at me with sad droopy eyes. "Don't make me beg."

I lie down like a zombie beside him.

"Come on, don't be so stiff. Come here." He unfolds his one good arm to take me in.

I am drawn to Wish and let myself be enveloped into him. He wraps his arm around my body and pulls me closer to him. Now my whole body is pressed against him and damn, he feels good. His skin is soft and I get a whiff of his cologne. Normally I don't like the fake smell of cologne, but whatever he is wearing is light and faint. He smells clean and fresh, and a little woodsy. It's absolutely perfect for his brawny look.

"Hi." He turns to me, opens his eyes and smiles. "I'm feeling much better already," he whispers.

I plop myself up on my elbow, "Are you faking?"

He leans up to kiss my cheek, "no, not at all. I'm happy to see you. Besides feeling like crap all day, I've also been nervous at the thought of seeing you."

I keep his sensual gaze for what feels like a few minutes, then let myself melt into his arms. His face is close to mine. I can feel his breath on my skin. It smells like the breath of a baby – part sweet and part milky. Or is that my imagination?

The rhythm of his breath is soothing. Slow inhalation. His diaphragm expands. Slow exhalation. We lie together in silence as he dozes off and I soon follow.

I wake up to soft, luscious full lips pressed against mine. My eyes are shut. I part my lips to let his tongue wander in. Warm. Smooth. I inhale his breath. He presses me harder against his body. I let out a light moan. And then thoughts rush in. Oh my god, he feels so good. What am I doing? I shouldn't do this. I don't want him to let me go. I push him back.

"I can't do this." I can't even look him in the eye. I stare at the white comforter. I cover my face with my hands and pull my hair back, "this is not a good idea, Wish."

"You don't have to say anything," he mumbles. I don't know whether he doesn't want to hear the rejection or can already predict what I'm going to say.

"I do." I'm determined to vocalize my objection.

He rolls his eyes at me, and shakes his head, "I know what you're going to say. " He sits up on the bed. "Yes, I know I'm married. You don't have to remind me."

"Ummm. Ok." I'm confused by his annoyance, but decide not to probe. I turn my back to him to get up, but I don't want to leave, so I end up sitting there in silence.

He puts his hand on my shoulder, "please look at me."

I slowly turn to face him with droopy eyes.

"Nikki…I like you… a lot… but I understand, and can respect your wishes."

"Thank you." I look away.

"I'd like us to be friends."

"We can…" I give him a half smile. "Sure we can be friends." I shrug. "As long as you don't try to get in my pants." I laugh out loud, wanting the awkward moment to pass as quickly as possible.

"I promise," he responds as he sits ups, and smiles at me.

"Do you need anything before I leave?"

"No. Just let me know you got in ok."

"Ok." I give him a quick hug goodbye, even as he tries to hold on longer.

On my way out I stop by the bathroom and it's like something I've never seen before. The full marble bathroom has a deep soaking tub, a glass-enclosed shower, a television and a foyer area for changing. It's almost as big as Peter's Tribeca apartment. I stare at my disheveled self in the mirror. My hair is frizzy and my side part is all over the place. The light pink Burt's Bees combination Chapstick and lip color is worn off and is smeared on my chin. My black eyeliner has turned into black eye boogers on the inner corner of each eye. This is definitely not a very sexy look. I do my best to piece myself back together. I pull my hair back into a ponytail, and put on a dab of lip color.

I can smell Wish on my skin and clothes, so I spritz myself with a lavender body spray and then I notice Wish's open toiletry bag sitting on the bathroom counter. It really wouldn't be appropriate for me to look into his bag, but I want to know what his cologne is. So, all of a sudden I forget that I have to use the bathroom and being the curious or rather nosy person that I am, I reach over and peer into the bag. I see his Jean Paul Gaultier's blue Le Male cologne bottle. I pull it out and take a long whiff, then try to return it undisturbed. As I pull the bag open again, I see a pack of Trojan Condoms.

***

CHAPTER 9

The next week at work, I have a board of directors meeting to manage. Chester has been nervous about the upcoming meeting. Chas Chandler V, our new chairman and a very wealthy blue blood, will be in attendance. Chester wants to impress him with an announcement about the upcoming Summit. The Center will have a new board member joining, a Black woman, who is CEO of a major media company, Nancy Pattison, someone Chester has been courting for a long time.

The Board is full of thirty antique, almost dead, balding white male CEO's of various large corporations, and for a long time now, Chester has wanted to add more women and more color, as he puts it. For him snagging Nancy Pattison for our board is a two for one deal. He thinks that Nancy will contribute in valuable ways beyond money by attracting more diversity to the organization and by reaching out to the African-American community.

The day of the meeting I go in early to the building named after Chas Chandler V and his family, Chandler-Hill. From the outside, the fifty-five-story building looks like a LEGO representation of a prison with its gray stone exterior and gray light reflecting glass windows. It makes me wonder why all offices use the same variation of a few color schemes of gray, blue, and white. As I take the private elevator to the fifty-fifth floor, I find myself excited about the upcoming meeting. Usually the board meetings are quite boring and my role consists of setting up for the meeting, making sure everything runs without a glitch, and taking notes. But Chester's planned announcement about the Summit and my involvement has me a bit nervous.

The elevator opens up to a large hallway lined with a deep rich walnut wood, and dark beige carpets. The conference room is absolutely beautiful with two walls of floor to ceiling windows overlooking midtown. I prepare the room, test out the audio and Chester's PowerPoint presentation, make sure the caterers have set up properly for breakfast and lunch, and mentally prepare myself for the all-day meeting.

It's 9:20am and Board members are slowly limping in with as much gusto as they can muster, and with much ado about nothing, in walk three of Chas's handlers.

Chas Chandler V is the Chairman of the Board of The Center on Ethical Business. His father founded one of the largest news companies and Chas manages and runs all day-to-day operations. Chas is just over 5 feet tall, has perfectly coiffed plastic golden brown hair, something of a cross between Ken (of Ken and Barbie) and Donald Trump. It may be bad hair plugs or a bad toupee, and is somehow super-glued in place so that even in a tornado it wouldn't move out of place. Chas is in his 60's but it's obvious that he has had way too many plastic surgeries. The skin on his face is smooth from the obvious laser and chemical peels, and he looks like he is in his early-40s. He always wears turtlenecks or fancy Hermes scarves to hide his prune neck. You would think with all that money, he would have some kind of neck lift surgery.

Chas is a serious germaphobe, and goes everywhere with an entourage of three people – two of whom clean, spray and wipe down anything that Chas has to touch, including chairs, tables, cups, forks, pens, writing pads, etc. The third handler is there as an extra, just in case Chas needs a cup of coffee, a glass of water, or someone to wipe his nose. He gives these people fancy Director and Vice President titles, to make them feel important, but in essence they don't have much to do. His entourage has to constantly prove that they are worth their hefty salaries. Before every board meeting they want to approve the meeting notes from the previous meeting, and want to define the agenda for the meeting. In essence, they have no idea what they are doing. I once listed one of their titles as, "Director of Corporate Social Responsibility," and the woman, Pat, whom by the way, Bren is having a love affair with, sent an angry email to Chester, and cc'd me and Bren about how I got her title wrong and it should be, "Senior Director of Corporate Social Responsibility," note the Senior. Bren made sure that plenty of light was brought upon that particular mistake.

After the wipe down, the Board meeting starts and Chester and Chas welcome the thirty stiffs. Chester begins the meeting.

"I am so happy and honored that Nancy Pattison has agreed to join our board." The thirty white men do an obligatory round of applause and welcome Nancy Pattison.

Chester continues, "She is the CEO of Stygian Corporation. Under her direction, the company's profits have increased by thirty five percent over the past two years. She is very articulate. Please welcome her to our board."

Various members smile and welcome Nancy. Chester turns to face Nancy to give her a hearty smile. "I am so happy you are here," he broadcasts from the podium. "You know, I grew up in Atlanta at the height of segregation."

Oh no, I think to myself, wondering where he is going with this story. Chester in his own innocent way can be a bumbling buffoon who says inappropriate things. I find myself many times, wanting to follow one of his politically incorrect statements, with a 'what he meant to say' clarification. I'm beginning to think this may be another moment.

He continues, "--In a wealthy white area. I was never exposed to many blacks, and I am so honored to introduce Nancy as The Center's first-ever Black board member."

I stop breathing as he finishes his statement, and wonder how I can correct this situation from my where I am sitting. I think and think, but am at a loss on what to say or even how I can jump in front of all these people, and besides, I don't even have a microphone. I quickly glance around the board table at the faces of the old white men, and realize that none of the of them have noticed the tasteless and beyond inappropriate comment.

Chester continues as he faces Nancy again, "You know, Nancy. In some weird way, I feel like I am at the forefront of the anti-segregation movement."

He throws his hands up in the air with an air of excitement. "I can only imagine what it might have felt like."

Nancy looks around the room making eye contact with everyone with a closed lip smile.

At this Board meeting, Chester's big plan, to impress Nancy, is to introduce our new publication that he is oh so proud of, *Outsourcing*, on the ethics of corporations using third world country labor for western world production and consumption.

After reviewing the Center's usual business and finances, announcement of the Summit, and after our lunch break, Chester proclaims, "This is our biggest accomplishment to date." His eyes are gleaming. "All of you will find a copy in your Board packets of *Outsourcing*, brought to us by the generous support of Chas Chandler and Chandler-Hill." Chester is like a kid that's been given his favorite toy as a gift and he wants to show it off to everyone. "To give you a brief summary, *Outsourcing* is about how the west can exploit, and as an aside, I want to add that the word 'exploit' is not necessarily a bad thing, as you will read."

Chester pauses to let the old men pull out their copy of *Outsourcing*. Some of the men begin to smile as they take in the hefty book and flip through its pages.

"Where was I?" He continues. His eyes beam with excitement. "Oh yes. The book is about how the west can exploit the resources of the third and developing world and why it is mutually beneficial to all parties involved – that includes the child laborers and those who work in sweatshops." Some of the men shake their head in agreement. "We can have our cheap products, and these other countries can build their economies. I mean look at China." At this, everyone but Nancy Pattison burst out into a round of loud applause.

The Outsourcing book looks impressive, that's if you believe that size matters. It's approximately four hundred pages and the cover shows a majestic illustration of the earth held in the palm of a generic white hand.

My God, these men are all stuck in the days of colonialism is all I can think to myself.

I look at Nancy Pattison. She is dead silent with absolutely no expression on her face. She looks around the room studying the men in silent exasperation. When she gets to me, and realizes that I've been watching her. I quickly look away as I continue to feel her gaze on me.

After a few seconds of feverishly hitting random keys on my laptop, I keep my head down to not draw her attention to me again, but from my peripheral vision can see her flipping through the book with a twisted and furrowed look on her face.

After the board meeting, I pack up my laptop, nametags and all the *Outsourcing* books that people left behind into my little suitcase, say my goodbye's to the various lingering board members and make a mad dash out of there. New York City in the middle of winter is no fun. The damp cold wind cuts through my long down coat, into my black cashmere cardigan, through my dress and tights and goes straight into my bones. Chandler-Hill is only a ten-block walk from my office, so despite the freezing weather, I decide I need some fresh air after the stuffy board meeting. I pull my hat further down on my head to cover my ears and wrap my scarf tighter around my neck. My hands are freezing as I lug the heavy suitcase behind me, almost running to get to the office. Today is the big day. Zuni's flight should be arriving at any moment, and I want to stop by Trader Joe's on my way home and have dinner ready for when Peter brings her home.

At the grocery store I think back about some of her past visits to New York. Peter in his usual meticulous manner would prepare every tiny detail of her visit and plan their activities down to a tee. He would take Zuni to a Yankees game, or to one of the many great Museums of New York City, The Metropolitan Museum of Art being one of their favorites for its massive size and impressive collections.

Zuni also loves Chinatown for all the inexpensive clothing, bags, and various girly rhinestone decorated belts and hairclips. And even though Peter hates shuffling around Chinatown dodging tourists and avoiding pushy salespeople, he would often take Zuni, just to make her happy. On rare occasions, even though I tried to avoid it, I would join them for lunch or dinner for Zuni's favorite food, hamburger and fries. There is only so many burgers and fries a girl can eat, or so I thought. As I watched her wolf down another burger, I never understood how Zuni didn't get sick of always eating the same crap. I thought the girl would grow a fry out of her stomach.

At Trader Joe's, I want to ignore Peter's advice, and think about making hamburger and fries for dinner. But then, Peter knows Zuni best and earlier in the day had given me some very specific suggestions on what to make besides hamburgers and fries. I pick up the groceries and rush home.

While the food is cooking, I tidy up and straighten pictures and photo frames, books, and various decorative doo-dads around our apartment. I even pull out the duster and begin dusting.

Zuni is a nice kid overall, I think to myself. I've spent time with her in the past, so everything should be ok. But then I don't know. What am I getting myself into? I hope this is not going to be a disaster. What do I know about raising a teenager? She probably secretly wants her parents to get back together. She's going to hate me. I hope I don't hate her living with us.

The jiggle of the keys snaps me out of my delirium, and I quickly run towards the front door and stare as if I've been caught doing something wrong. I hear their chatter as Peter unlocks the door, and as they walk in, I take a big heavy gulp of air and rush over and give Peter a kiss and hug Zuni.

"Hey, welcome to your new home," I say with forced cheeriness.

"Thanks," replies Zuni as she quickly pulls back from me and drops her backpack onto the hardwood floor with a loud thud.

Aaaah...the gruff attitude of a teenager. Before me stands a stranger. Zuni is no longer the sweet, pink crystal-studded girl with long curly strawberry blond hair, but instead a creature out of a vampire movie. Her bouncy Rapunzel-like hair is replaced with a jet-black bob that is jagged and uneven. It looks like she may have taken a razor to it in the middle of the night. There are random streaks of a bright blue color peeking out of the black mass on her head, which I assume is some type of Manic Panic hair color. Her eyes are lined with thick black eyeliner and a purple glittery eye shadow that gives her soft hazel eyes an eerie transparent glow. Like she can see right through me.

Zuni has a small stud piercing through the left bottom corner of her lip, and is wearing a black t-shirt with a picture of blood dripping from a red rose. Her black skinny jeans are practically painted on her pubescent legs and budding hips. Her dark gray Skechers have drawings and writings on them that I can't decipher.

Oh my God, she is going to hate the pink berry forest that is her room is the only thought that runs through my head. I wonder if it's too late to paint the room all black or vamp purple.

How was your flight Zuni?" I ask, ignoring her attitude and my shock at her new look.

"Long and cold. Then there was an accident on the Brooklyn Bridge," she answers as she rolls her eyes.

"Oh by the way, I'm going by 'Z' now. Don't call me Zuni anymore," she says as she crosses her arms and chomps on her pink gum.

"Ok." I shoot Peter a nervous look. He doesn't seem distressed by this whole interaction or by the little vampire standing before him.

She looks around, "so which room is mine?"

Peter steps in and picks up Zuni's backpack, "come on 'Z'. He puts an extra emphasis on 'Z'. "I'll show you. We've decorated it really nice and I think you'll like it."

Hello…what the hell is wrong with him? Can he not see that the little innocent pink girl he knew no longer is? Peter's optimistic attitude sometimes makes him blind.

As they walk down the hall and into Zuni's room, I strain my ears to hear their conversation. My own breathing seems loud, so I hold my breath.

"What do you think?" Peter asks desperately wanting Zunis' approval.

"Dad, it's PINK," she exclaims.

"Well, I didn't realize you didn't like pink anymore, until you showed up today."

I can't help but smile. This would be funny if it was happening to someone else.

Peter's voice sounds higher than normal, "Your mom didn't say anything to me about your new look."

"Dad, " Zuni whines, "It's kinda like too small for me."

I wince as I hear the floor creak under my footstep to get closer. Luckily they don't hear me.

She continues in her high-pitch whiny voice, "I'm not like eight years old, Dad."

Peter lets out a big sigh, "Well, my sweetie, my darling, this is all we have."

I hear a loud thud. I assume Zuni drops something on the floor.

"Where is my TV?" Her voice clearly sounds irritated.

I hear Peter's footsteps.

"I know that with your mom, you had a TV in your room," says Peter in a forced calm and zen voice, "but now, I don't think it's such a good idea."

"Dad, I'm going to be bored. Where am I going to watch TV?"

"I don't want you spending so much of your time watching trash."

Awkward silence. I can only imagine the death look she is giving him.

"Why?" Zuni finally asks.

"Look, we'll talk about everything later."

"I already hate it here," says Zuni. "And my reality shows are not trash dad!"

Uh oh. I wonder how Peter will handle this.

"Look sweetie. Everything will be ok. We will work something out for you ok?" His voice is pleading. "Let's get you settled."

"Can I put up a basketball hoop in my room?"

"You want to put up a basketball hoop? What for?"

"It helps me think."

Think about what? Which color to choose for her hair? This little girl is a full bag of contradictions, with her vamp look, her love of reality TV, and now a basketball hoop. I feel so bad for Peter.

"There are basketball courts down the street that you can go to. I know you're used to living in a house with a yard, but this is New York City, and we will all be living together in a confined space. I don't think bouncing and throwing a ball around is such a good idea."

As I listen to their conversation, my chest becomes tighter and tighter. I decide to walk away and set the table for dinner before I implode due to stress.

I yell towards Zuni's room, "ok guys. Dinner is ready."

Peter and Zuni both come out looking a bit drawn and uneasy.

"Are you hungry?" I ask with a big smile on my face, and a spatula in my hand. Oh lord, I must look like a creepy Stepford wife.

"Yea…..I want mac and cheese. I like Velveeta." Zuni walks towards the dining room chair, pulls it out with force, and slams herself into the chair. "My mom makes the best mac and cheese." She turns her head towards me in the kitchen. "Can you?"

Oh my word, Lord…Jesus…. help me now. I didn't know people still ate that chemical concoction, let alone feed it to their kids.

I glance at Peter, but he refuses to make eye contact with me. Ok, I guess I'll handle this on my own.

"Oooohh…..well, unfortunately we do not have mac and cheese. We're not a mac and cheese kind-of-house."

"Ugh…whatever." She puffs up and crosses her arms.

"But Z, check this out. I've made something new that I think you are going to love. Quinoa with roasted pine nuts and lamb and feta kabobs."

"Huh…..What's koooonia?" She bunches up her face and shoots me a dirty look. "And I don't like lamb. It stinks."

Pardon moi Princess Zuni. It was Peter's idea to cook quinoa and lamb kabobs. He wanted to introduce Zuni to new experiences and expand her palette, and what better way to do this than at her first moment of arrival. Peter dismissed my hamburger and fries suggestion.

Peter squirms in his chair and lets out a low chuckle, "Zuni, excuse me, 'Z', why don't you give it a try. Please?" He reaches over and takes the plate from me and places it in front of Zuni. "You never know, you may like it." He reaches over and picks up her fork. "Remember that time you didn't want to eat a tomato and when you finally tried it, you liked it?"

The kid doesn't look convinced.

"If you don't like the food, then I'll make you something else," I say.

I eye the food on Zuni's plate. The quinoa, lamb kabobs, and the steamed kale look delicious, but it is obvious this is alien food to her.

"Is this the koooonia?" She asks as she turns up her nose and pushes the plate back towards Peter.

"Try it. I betcha you'll love it." I give her my best cheesy smile.

"I don't know about that," she throws me a dirty look like 'how dare you tell me what I'm gonna like. You don't know me.'

"Come on sweetheart," says Peter. He proceeds to take a forkful of quinoa and a piece of kabob towards Zuni's mouth."

Zuni sits there with her arms crossed and her mouth closed tightly. Peter is frozen in mid-motion with his furrowed smile and his extended arm.

"Come on baby poo. Open up. For Daddy," Peter says in his best baby talk voice.

At the sound of baby poo, Zuni opens up her mouth and pinches her nose. She reluctantly takes in the food, and shakes her head in affirmation as she slowly chews it all up.

"Hmmm... not bad...this is tasty," she says.

I look over at Peter and see him beaming with happiness. Peter smiles at me. I look at him and remind myself to smile back.

"This is what I've wanted for so long. I have my family all in one place. Z, even though Nikki and I are not married, I think of her as your step mom," says Peter.

I don't know if I'm ready for all that, but decide that this is not the best moment to say anything. The rest of dinner goes smoothly and mostly consists of Zuni and Peter telling me about their travel misadventures. There was the time they went camping and had to put up a tent in a torrential downpour and windstorm. Finally after having their tent blown away for the third time, and being completely drenched to their bones, they figured out how to secure it. There was the time they took sailing lessons and somehow Zuni managed to fall out of the boat. They were both grateful that Zuni had on her life jacket. And then there was the time in Paris where they walked up the Eiffel Tower, all 674 steps to the second platform, and how at one point, Zuni faked a fainting spell so she wouldn't walk anymore, but Peter didn't fall for her trick, and somehow encouraged and cajoled her to go up the stairs. I assume probably by calling her baby poo.

After Peter and I clean up the table and wash the dishes, we get ready for bed. Peter approaches me as I lie in bed with my latest Eckhart Tolle book, *A New Earth*, sitting closed on my lap. I'm reading this week's issue of Us Magazine highlighting Celebrity workouts and diet tricks. All the rage seems to be juicing and eating Raw. I don't think I'm ready to give up my cupcakes for green juice yet.

"Nikki, do you mind letting Zuni sleep in our bed and you sleep in her room?" Peter says.

I look at him perplexed, "But she's thirteen years old!"

"She's feeling a little scared."

"But she's stayed with you before. It's not like it's her first time."

"I know, but it's her first night here as her new home. Just this one night. Please."

"Peter! It's a little weird to have your thirteen year old daughter sleep with you."

"Oh stop it. Don't even go there. She's my child and she's scared. She comes first in my life."

I grab my book and magazine and go to the pink chambers. I throw down the Us magazine, and decide to read my book. Maybe something spiritual will make me feel like a better person. I lie in the pink loft bed, positioning myself just so my head doesn't hit the off pink ceiling. As I lie in bed, I feel like I am in a strawberry shortcake cartoon. All that is missing is me wearing a bonnet with strawberries. I keep reading the same line over and over again - *Trying to become a good or better human being sounds like a commendable and high-minded thing to do, yet it is an endeavor you cannot ultimately succeed in unless there is a shift in consciousness.* That sounds deep, but I can't focus on such deep life lessons in this moment. I throw down the book to the floor and it lands with a loud thud, turn off the lights, and plop myself down on the pink sheets and cover my head with the cherry blossom comforter, hoping tomorrow will be a better day. That's a conscious thought, I think to myself. Well, just that one night of Zuni sleeping with Peter, turns into the rest of the week, as I get relegated to her room.

***

CHAPTER 10

"Niiikkkkiiii?" yells Chester from his office.

Sigh. "Be there in a sec."

As Chester's assistant I constantly deal with him and his needs. I find myself a lot less patient these days.

"Do you need something?"

"Aaah..yes." He can tell that I'm not in a good mood. "I'm sorry to bother you with my personal things. I know you are busy with the Summit." He looks at me with big sheepish eyes.

"It's ok. What do you need?" I feel guilty for snapping at him.

"I want to print the pictures of my new grandchild from this email. Can I do that?"

"Sure." I fake a smile and proceed to show him yet again how to open an attachment and save it on his computer. I open him an online account and send his pictures to print.

"Voila. It's that easy," I say.

"Thank you. I would be lost without you...May I ask? Is everything ok?"

"My plate is really full with all of my routine work, add the Summit, and all of the changes going on at home."

"Oh." Chester is concerned. "Do you want to talk about it? Is everything ok with you and Peter now that his child has moved in?"

"Yes, I think so. It's just a lot to deal with."

"Kids can be difficult to deal with and it changes your life. You have to be prepared for that."

I'm reluctant to go into more detail about my home situation, simply because I don't know what the hell is going on. I remain silent and Chester notices my discomfort and changes the subject.

"Well, I know things are very busy here. If you think you need some extra help, why don't you get a temp," he says.

"Really? Can I? I didn't really think to ask you."

"This Summit is very important and I want you to have all the support you need. God knows I keep you busy enough. Get someone really top notch and professional."

I rush out of Chester's office to call the placement agency for my temp. This will be my first time being a supervisor.

***

"Hello. I'm Consuela Roberta Olalla Wilfredo. The temp agency sent me over."

In front of me stands a petit girl-woman, no taller than five feet. She has long crinkly sand colored hair that is all one length. Her skin is pale. It appears that she is not wearing any make up. Her face is round and has the fullness of a child's face. Everything on her face is cute and small. Small mouth. Small nose. Small eyes. Her shoulders are stooped. She is wearing a simple cream-colored button up shirt with a gray knee length skirt and some black clogs.

"Hi. Very nice to meet you." I shake her hand. It's limp and damp.

"Gracias. It's nice to meet you too," she responds in a soft voice.

"Oh great, you speak Spanish."

"Yes, I am fluent in three languages, Spanish, Dutch, and English."

"That's great. Maybe we could use your language skills around here. Let me show you where you will be sitting."

I take her to my old gray cubicle, which is a few feet away from my office.

"Hmmmm." she mutters under her breath.

"I'm sorry."

"De nada…oh nothing." She smiles.

Back in my office, I proceed to tell her about the Summit and the importance of the event, and put her to work researching event venues and hotels in Washington, DC, where we will hold the Summit.

"Not a problemo," she mutters. "I can do these things with my eyes closed."

"Great," I reply. "I'm happy that you can take direction and run with it. Let me know if you have any questions."

"Well you know that Frida Kahlo, the famous Latin artist, paid so much attention to detail. Her paintings were amazing. Like her, I do the same."

"Oh, you paint?"

"Mi Dios. No." She smiles, "I pay close attention to detail."

"That's exactly what I'm looking for." I am happy the agency sent over someone competent. "If you have any questions, feel free to ask me or Chester."

There's something about Consuela that I find endearing, even though half her sentences are in Spanish. She seems shy, and she must be smart if she is fluent in three languages. I think we will work well together.

As the days progressed, so did Consuela's outfits. After the first few weeks of wearing demure and unassuming work attire, her clothing on both ends, shrank towards her belly. The tops became increasingly low cut, the skirts became increasingly shorter, and the colors of both became brighter. Since I am her supervisor, I decide that it would be good for me to get to know her better. I take her out to lunch one day.

At O'Brien's Irish Pub, we take a booth at the back of the dimly lit restaurant. I order a soup and a veggie wrap since I have not made a dent on my goal of losing ten pounds. In fact, I may have even put on a few. Consuela orders mozzarella sticks and a burger with bacon and blue cheese, with shoestring fries on the side, my favorite.

"So, Consuela, how is everything going?" I eye her mozzarella stick.

"Very well. I like working at the Center very much." She takes a bite of her mozzarella stick and pulls off the cheesy goo with her hands.

"Good. That's great. I'm glad you are happy here."

"How about you?" She asks. "Do you like working at the Center?"

"Yea. I love my job." I watch her finish off another Mozzarella stick. "One of my rules is to have a purpose in my life, and work for something I believe in. The work of the Center is really important especially in these days of corporate greed and bad behavior."

"You know, Carlos Castaneda said that 'all paths are the same: they lead nowhere. But a path without a heart is never enjoyable.' What's important these days is the bottom line, and not people or our planet…," she says.

I push my bland vegetable soup away. "Yes! Oh my God. You are so right. That's why I like being here. The Center is working to change the corporate "me" culture to a "we" culture. And since Corporations rule the world and politics, it is the only way to bring a little more heart into the equation."

Consuela ponders a moment in silence over my words as she dips her fry in ketchup. "Si. Si." She shakes her head and waves her fry in the air, as if to taunt me. "They are the ones with the big bucks." She throws the fry into her mouth.

I find out that she is half German and half Argentinean. She has a Master's Degree in conflict resolution, and studied the effects of post-traumatic stress on victims of war. She recently moved to New York to take care of her ill grandmother, whom she lives with.

"Nikki. Can I tell you something?" She looks worried.

"Of course."

"I don't have any friends here and I feel like I can talk to you. Can you keep a secret?"

"Yes."

"Well. I had an affair with a priest."

"Whoa, are you serious? You had an affair with your priest?" I ask.

"Si, era una locura." She glances off into the distance.

I wish she would stop speaking Spanish. I have no idea what she just said. "But you know what? He showed his true colors after I slept with him." She finishes off her burger, as I move the vegetables around my plate.

"Like all men. He was no different because he was a priest. He was an asshole."

I let this sink in as we sit there in silence watching our waitress clear off the table. There is nothing left on Consuela's plate and mine is full of a sea of vegetables floating on a white plate. Consuela orders an apple pie with whip cream and a cappuccino.

"That's all I have to say about that. Está terminado."

"Nikki. Is there any way for me to make more money? You know temping doesn't pay much."

"Well we have a fixed budget for temp help, but why don't you wait a few weeks until you've been here a little longer and then talk to Chester about it. Maybe there will be some positions opening up in the future."

So begins my working friendship with Consuela. The work I often give her is administrative. In addition to researching venues for the Summit, I ask her to make travel arrangements for Chester, type up his letters and emails, and maintain the filing. Our lunches become routine and every now and then Weston joins us. One day, Weston comes into my office and closes the door.

"I need to talk to you." He throws himself on the chair. "Look. I've been wondering if I should say something to you about CROW."

"What the hell are you talking about? Who or what is CROW?"

"Oh. I didn't tell you." He rolls his eyes. "That's my nickname for

71

Consuela."

He has my full attention but I don't respond.

He fidgets around in the chair and can't seem to make eye contact. "I don't know how to say this except to just say it."

"You're making me nervous. Will you just spit it out for God's sake," I say.

"There'ssomethingaboutConsuelathatIdon'tlike," he spews out.

"Ok?" I don't really know how to respond to him.

Weston lets out a deep sigh, "there, I said it. He throws his hands up in the air.

"Do you want to be more specific?" I ask.

"You're not mad at me?"

"No. I think she's nice. If you don't like her, that's your business."

He sits upright, "well, have you seen the way she dresses?"

"Yea. I admit she dresses a bit provocative. So what? I don't think it's a big deal."

"It's not just her clothes." He's almost shouting at me. "It's the way she flaunts herself around here."

"You think she flaunts herself?"

"Hello? Are you telling me you haven't noticed?"

I give him a blank stare.

"The other day, we had a program conference call and Chester asked her to join the meeting to take some notes."

"Yes, I'm aware of that. I couldn't attend because I'm working on the Summit." I cut my eyes and cross my arms.

"Don't give me that attitude. You weren't there. She kept finding excuses to get up and reach across the conference table, hike her ass up in the air with her short little skirt and lean on the table so her boobs were hanging out all over the place."

"How do you know she was doing it on purpose?"

"Because she was!" He yells. "She did it like four times. Once for a pen, then for a notepad, then to increase the sound on the phone, then to pass something to Chester."

"Ok, you need to calm down," I say. "And what's up with calling her CROW?"

"She went from wearing no makeup to a weird matte color that makes her skin glow orange and highlights her massive crow's feet. So, **C**onsuela **R**oberta **O**lalla **W**ilfredo is now CROW."

"That's sort of mean, don't you think?"

"Yes, but I don't care."

"She told me that the reason she didn't wear makeup is because her boyfriend didn't let her. She apparently was madly in love with her Argentinean boyfriend. They were together for ten years and he left her to become engaged to a blond American women."

"What does that have to do with her orange makeup?" He gives me an evil look.

"He was controlling. So now she's just trying to find herself. I think that's why the experimentation with clothes and makeup."

"And what's up with her walking around speaking Spanish and quoting Latin artists and shit?"

Consuela loves Pablo Neruda, Chilean author; Carlos Castaneda, Peruvian author; Frida Kahlo, Mexican artist; Simón Bolivar, Venezuelan Statesman, Writer, and Revolutionary General; Evita Peron, Argentinean president; Salma Hayek, Mexican actor; Gloria Estefan, Cuban Musician – well you get my point – all things Latin and Latina.

"I guess she's proud of her heritage," I say.

"She's not the only Spanish person in this office. There are three other people that come from a Latin background and are fluent in Spanish. She acts like she's special."

"You're right about that."

He gets up and opens the door to leave. "Just watch your back with you-know-who." He gestures with his thumb towards Consuela's empty cubicle as he walks out the door.

Weston has a point about Consuela's skimpy outfits and Latin obsession. She may be experimenting, but it's not professional behavior. As her supervisor, I wonder if I should say something to her. But what? I wouldn't even know where to start. I need to get back to work, but decide that I will think about how best to handle the situation.

I pick up the stack of letters that need Chester's signature. As I walk down the corridor, I hear loud giggles and laughter from the direction of his office. I don't recall him having a meeting. Maybe he's in with a staff member. As I reach the door, the scene before me unfolding in slow motion dumbfounds me. Chester has his chair pushed back and Consuela is practically sitting on his lap. She is leaning over his desk and has her rear end in his face. Her black mini skirt is so short that the bottom of her ass is hanging out. She has a low cut V-neck top on and her big boobs are resting on his desk.

Chester has a Cheshire grin on his face. I clear my throat.

"Oh, Nikki. I didn't see you there." He sits upright and stops recklessly eyeballing Consuela's ass.

"I have some letters that need your signature."

"Ahh...ok. You can just put them on my desk."

I walk over expressionless and set the papers down.

"Consuela was good enough to help me with my computer," he says to me impishly.

I give him a closed lip smile and shake my head. "I can see that."

"She is very good with computers."

Consuela, still bent over, turns her head around, tosses her hair to one side, looks at Chester and says, "El Placer fue todo mio (the pleasure was all mine) …Hee..hee…hee…hee."

Never mind that Chester doesn't speak Spanish. I decide to avoid Consuela as much as I can over the next few days. I communicate with her mostly through email. This situation is beyond me and unfortunately there isn't anyone in the office to give me advice on how to handle it. And then one day, I receive an surprising email from her.

Nikki - Can you please reserve a car for Chester and I for 11 am Wednesday to take us to Chandler-Hill. I would like the car to wait for us during our meeting, then bring us back to the office.
Muchos Gracias -- Consuela

I respond.

Consuela - I am aware of Chester's meeting with Chas Chandler and have already reserved a car for the meeting. It is a sedan. So, there will be plenty of room for you. Also, just so you know, this is standard practice for all of his meetings. But thank you for the reminder -- Nikki

Her Response.

Nikki – be sure the car is for ME and Chester.
Aprecio su fuerte empeno - Consuela

I go to Google Translator, copy and paste her words and click on translate

- *"I appreciate your hard work."*

My fantasy response to her, thanks to Google translator.

Eres una perra (aka Bitch)

Instead of responding to her last email, I approach Chester regarding Consuela's change of attitude and behavior.

"I received an email from Consuela asking me to book a car for the both of you for a meeting with Chas Chandler?"

"Ahh, yes. I'm glad she took the initiative to do that."

"Well, I wasn't aware that you and Consuela were going to the meeting, and also, as the Director of Communications, shouldn't I attend the meeting?"

"Oh, I'm sorry. You've just been so busy with the Summit that I asked Consuela." He takes a long pause. "Well Nikki, you know, she's just so bright and the administrative work is beneath her."

"What do you mean beneath her?" I am still standing and take a step closer to him wanting to pounce on him.

"I mean that she is overqualified for the administrative work and is a little bit bored with it."

I want to scream but she's a temp here to do administrative work and help me with the Summit.

"She was curious to meet Chas Chandler, so I invited her along, but don't worry, I'll have her back soon so she can help you."

"Ummm...ok. Well, do you need me to come along?"

"No. You have your hands full here, and besides, three's a crowd."

"Ok." I walk out of his office not quite sure what to make of the situation, and wonder why I am so upset by this whole exchange.

Soon after, Consuela begins to ignore me and go directly into Chester's office and close the door behind her with a loud thud. I would often overhear both of them giggling together, "heeee…..heeee…..heeee."

***

CHAPTER 11

Over the past few weeks, I've worked closely with Wish and his Foundation to plan the Summit. Most of our meetings are over the telephone, but when they are in person, I take a little extra time to put myself together to appear professional, mature, and did I mention attractive. I normally don't wear much make up, just a little bit of Nars Casino Bronzing powder strategically placed on my face, and a single stroke of brown eyeliner, but anytime I have a meeting with Wish, I get heavy handed with my makeup. The subtle brown eyeliner turns to black. I even go as far as applying a smoky charcoal eye shadow to highlight my hazel eyes. My lips turn a reddish pink, and I use my recently discovered lotion, vanilla chai, to add a light whiff of sexy. I usually am too lazy to do anything with my hair except wear it in a ponytail or leave it a loose mess, but for the Wish meetings, I run some Infusium 23 Leave in Treatment through my hair and then to control the frizz, some BioSilk Therapy drops. This stuff is liquid gold and leaves my savage hair feeling soft with loose waves and smelling absolutely yummy.

When we meet as a group, Wish is always professional and focused on the business at hand, but when we're alone, the conversation, at some point, always turns personal. At one of our solo lunch meetings, he becomes pensive and the conversation drifts to him and his life.

"You know, one day I would love to have kids, although I wonder about the amount of responsibility." He is furrowing his eyes and I can see the small creases beginning to form around them.

"Kids are a lot of work." I smile. "Trust me I know."

"You don't have kids, do you?"

"God no." I throw my hands up in the air. "I've just raised enough of them in my life to know the amount of work it takes."

"It is work." He shakes his head in agreement. "But I'm also responsible for a lot of people. I have one hundred people on my payroll, and I can't imagine the added responsibility of a child."

We are sitting in a semi-circular booth at the Capital Grill situated beside the Chrysler building. The walls and ceilings are made up of slanted glass held up by large beams of steel, jetting in different directions. All around us are men dressed in ritzy suits with expensive ties and shiny cufflinks. Their hair perfectly cemented with gel, as they dig into their thick slices of steak. The few women present look like super businesswomen that just stepped out of the cover of Fortune Magazine.

I put my arms on the table and lean in to give him more of my attention. My knee touches his.

He continues, "So many people count on me. I have to come up with their salaries every two weeks and I feel that pressure." He leans in towards me. His face is about a foot away from mine. I feel my heart thumping against my chest like one of those cartoons. I want to say something, anything, but the loud beating of my heart makes it difficult to think. He looks down and rubs his wedding ring. "I feel the pressure."
Ok, maybe if I focus on my breathing, I can think of something to say.

"Is there anything you can do to take care of yourself...Are you doing anything?"

"No. Not really?" He looks at me with deep coffee colored eyes that just make me want to drink him up. "I'm so busy, I can't keep up with myself."

"How can you take care of others, if you are not well or low on energy?"

"You have a good point," he responds and smiles at me. I lean back, wondering if all this bright light is highlighting my large pores.

"Go treat yourself to a massage, or just turn off your cell phone, and computer for a day. You know, take time for you."

He looks at me with a smile that feels like it lasts an hour.

"What? Why are you looking at me like that?" I ask.

He is still smiling, "I'm smiling because….spending time with you, talking to you, energizes me." He places his hand over mine.

I feel my whole body heat up, from the tip of my fingers to the top of my head to my cold-ass feet.

"I like talking to you too." I smile back.

"I mean it. Even if we're talking about the Summit, I enjoy being around you."

"Thanks." I feel his wedding ring and pull my hand away and flip my bouncy wavy good smelling hair back.

"You are meek on the outside, but on the inside, you're extremely smart and wise."

Meek? Meek like a mouse? Who wants to be described as meek? I get a vision of myself with my head on a little white mouse body sniffing around the office with pulled back ears and moving my whiskers from side to side.

He keeps jabbering away, while I'm still fixated on the meek mouse image.

"Having to go through what you have builds character. You should believe in yourself more."

While I know I have a few insecurities, his ability to see them and be so direct with me, makes me uncomfortable, like I'm bad for feeling bad about myself. Go figure that one out.

"Well, everyone didn't have the loving mother that you did," I sit back and snap at him without meaning to.

"Nikki, I'm not judging you." His voice is calm.

"I'm simply saying that you've got a lot going for you. Hold your head up high."

"Ok. Thanks for letting me know." I want to get away from here right away. "I'm not as insecure as you give me credit for being." I reach for my coat.

"I'm sorry if I offended you."

"You didn't offend me. I don't get offended that easily." I shimmy out of the booth. "It's ok. Look, I need to get back to the office." I stand up and put on my coat.

Wish looks confused at the quick turn of events.
I give him a big cheesy smile. "I'll send over my notes from the meeting to you later today."

I pick up my note pad, and quickly shake his hand before he even has a chance to get out of the booth. "So, we'll chat soon." I turn around as composed and as classy as the super businesswomen and strut out of the restaurant as fast as I can. The freezing New York City weather hits me in the face like a hard slap.

"Nikki? Wait." Holy crap! He's come out running after me.
I turn around to face him. It's so cold that I can see his breath as he exhales out each word.

"Can I give you a hug goodbye?" He asks.

"Uhhh…sure, I guess," I say.

He puts his arms around me and pulls me to him. I wrap my arms around his shoulders, maintain upper and lower body distance and pat him on the back. I pull away, but he doesn't let go. He pulls all of me into him and squeezes harder. I can feel the bulk of his chest through his wool coat and suit, and his body warms me all over. I rewrap my arms around his shoulders and let him hold me for one one thousand, two one thousand, three one thousand, four one thousand. He squeezes me harder. Five one thousand, six one thousand, seven…"

"I can't breathe," I manage to wheeze out.

"Oh, sorry." He laughs and releases me from his death grip.

We hold each other's gaze for an awkward moment.

I rear back, brush my hair off my face, and say, "Ok. It's cold out. I better go," and turn around and make a mad dash towards the direction leading away from my office.

***

CHAPTER 12

Now that Zuni lives with us, I see a side of Peter I never have seen before. And let me tell you, dating a dad is definitely not sexy, at least not for me. I know there are women out there who wouldn't mind dating a man with kids, but I am not one of them. Our life is completely different now. Hanging out on some weekends with Zuni was do-able, but having her day in, day out, twenty-four hours, seven days a week, every second and nanosecond is a whole other story.

Overnight, Peter and I transform from a young, happening couple who enjoy all the great things New York City offers, from art movies and documentaries, Broadway plays and various gallery shows, to a ripened, passionless, placid, and humdrum old couple. We stay home every night in a monotonous routine. Every day Peter calls me at work to ask me what I want for dinner, and proceeds to read me his menu for the evening. While I think this gesture is sweet and considerate, it also drives me insane. He usually calls mid-afternoon around two-ish, just like clockwork, and we repeat the same conversation and corresponding emotions. It's like a bad version of Groundhog Day. Our typical conversation goes something like this.

"Hey love, what time are you coming home?" Peter asks.

"I'm not sure. I'm having a busy day," I reply.

"Just wondering when to have dinner ready?"

"Ok. I'll be home around six or seven."

"Can you be more specific?"

"I'll be home at seven," I answer through gritted teeth.

Peter continues to throw out the relevant and important questions.

"Do you prefer broccoli or green beans?"

"I don't care, Peter. Whatever you and Zuni like?"

"Ok. I'll make some broccoli. Do you care if it's steamed or sautéed?"

I wish someone would put me out of my misery.

"No I don't. Like I said…whatever you like."

We have dinner together as a family every night, and try to engage a crabby teenager in conversation. Peter wants to know everything about Zuni's day, such as who her friends are and what they are up to, what she's learned in school that particular day, and if she's done her homework.

While I logically understand these are the things that make one a parent, the reality of dealing with this type of life on a daily basis is difficult for me and it's not what I signed up for. I even find myself feeling a little jealous of Zuni for all of the time that Peter commits to her and her feelings. I beat myself up on a regular basis for my feelings of jealousy and try my best to hide it from Peter. I am the adult here and I shouldn't feel jealous of a kid, right? If Peter gets a whiff of that, he would totally flip out on me and think that I am an immature brat.

My other issue is that I don't like the fact that he uses the same term of endearment for the both of us. Since Zuni has moved in, he has started calling us by the same nickname, 'baby cakes.' I'm sure something Freudian is going on there and I find the whole thing weird. I find myself slowly wafting by the wayside, and my mind wandering to Wish more and more.

One evening as I get home, I find Zuni on the couch with two of her friends screaming into the television, which by the way, Peter bought against my advice, to appease her. Peter does his best to engage me and keep me involved by talking to me about his concerns about Zuni, but then dismisses my ideas or suggestions, not necessarily by saying anything, but by doing whatever he had decided to do before he asked me for advice. When it comes to Zuni, Peter's made it obvious that he is the parent and that he knows best. After all, Zuni is his kid, not mine.

My apartment reeks of musty teenage funk. As teenage girls, I would think they would care about being clean, but Zuni has gotten herself into some weird group at her new school and by the assault on my nose, I can tell that a few of those kids do not shower on a regular basis. Their black Skechers and Converse shoes are strewn all over the living room, coats are thrown over the couch and on the dining room chairs. Empty cups of some red sticky juice are littered on the dining room table, and dirty plates fill up the sink.

"Hi everyone." I smile through gritted teeth, reminding myself that they are only kids, and that if I don't stop gritting my teeth I am going to damage them.

Without looking in my direction, they all reply in unison, "Hi."

I am too upset to even care what they're watching, so I walk into the bedroom to calm myself. I hear Peter in the adjoining bathroom taking a shower. Ok, I will let him handle this. I am not in a position or mood to say anything to Zuni and posse.

I push all the square, rectangle, and round decorative pillows onto a cream and tan pile on the floor, and throw myself face down on the bed. I can smell the lavender laundry detergent on our freshly washed taupe duvet cover. I am too exhausted to take off my coat and shoes. I simply lie there, smelling the sheets and wondering what my life has come to? Growing up we were three kids with both of our parents working two jobs, and barely at home. As the oldest, it fell upon me to be the surrogate mother to my siblings. From the ages of ten to seventeen, I raised my siblings and myself. Now it was supposed to be time for me to live my life on my own terms. And yet here I am again, feeling like I am living a life that someone else has chosen for me against my own will.

Peter's voice jolts me out of my thoughts.

"Hi baby cakes."

I let out a deep moan and slowly roll over, and lie spread eagle on the bed

"I didn't know you were home," says Peter, "but, I'm happy to see you."

He stands before me with a white towel around his waist. His body is muscular but lean and more on the skinny side. I watch the beads of water roll off his shoulders, and somehow find myself underwhelmed at the site of his naked body.

"I guess it would be hard to hear anything over the girls screaming," I say as I take my gaze to the ceiling.

"Zuni asked if she could have some friends over to watch some reality show on MTV. I thought it would be good for her. You don't mind do you?" I remain silent and study the cottage cheese white paint finish on the ceiling. "Well, this is not just your home Nikki," Peter says.

I always hated that cheap look. It looks like somebody vomited white paint on the ceiling.

"It's Zuni's home too," Peter trails off as he heads back into the bathroom to finish drying off.

I guess there is nothing I can say to that. My home, my oasis is no longer my own. I am even careful of how I walk around. No longer can I be naked or simply just wear a t-shirt.

I continue to lie motionless looking around our bedroom. The bedroom is decorated sparsely with white walls and with a dark wood framed 16x36 print of Klimt's Tree of Life. We have an imitation mahogany dresser from IKEA that Peter bought when I moved in to accommodate my clothes. There are some photos of both of our families in silver and wooden frames on the dresser. A black and white photo of Peter and Zuni with Peter's parents stands out. They seem so happy standing arm in arm with Zuni strategically placed in the front, like a happy German family that stepped out of a shampoo commercial. Their hair bouncy and their bright white smiles match their white clothes.

Peter sticks his head out of the bathroom. "Hey, I need to talk to you."

I really don't feel like having a conversation at this moment in time, "what's up?" I reply as I continue lying plopped on the bed, arms outstretched noticing the wooden frame that holds a picture of my mom and dad standing like two wooden figures out of American Gothic by Grant Wood. They are looking into the camera with fake smiles and big eyes.

"Have you noticed anything funny about Zuni?"

"I can think of a few things." I let out a laugh, thinking that maybe I should put up a picture of my two sisters and brother.

"I'm serious. Have you noticed that she's been eating a lot more lately?"

Have I ever? The kid eats like she's got a tapeworm. Our grocery bill went from $200-$300 a month to $200-$300 a week. Peter wants to expand Zuni's taste buds and buys nothing but the best for his kid, and of course, all organic. Needless to say mac and cheese is not on our menu. Her favorite foods now are – lamb chops with fresh mint chutney, braised fingerling potatoes, wild pacific caught salmon, duck l'orange, and organic Knudson's Pomegranate juice.

To teach her responsibility and accountability, Zuni has to keep her room clean, and wash the dinner dishes, which consists of three forks, three plates, and three glasses. Her response to all this work, "I feel like Cinderella."

I don't think Cinderella ever ate duck l'orange.

Peter comes out of the bathroom and stands over me. His face is twisted and he is clearly upset. "Earlier today, when I was doing laundry, I found a condom and the remnants of a smoked joint in Zuni's jeans pocket."

I'm surprised that she could fit anything in those tight sprayed on jeans. I sit upright. "Are you serious?"

"Yes. Unfortunately." He snatches a pair of boxers from the dresser and hurriedly puts them on. He rummages in the closet and comes back with a white t-shirt and a pair of black sweats.

"I want us to talk to her during dinner."

That's not exactly how I want to spend my evening. "Do we have to do it tonight?"

He pulls the t-shirt over his head and shoots me a surprised look.

"Together, I mean...maybe you should talk to her privately." He jams his legs into the jogging pants.

I continue, "You know...she may be embarrassed."

"No. I want you there. It's important to have a woman's perspective."

Crap!

I push myself off the bed and let out a big sigh. Begrudgingly, I take off my coat and shoes, and head into the bathroom to change into something comfortable.

"I don't really feel like cooking tonight," he yells after me.

"Ok. Well, why don't you send her friend's home and I'll order some Thai." Even though I don't want to deal with this situation, I feel the need to help Peter, and maybe this could be a way I can connect with Zuni.

"Ok. Thank you." Peter runs over to me in the bathroom and gives my naked body a flash hug, one that doesn't even last two seconds, and definitely very different than Wish's hugs. "I appreciate it," he says and rushes to the living room.

Compared to Peter's cooking, the Thai food tastes like hot and spicy cardboard. As we pick through the food, trying to salvage something edible, Peter begins his inquisition of Zuni.

"Zuni, is there anything you'd like to talk to us about?" Peter says.

"No Dad. You know everything about my friends and school." She rolls her eyes at him. "And you forgot to call me Z, remember?" She goes back to eating.

Peter is silent. His jaw is locked and his eyes fixed on Zuni. He puts his fork on his plate, slowly reaches for his glass and takes a sip of his pomegranate juice. Returns the glass to the table, then pushes everything away. He leans on to the table with his elbows.

"I found a joint and a condom in your jeans today." His voice thunders.

Zuni freezes mid motion, as if someone paused the DVD player. She blankly stares at Peter, her mouth pursed with half of her rice noodles in her mouth and the other half hanging out onto the plate. She takes her gaze off of Peter and looks at her food. She bites off the rest of the noodles and slowly chews and swallows. She challenges Peter by directly looking at him.

"Why are you going through my shit?" She slams down her fork. This child clearly thinks she has been wronged.

"Well, first of all, I was not going through your shit. I was doing laundry." Peter is waving his finger at Zuni. "Second of all, watch your tone and language with me." He has no patience in his voice. "And thirdly, you don't own anything in this home."

Zuni is glaring at Peter.

"Don't give me that dirty look like I'm the one in the wrong." Peter's voice is straining.

I've never seen him like this. I reach over and touch Peter on the arm. "Look, I know this is upsetting, but try to calm down," I say.
He pulls his arm away and ignores what I said.

"You are carrying around pot. You could get arrested. What the hell are you thinking? And who are you having sex with?"

"Dad. Don't hassle the Hoff, OK. It's not a big deal."

"Don't hassle the who?" Peter contorts his face. "What are you saying?"

Zuni lets out a roaring laugh to the shocked face of Peter. "Look Dad. Like, I'll tell you the truth…"

"I would appreciate that," Peter responds.

Zuni continues, "I like smoked some weed last week after school, and I sort of like fooled around with a boy too."

By now, we all have stopped eating. I shoot Peter a worried look of bewilderment.

"Look Zuni, I'm glad you feel comfortable enough to admit that to us," says Peter, his voice calmer.

"But you don't think that smoking pot and fooling around with a boy is a big deal?"

"Chill, Dad. I didn't like smoking weed. It was like my first time. It was gross. Everyone was like passing it around and putting their nasty lips on it. I was like last, so I got everyone's spit, and lip-gloss marks. I had to like wipe it down first." She gestures wiping off the joint. "Like don't worry. I'm not going to do it again. I was just like trying it."

"And why were you carrying the joint around with you?"

"Well, my friend Jenny didn't want to take it home. So she asked me to take it."

"And why didn't she want to take it home?"

"Cause her mom like goes through her stuff and if she found it, she would be in a lot of trouble."

"So you volunteer to carry it?"

"I didn't like volunteer. It just, I don't know, sort of like happened."

"Ok. In the future I want you to think about consequences. If something were to happen, you would be the one to get in trouble for carrying around pot. Do you understand me? Jenny would be running around free and you will get arrested and go to jail for drug possession."

Zuni is silent. Her face collapses as this sinks in.

"Do you understand?" Peter says.

Zuni shakes her head in the affirmative.

At this point, I wonder if maybe I should jump in the conversation. "And who is this boy you are fooling around with?" I ask.

"Mind your own fucking business, Nikki," she snaps with a head roll.

I rear back in shock at the force of her response to me, and look to Peter for guidance.

"Please don't speak to Nikki like that," says Peter.

Zuni crosses her arms in defiance as Peter continues, "Nikki is an adult in this house."

Funny. Sometimes I don't feel like one.

"And if I'm not around, she's responsible for your welfare."

"Well, like she's not my mom and I don't have to answer to her."

I give Peter an uncomfortable look of raised eyebrows and a closed half smile. True I am not her mom, but from what Peter told me, Zuni was speaking just as disrespectfully to her.

"Well, that's something we can talk about later. I want to stay on the subject."

"That's cool by me," retorts Zuni.

"So, who is the boy that you fooled around with?" Peter asks.

"David. He's like hot and he's a senior." I guess she gets a picture of him in her head because a smile spreads across her face.

"Where did you fool around?"

"In the school bathroom," replies Zuni.

I guess nothing says true love like fooling around in the school bathroom.

"Is he your boyfriend?"

"No…I guess." Zuni pushes her plate away and drops her head on the table in frustration. "I don't know what we are…we just sort of fooled around. Ok?"

"Have you had sex yet?"

Zuni's head is still on the table and she mumbles something.

"I can't understand you."

She lifts her head up and rests her chin on her hands. "Not yet."

"No? Not yet? What have you done then?"

Peter is relentless and keeps peppering the poor girl with questions. He should have been a detective instead of a chef.

Zuni sits upright, begins fidgeting in her chair and turns red.

"We just like fooled around? You know, like felt… each other, but we didn't have sex. I got a condom from Jenny…just in case, but it's not a big deal."

"I'm not sure I like Jenny too much," I chime in. Peter shoots me an uncomfortable look.

"Shut up! No one asked for your opinion," Zuni screams at me and slams her hands on the table.

That's enough to silence me for good and let Peter handle this awkward situation. I'm just trying to help him. Why should I care who she fools around with?

"Zuni. Calm down. Nikki cares about you and is trying to help." Peter has switched to robot mode. He does not radiate any emotion. Zuni falls silent.

He continues, "If he's your boyfriend, I'd like to meet him."

"No," Zuni shouts. "No, I don't want that."

"Why not?"

Zuni stares at the ground.

I decide to make one last attempt here. "Are you afraid we'll embarrass you?" I reach over and touch her arm.

She pulls away, completely ignores me and looks at Peter, "I just don't think it's like that big of a deal. It's not like I'm having sex. When I like do it with a boy, then you can meet him."

Peter lets out a loud laugh.

"So, whenever we finally meet one of your boyfriends, I'll know you're having sex?"

"Yup. Basically. A boy should be honored to have sex with me. That's when I'll introduce him to you."

"Is that right?" Peter responds.

"Yup. I'm a good catch."

"Well Zuni, It's good that you have a healthy self-esteem. But this is something we need to talk about. Sex is a serious thing and there are a lot of repercussions."

"Do you know how to use a condom?" I ask in a soft voice.

"Ok. This conversation is getting like totally weird," she retorts. She turns around and looks at me directly with her penetrating eyes. "Nikki, like shut up. I don't want to talk to you of all people, like about sex. This is a conversation between A and B." She points to herself and Peter. "Why don't you like C your way out of it."

All of a sudden I feel the heat in my chest. I clench my jaw and swallow hard. I want to strangle this little bitch.

"Ok. I'll mind my own business," I say. Why am I letting her get to me?

"Good, because that's so nasty. I don't want to talk about condoms with you Nikki. I mean like it's nothing personal. I'm just saying like...You. Are. Not. My. Mom."

Peter jumps in, "Well it's important we have this conversation. If you get pregnant, you are on your own. I'm not taking care of you and a baby."

"Geez. I'm not getting pregnant. I'm not even having sex yet." Zuni is getting whiny and exasperated. "Besides, it's not like anybody's fucking business what I do with my body."

As she says this, Zuni slams her chair back and stomps to her room, slamming the door behind her.

"That didn't go too well." I try to make light of the situation as I lift my fork and begin moving around the food on my plate.

"No...duh...Thanks for the analysis Einstein." Peter stares at me combatively.

"Sorry...ummm...I was just...." I shake my head. "Never mind...sorry." I respond.

He lets out a heavy sigh, "I'm sorry too." Peter reaches for my hand. "What should we do?"

"Let's finish dinner, and give her time to cool off," I say.

"Ok."

"Then you have to go talk to her over the next few days."

This is the first time Peter has taken my advice about Zuni. So, even though I wish he had defended me when she snapped at me, I don't dare bring it up.

Of course all this parenting and stress kills Peter's sex drive. He is tired and cranky most of the time. I am just cranky! I decide to approach the topic as we go to bed. I wear my black silk and lace teddy with the plunging neckline and a high slit. If this won't get him in the mood, nothing will. As I come out of the bathroom all dolled up, I see that Peter is already cozy in bed reading his latest issues of Bon Appétit. He doesn't glance my way, so I decide to get in bed and snuggle up to him. I pull his magazine away and kiss his neck.

He yanks his head and neck away from me and pulls the magazine back up.

"I'm sorry, I'm not in the mood." And still no glance my way.

What the hell is wrong with him? He has a semi-naked woman in bed with him, and he's not in the mood? I take a deep breath in.

"OK….sweetie, I know being a full time parent is hard. I'm having a difficult time too, but it's killing our sex life."

He puts the magazine down, "Zuni doesn't want to really be here."

That's not the answer I was hoping for.

"I have to spend more time with her….you know?" He looks at me with deep consternation. "Maybe do things after school." He smiles to himself thinking that he's found the solution to all of our problems. "Or maybe we can do something as a family once a week. Like bowling or a movie."

He is obviously not hearing me. I'm cringing inside.

"Well, we can talk about that later," I respond. The kid conversation is a total mood killer, but a girl's got needs, so I try to kiss Peter.

"Sweetie, I said, I'm not in the mood. You look great, but I'm exhausted." He pushes me away.

"What do you mean you're not in the mood? You're a guy, you're supposed to always be in the mood."

He gives me a dirty look and turns over.

I soften my voice and try to have him turn towards me. "You don't have to do anything. Just let me get you in the mood. I'll do all the work."

He's like a log and doesn't budge. His back is still to me. "Not tonight. Goodnight sweetie."

Goodnight my ass – well, maybe not such a good night for my ass.

"I'm going to read a book."

I walk out into our small living room and plunk myself on the couch. I am so tired, drained of energy, and not to mention, horny that I can't sleep. It actually feels good to be alone in the quiet room. I don't have any mental space here, and there is definitely not enough space for three people. Peter's living room has a dark contemporary feel. I look around the small two hundred fifty square feet living room that is filled up with a dark brown ultra-suede sectional couch, a small butcher block type coffee table with a frosted glass top that Peter had custom made sits on top of an antique burgundy Persian rug with a sapphire blue border. The cozy rug is my favorite piece. There is a small flat screen TV and stand, and a bookshelf full of books and framed pictures of Zuni as a baby, Zuni as a toddler, Zuni at her first day of school, and Zuni as an angelic pre-teen.

The rest of the pictures are of Peter and I at the various stages of our relationship. Even though I pay half the rent now, when I moved in, Peter had already decorated his apartment in his own manly way, and I didn't really mind it. But to make it feel more like my home, he littered the living room with some pictures of us. The picture that most stands out is the silver framed picture of us on the Coney Island boardwalk posing with big smiles and laughter with two very colorful performing artists on stilts. We looked happy then.

I am brought out of my coma by a single beep from my phone, indicating that I have a new text. It's 11:30 pm. I wonder who would text me at this hour?

Hi You. Thinking of you. Are you awake? This is Wish.

My heart just stopped beating. I hold the phone tightly in my hand and stare at his text until my screen goes black. I push the message pad. Watch the screen light up again. I reread his text and stare at it again, wondering what I should do. I respond:

Hi There. I am awake. Why?

I sit there for what feels like long painful hours wondering if he will respond and if he does respond what will he say? I get a beep.

I know it's late in NYC. I'm in Zanzibar. Speaking at a conference later today. Thinking of you and wanted to chat. Can I call?

Zanzibar. I didn't even know that was a real place. Can he call? Can he call? There is no way I can have a conversation without waking up Peter.

Zanzibar is amazing. Not a good idea to call this late. But, can text. What are you thinking about?

I stare at the phone waiting for his response.

Early morning here. Lying in bed looking at the amazing sunrise on the ocean. Wish you were here. Look at this beautiful picture.

Attached to his text is a picture of a beautiful ball of light surrounded by hues of amber and carnelian across a dark lapis blue sky and ocean. It's absolutely breathtaking.

Wow. You should've been a photographer. I'd like to be there instead of here. It's freezing. Look at the Hudson.

I attach a gray and depressing snap of the Hudson river with mini icebergs floating all over. Another beep.

Not a day has gone by that I haven't thought of you. I miss you.

Hmmmm…

I've thought of you too, a lot.

No…I erase my message…

I've missed you, occasionally.

I erase and try again.

I think of you all the time!

Definitely NOT…

I like talking to you.

That was lame, but I hit send and then quickly send a follow up text before he responds.

It's late. Gotta go to bed. Good luck with your speech and enjoy Zanzibar.

Mental note to self - Google Zanzibar at work tomorrow.

Sweet dreams. Think of me. I'll be thinking of you.

"What are you doing?" I hear Zuni's accusatory voice behind me. I jump up out of the chair to face her, my phone still in my hand.

"Excuse me? Shouldn't you be sleeping?" Nothing like a good offense.

She rubs her eyes, "I had to use the bathroom." She looks at me funny.

"Who are you texting this late at night?"

The little nosy sneak. "Oh, a friend of mine. You should go to bed," I say. We both stand there like two cowboys staring at each other, ready to draw out our guns. I decide that this is stupid and walk towards my bedroom.

"I'm going to bed. Goodnight."

"You're weird," she says behind me.

I turn around to face her. She gives me a smile and walks to her room. I wonder if Peter would agree to have her wear sunglasses inside the house. Her ghoulish eyes creep me out.

I decide to go to bed and spoon with Peter.

***

CHAPTER 13

It's Monday morning...I'm already wishing it were Friday. I walk into Chester's immaculately furnished sunlit office to go over our week to come. Chester sits glassy-eyed in his large mahogany partners desk as I clear the thicket of papers strewn all over his desk to make room for my writing pad. His desk is always a mess. Piles of papers yearning to be free are the norm. I know how they feel. He creates the dumpster on his desk to give us, the impression that he is working hard and is overwhelmed.

Chester expounds on all the work and maintenance involved for Chas Chandler V, and how careful I need to be in my treatment of him and his people for the upcoming Summit. I take down my notes meticulously and like a quickie, the meeting is over, but only in my mind. Chester is unstoppable, he drones on and on, babbling a never-ending string of yawn worthy phrases.

"Nikki, we need to carefully sail our ships into harbor with Chas Chandler."

"I think our past problems with Chas are water under the bridge."

All this talk of water makes me want to pee.

"There is good synergy between him and the Center."

"I want us to drill down on the issues."

"Let's create a matrix that outlines our connection."

Speak English for God's sake.

"His impression and opinion of how we conduct this Summit is important. Can you share with me your thoughts?"

No. I don't feel like sharing.

"Uhhh...I think you're right....sure. I also think that if Chas is impressed, he would help us get funding."

"Nikki. I didn't think of that," his eyes light up with excitement. "I always knew you were smart. I trust that you will pay attention to all details when it comes to Chas."

No Chester, you can't trust me to pay attention to any details. That is why you hired me.

My mind wanders back to the good old days with Peter. God, how quickly things can turn sour. Over the weekend, I played house with Peter and Zuni. Saturday we spent cleaning our apartment as a family, then went on a fun trip to the Union Square Farmers Market and Trader Joe's, where Peter tried to teach Zuni the fine art of conscious and healthy grocery shopping, and where the bill came out to $250 of which I paid half. Peter made sure to deduct an $6 toothbrush I bought for myself from his half.

That evening we cooked dinner together. Zuni cut the tomatoes for the salad. Peter poached the salmon and I set the table and poured out the infamous pomegranate juice. We topped it all off by watching The Sound of Music, one of Peter and Zuni's favorite movies.

Back in Chester's office, I hear him drone on and on. Mercifully, I lose eye contact with him and my gaze wanders to his oh-so impressive collection of books that he keeps to impress people. Even though he's a former English professor, I wonder if he has read any of the books or knows much about the authors and poets on his shelf.

And then it happens. I catch something out of the corner of my eye, something lying on the floor.
Oh no! My heart, races like it's running a marathon, and my throat is the finish line. I stare, panicked, at Chester. His mouth is moving. All I hear is, "blah, blah, blah, blah."

I wonder what should I do? Should I get up? Should I walk out? Should I say something?

In the meantime, Chester continues to flap his gums, "blah, blah, blah, blah."

A police siren sounds in the background.

Man, he sure loves to hear his own voice. I am going to do it. If I don't say anything, someone else will.

I take a deep breath and dig the nail of my index finger into my thumb to jolt myself out of my shock and calm my nerves. It's like my shot of Tequila. I raise my head slowly and make direct eye contact with Chester.

He continues, unabated, to blabber on and on, "It's important with Chas Chand--"

"There is a used condom on your office floor," I blurt out as I cut him off mid-sentence.

Chester is a deer caught in the headlights, a trapped bewildered animal with a paunch. I think he even stopped breathing for a few minutes. His eyes have morphed into big, wide orbs.

"Wha-a-a-at?" he manages to gasp.

"There is a used condom on the floor in your office," I sputter out. There is simply no poetic way to deliver that kind of information to one's boss.

Chester gets up from his chair and lumbers to the front of the desk.

"My lord," he gasps. "How did that get there?"

Can someone please poke out my eyes?

"I don't know," is all I can manage to whisper out from under my breath.

"The cleaning people must have dragged it in on their shoe," he says.

"Hmmm...Probably."

Chester shuffles around his desk, gingerly grabs a Kleenex and with a look of contrived revulsion, picks up the condom and disposes of the nasty.

Somebody shoot me now.

"That's disgusting," he says.

And Chester sure as shit knows his way around disgusting. There have been times in the past when I had to discreetly clean the ear wax build up from his phone headset or close his office door when he's been cutting his nails. But this, this is just too much. He has gone too far.

I stare at him without expression, and look back at my notebook. I want to forget about this incident, like now. I feel traumatized. I will forever have a visual seared into my brain. Yuck!

"Ok, where were we?" I ask oh-so-innocently and unfazed. We go over a few more clichéd sayings regarding Chas Chandler, and I get myself out of there as quickly as I can.

I always find used condoms so depressing. There they are after the fact, usually a clearish cream-colored piece of rubber with a drop of jism at the tip, either thrown haphazardly on the floor, in the toilet, or in the trash. So sad and pathetic that so much of life revolves around that dollop of love juice.

I walk into my office, close my door, plop myself into the hard chair I keep for guests and put my head into my hands to calm myself down. This is such a weird position to be in.

No pun intended.

My God, even if he can be the world's biggest buffoon at times, he is the CEO. I knew that he was a seventy-year-old lover boy, but never guessed that he would take it to this level in the office.

After about ten minutes of sitting there, I muster up the courage to open my door and try to attempt to get some work done. Just as I sit down at my computer, Chester walks by my office and disingenuously says, "Look Nikki," as he points to the floor in front of my office door.

Now what is this knucklehead up to?

I get up and walk around the chair towards my office door. I follow the direction of Chester's grubby little finger, pointing towards the floor, and there it is, a freshly unwrapped band-aid.

With utter disgust and disdain, Chester says, "Those cleaning people are really careless. Now there's a used band aid by your door."

I know what a used band-aid looks like and my rotund friend that sure ain't it.

"I am going to report them to the office manager, " I say.

"No, no, no, no. Don't do that, it's just too embarrassing," says Chester.

He picks up the band-aid and waddles into his office.

Why do I protect him? Why do I care so much?

I feel like I am in some weird version of Nikki in wonderland. Every day is a crazy day, either at home or in the office, and today is no exception. Thank God plans for the Summit are moving along well. It's going to be a full-day event with over five hundred attendees and twenty-five high profile speakers, from heads of major corporations and nonprofits, along with major media outlets.

I've been working unusually long hours. Generally, I'm in by eight in the morning and out at seven at night, and I've started to come in on a few Saturdays to make sure this show happens without a glitch. Needless to say, in addition to Zuni being with us, my job has put an additional strain on my relationship with Peter. But I don't mind it so much since it keeps me out of the house and away from the bratty kid and the father-knows-best Peter, who is still by the way, too tired to have sex with me.

It's 5:30 pm, and I've been pulled in so many different directions. Today I spent all day calling people, trying to confirm space, hotel for attendees, speakers, and all the minutia of planning such a high caliber event. Most of the speakers are CEO's and famous philanthropists, aka, super high maintenance people who come with two to four handlers, which means I tread that almost invisible tight rope between kissing ass and maintaining my own dignity, and am never really sure how I am doing. This has been the single most stressful thing I have ever worked on, and at this point, I've lost all of my initial excitement and passion. Like bad sex, I just want it to be over. And forget about getting help from Consuela.

The InCare PR people have been on my ass and driving me crazy. They want their one million dollar investment in the Summit to be their big debut into the world of ethical business and corporate social responsibility. Every major decision, like the panel, speakers, speech topics, and the whole visual look of the Summit has to be approved by InCare first. Whatever happens at the Summit, the end result and my job is to make InCare look good.

I am physically calm and give off the appearance of being cool and collected, but truth be told, my intestines are knotted up; my shoulders are harder than bricks; and I've been waking up at the witching hour of 4am the past week. This event can make or break my career, and there is still so much more work that needs to be done.

I close the door of my office and plop into my chair to open my email. There is a message from Bren.

The subject line reads, "URGENT/EMERGENCY", and there's the red exclamation mark, to show that it is super-duper uber important. In the cc box, I see that she has copied Chester, Henry, the Executive Vice President, and the four other department heads. My heart begins its slow jog. Anytime Bren cc's the whole world on an email to me, she's out to fry me. The email reads:

I don't mean to undermine your job as the Director of Communications,

Sure you do Bren. There is no need to lie. As I continue to read her email, my heart races faster and faster. It continues;

Nikki, in your monthly newsletter that you wrote and sent out yesterday, you called the GOLD foundation, GOLD corporation. You've made a big mistake and they will be very upset when they see this. This is a big problem!

I am starting to sweat profusely.

I know you have a lot going on now, with the Summit and all, but I don't care. This is urgent and needs to be quickly fixed. You need to re-write the whole newsletter for this month, acknowledge the mistake and resend it ASAP to the 10,000 names that were on the first list. And I don't understand why I don't see these things first. Answer me that!

I begin to shake out of fear and anger.

Don't you think there needs to be some process in place, so that you don't make these kind of mistakes anymore, especially now as the new Communications Director?!!!

My whole body starts to vibrate. My hands tremble. My thoughts race.

Did I make a mistake? I don't know. What can I do now? Should I say something to her? What should I say to her? Who the hell does she think she is anyway sending such a nasty email?

I try to calm myself, but can't stop my hands from shaking. I wish I could choke the shit out of her. Ok, Nikki, get a hold of yourself. Big breath in, slow breath out. Big breath in, slow breath out. Big breath in, slow breath out. Oh my God…I'm nauseous.

My stomach starts to churn. I feel myself getting queasy. And, voila! There it is. My lunch of chicken noodle soup is spread all over my desk in a goop of white indecipherable mess. There is vomit on my dress and on everything on my desk.

I rummage around my office and somewhere in the deep bowels of my desk drawer, under crumpled up shopping bags, I find a pair of pink yoga pants and a bunched up black t-shirt. I'm not sure if yoga pants and a t-shirt can pass off for work clothes but I guess it's better than walking around with puke all over myself. After cleaning up the yuck, changing, and salvaging some of the papers from my desk, I am still in terror of what will happen next.

This is what I get for trying to be perfect. Note to self: Trying to be perfect is boring and borderline insane. I need an intervention. I need someone to slap me into reality, and as much as Bren would love to be that person, I definitely don't mean her.

"Hey Wes, can you stop by for a sec. I need your help on something. Bren is at it again," I say in a hushed quivering tone on the phone.

"Again? Doesn't she ever get tired? I'm exhausted just hearing about it from you," he says.

"No. Being the devil reincarnated is like breathing for her. Just come here, will you?"

As he walks into my office, he is simultaneously shocked at my panic stricken face and aghast at the attack on his senses. He turns up his nose in disgust, "Eeewwww...what's that smell?"

"I puked all over myself," I say in embarrassment. I jump up and crack my window open and let in a gust of cold air.

"Bren sent me and the whole world another one of her nasty and accusatory emails, telling me how I fucked up." I ramble out the rest of my story in sequential order, down to the grossest detail.

"What an unholy shrew," he rolls his eyes. "You know what her problem is?"

"Please enlighten me because I've tried to figure that one out for a long time. She hates me and I don't know why," I whine with my best, exasperated victim look and voice.

"She needs a good stiff one," he declares with the utmost confidence, and gestures with his arm.

"What are you talking about? They don't come any manlier than her. She has more balls than you and Chester combined, and if it wasn't for her long hair, I'd think she was a football player. I mean, look at the way she lumbers around like she has horse gonads swinging between her legs."

"I'm telling you she wants a dick. Either she wants to be a man and have all of the privileges of being a man or she simply needs a really good hard dick."

"You are too much," I manage to say through my laughter. "I don't think it has anything to do with her sexuality. She is just an unhappy person."

"Well whatever it is, that unhappy person is making your life miserable," he says as he comes around my desk. "Move over." He shoos me away, and sits in my chair.

"Did you sanitize with Lysol?" He asks.

"I cleaned up."

"I don't know why Chester lets her get away with such horrendous behavior. Do you?"

"I guess because she is the fundraiser, and brings in the money," I say.

"Oh please...she's not that great of a fundraiser." He begins typing as I look over his shoulder. It reads,

Bren - You dirty old hag.

I understand your concern regarding the newsletter that went out and GOLD being referred to as a corporation and not a foundation. It's not a big deal, so chillax babe. And frankly, I am tired of your stank actions and your thinking that you're better than those around you.

We're both rolling hysterically. He continues,

Bren, on another note, I am truly concerned about you. If you're not careful with your obsessive anger, all of those manly breakfasts of bacon and hearty lunches of meatloaf, augmented by your a pack-a-day smoking addiction, you are going to give yourself a heart attack at the prime young age of forty five. And we all CERTAINLY want to be blessed with your loving and warm presence for as long as possible. You are our inspiration. By the way, what makes you think the CEO reads his own emails?

TTYN (Talk To You Never), Nikki

I love him.

"I think you should send this in response to her and to everyone in the world that she cc'd." He's insane.

"I wish I could," I lament with an impish smile on my face. "But you've made me feel better already. I will send her a nicer version of your response."

"Allll righty then," he furrows his eyebrows at me. "Well, I'm outta here. Don't work too late." He hugs me and leaves me to send the final email to the unholy shrew. I delete Weston's message and hit reply all, and begin typing.

Bren – I will talk to Chester to decide the best way to handle this. Rest assured there is a process in place for the newsletter. After I write the newsletter, Chester and Henry both read, edit, and approve it before it is blasted out to our email list.
-- best, Nikki.

So go fire your stink torpedo someplace else. I wish I could add the pizzazz and sharp tongue of Weston to my email, but I am either, (a) too scared of Bren and a big chicken (b) trying to be professional (c) don't want to sink to her level of bitchassness or (d) all of the above.

The need to be perfect has been conditioned into me all of my life. Mistakes have never been an option. Mistakes were never teaching moments, but more synonymous with punishment and being a failure. As a child, my mom usually compared me to some other little girl that in her opinion was prettier, smarter, thinner, or in some ways better than me.

By raising my siblings, I had to learn to do everything at a young age, cook, clean, laundry, my own homework, and make sure the kiddies did their homework. If one thing was out of place when mom came home, it would mean getting a verbal lashing. Needless to say, I always fell short.

And now here I was. At a job with a bully on my back constantly looking for me to make a mistake and if I didn't, she would make one up for me. I constantly take care of Chester. And let's not forget Peter. Mr. Peter Perfect and his little vampire angel. Disciplined, straight-laced Peter who thinks I'm fat. Sometimes I feel like I'm dating my mother.

More and more, I feel a strange tightness in my chest, like a habitual suffocating feeling, and constant knots in my stomach. I dread work, and I dread going home at night, and at times I walk the city streets window shopping and playing with make-up at Sephora. Sometimes by the time I get home, and after a little too much rouge here, a smidgen of red lipstick there, and a pinch of bronzer all over, I look like a clown with all the goopy colors on my face. I feel like I have become the husband who avoids going home to the wife and kids. On some nights, I even contemplate picking up some flowers for Peter out of guilt.

***

CHAPTER 14

The pressure of the Summit is on me full force, and I no longer have anyone to help me. Consuela, in fact, has become a major nuisance. She's like that one chin hair that you can feel, but have a hard time pulling out. Chester seems to be mute on the topic of Consuela anytime I've approached him about getting additional help. He simply brushes me off by saying that we will talk about it later. Then one mid-afternoon at the office I along with the whole staff of the Center receive an email announcement from Chester.

I am happy to announce that Consuela Roberta Olalla Wilfredo has gladly accepted the position of Director of Global Affairs. Consuela came to us as a temp and has quickly proven her talent and willingness to take on new positions, challenges and responsibilities. She has a Masters in conflict resolution and is fluent in Dutch and Spanish. Consuela will be responsible for expanding the Center's reach internationally. Consuela will be reporting directly to me. Please join me in congratulating her.

Director of what the fuck?

Chester then proceeds to move her out of the cubicle and give her the large empty office next to mine. After making a big raucous moving her few files and papers into her new office, Consuela breezes into my office, closes the door behind her, and makes herself comfortable. I continue to look at my computer.

"Hola, I need to chat with you," she says with a smug smile.

"I'm busy right now. Can it wait?" I give her a quick glance then look back at my computer.

"Look, I've been feeling a lot of aggression from you, and I don't need it. Comprende?"

I turn around to face her. As she sits in front of me in the guest chair with her ultra-short skirt, I can see her white granny Hanes underwear.

"What are you talking about?" Girlfriend, if you are going to do sexy, you need to do it all the way.

"I know you are used to getting all of Chester's attention and being his favorite and all, but things are changing, and you need to drop your attitude."

"You and I are not competing for anything." I am both disturbed and impressed by her audacity. "If you want to 'have' him, go ahead."

I can't even imagine what that means in her little disturbed world.

She leans in towards me, and her legs spread open even more. "Nikki, I'd like for us to be friends, you know, like we used to when I first got here."

I would like to tell her that we were never friends, but that would be mean and not true. In all honesty, I feel betrayed by Consuela, and have not handled the situation very well. For the most part, I have avoided her, which has been easy to do since she is no longer reporting to me.

"Sure, I'm sure we both can be professional," I respond.

That seems to appease her. "Cool. I'm glad we talked." She breezes out of my office as I watch her try to swing her nonexistent hips from side to side.

After Chester's email went out, Consuela's behavior completely changed. Working hours were nine to five, but for Consuela, it was a free for all. She would arrive at the office past 10 am, and sometimes she would even waltz in at 11. She would then disappear for a two-hour lunch and leave at 4:30. She did not even try to be discreet about her hours, but flaunted it by making a big production when she arrived by yelling out, "Buenos dias, everyone." Never mind that the majority of the staff at the Center did not speak Spanish. This became her routine, and of course did not win her any friends. Everyone in the office stopped talking to her and would shoot her dirty looks anytime they had a chance. Meanwhile, Chester was oblivious to it all.

Soon thereafter, she began taking fact-finding business trips together with Chester to places like Buenos Aires, Paris, and Acapulco. While I usually made Chester's travel arrangements for him, for all of his travels with Consuela, he asked her to make the flight and hotel reservations. In his own words, 'I'd like to lighten your load.' All I could think was, 'Yeah, I bet you're lightening your load buddy.'

I once mistakenly saw his flight reservation for Paris, two round trip first class tickets, one for him and one for Consuela. And then the hammer came down on me one morning as Chester walked into my office with an unhappy grimace on his pudgy face.

"Nikki, I've noticed this past few days you've been coming in about fifteen minutes late."

I stare, dumbfounded, and it takes me a few seconds to get my bearings.

"Well, I've been working late for months now, and even on some weekends. The commute this week has been hectic, but I'm usually here by 9:15."

More like I can't roll my ass out of bed in the mornings. I can't believe he lets Consuela come and go as she pleases and I come in fifteen minutes late a couple of days and he pounces on me.

"Well maybe you can leave home earlier so you can be here on time. Things jump off at nine on. The. Dot." As he finishes off his sentence, he points his grubby finger at me like I'm a child.

I watch him waddle off and wonder why he walks so funny. Both of his feet turn out and as he takes a step, and his whole body shifts to that side. He looks like a weeble wobble, and I wonder why I've never noticed it before.

That morning, my commute was especially interesting. As I sat on the train listening to my iPod and flipping through Us magazine, a mangy looking man got on after me and sat across from me. I didn't look up, but could see him staring at me and licking his lips. My man was burning a hole right through me with his stare.

"Damn girl. You sexy," he said.

I didn't look up.

"Hmmm...hmmmm....hmmmm. Will you be the gravy to my biscuit? I could sure sop you up. hmmmm!"

I don't budge and pretend I can't hear him. People around are starting to look up and stare at him and then to me to see my reaction.

"Girl. I know you can hear me. You better stop acting like you can't."

Oh God. This guy won't let up. Thank God the train is stopping. I'll pretend this is my stop and get off the train.

As I walk away, I hear, "Hmmm...damn. Look at that booooottttty. I hope to see you soon. You just made my week you fine thing."

***

CHAPTER 15

"OHHHHH MY FREAKING GOD!!!!!" Weston whispers, yells, and hisses simultaneously as he comes running into my office and slams the door shut behind him. "You've got to see this," he shoves a paper in my face. "No wait," he yanks it back. "Even better. I will read it to you."

"MY VENUS," he hisses then proceeds to shoot me an undecipherable look as I sit staring up at him, perplexed. He continues,

MY VENUS

"My Goddess,
you haunt my dreams.
Your creamy bosom enraptures me.
I dream of your wild untamed hair
wrapped around my body.

You are like Botticelli's Venus,
arriving at the seashore of my heart.
You take my love.

My loins ache for you.
My Goddess,
you arrive into me
igniting my passion.
I come in you.

All my love --- Chester"

"Oh My God. Where did you get that poem? Because I sure as hell didn't type it." I ask bug eyed, mouth agape.

Chester is a bit of a romantic and an aspiring writer, and sometimes while at work, he often handwrites poems about life, his observations, his travels, the people in his life, and gives them to me to type. I've read everything, or so I thought. Chester loves the idea of love. And he sure as hell loves women – tall, short, chubby, skinny, blond, brunette, redhead, young, old.

"Well," says Weston. "You know that CROW and I share a printer. I mean *just* her and I are connected to *one* printer."

"Are you serious?"

"That's right, Daniel-san. Him and the CROW are doing the do." He makes a lewd sexual gesture by moving his right index finger in and out of a circle in his left hand.

"I don't know if I'm grossed out more by the fact that he's having sex with Consuela or vice versa," I say, trying to not show my hurt.

"Hmmm....mmm," responds Weston. "Wait a minute, are you telling me that you had no idea?"

"I don't know what I thought. They've both been acting shady and I thought it was just a young woman flirting with an old lonely man, and him liking it. I can't even imagine them having sex."

I have been all too aware of Chester's gigolo ways, but simply didn't make too much of it until this whole Consuela situation. His womanizing had never interfered with work and besides, I rationalized, he's a single wealthy older man in New York City, and he has some degree of charm. It's like fishing in a barrel for him, and at the end of the day, whatever he did with his pecker, it was his private business.

"Everything makes so much more sense now. I suspected nothing like this, that's for sure. She walks around here like she owns the place.

Coming and going whenever she wants. Working from home! Nobody here works from home."

"Well that's how she does it. When you're screwing the CEO, you can get away with a lot."

"I guess everybody needs their pipes cleaned, but I'm sorry, I'm totally grossed out. She is thirty-five years younger than Chester. Chester is old. That's just plain nasty. He looks like a cross between Dick Cheney and Elmer Fudd. I mean how often can he even get it up at that age?"

"Have you heard of Viagra? Besides, even an old man needs his balls greased," responds Weston. "And what's better than to bang a chic that's thirty five years younger. I wonder if that was the condom you found in his office."

Oops. I did spill the beans to Weston about that traumatic incident. I mean I couldn't keep it to myself.

"Ewww...don't remind me."

"I am going to rewrite his poem. Tell me what you think." Weston begins to recite his own version of Chester and Consuela's love poem.

MY VENUS FLYTRAP

My Imitation Goddess
You haunt my dreams...literally
Your creamy bosom lures me like the sirens
I dream of your wild untamed hair
Wrapped around my body
Pulling me into the sea of destruction.

You are like the Venus Flytrap
The right appeal on the outside
But you'll eat me alive

Taking my money and soul

My loins burn for you
My Venus Flytrap
I think it could be
That you gave me an STD.

"Maybe you should take up poetry," I exclaim between snorts of laughter.

We laugh so hard that we are both crying. News of the poem spreads faster than the swine flu pandemic, and in the eyes of everyone there, it is the final nail on the coffin for Consuela. Consuela, however doesn't seem to care. She is unfazed, and continues with her routine. I wonder whether I should say something to Chester about their behavior in the office, but decide against it. It is none of my business, and at this point, I have no respect left for Chester. His behavior is beyond unethical.

***

CHAPTER 16

As I am calmly working away at my computer, I get an instant message from Bren.

Do you have a minute to come into my office?

Oh no. What have I done now? It must be serious. Since in the time I've worked here, the only thing Bren has ever sent me has been nasty emails, dirty looks, and accusatory words. This is the first time she's ever im'd me or has asked me to come into her office for aaannnyyything. Unfortunately, after witnessing the flurry of closed-door activities over the past few weeks, I have a nagging feeling that all is not well.

I reply,

Be there in a sec.

I take a few short breaths to calm myself and coolly walk into Bren's office. She asks me to close the door. I stand there trying my best not to shuffle my feet.

"Don't just stand there like a stump. Sit down." She points towards the chair.

"Nikki, I'm going to get right to the point here."

I don't think Bren is even capable of small talk even if her life depended on it. She continues, "Do you know about all this Consuela Roberta Olalla Wilfredo stuff?"

I'm not sure how to respond to her. Bren is not exactly someone I can trust. "I'm not sure what specific 'stuff' you are talking about."

"Come on, Nikki. You don't have to try to protect him. It is obvious to the whole office."

I let out a deep sigh. "Ok." I throw my hands up in the air. "Unhappily, yes I do. Why do you ask?"

"I had a little chat with her about her and Chester."

"You did? Why?"

"Listen, I don't like the person I've become in this job." She is looking me intently in the eye, and for the first time I notice she has black eyes. "And I know that I've been unbelievably cruel and mean to you."

No shit, Sherlock. "Yes, you ha--"

"I've become angry. Everyone here tells me how angry I constantly am. I don't mean to be like that. It's just that I have so much pressure on me."

Aaahhh...poor baby. My heart is bleeding. As if that justifies your unbelievably antagonizing and bullying behavior towards others and in particular me. Of course I don't have the guts to say this.

"I just want to give you a heads up about this Consuela situation. She is going around saying that you are spreading rumors about her and Chester. But I jumped to your defense and protected you."

"You did?" I ask as I contort my face in shock and awe.

"I told her that you have nothing to do with this and that you are not involved." She stares down at her desk. "Look Nikki, I know that I've been very mean to you," as she shakes her head in a disciplinary way at herself.

I guess this is her way of apologizing. I'll take what I can get.

"I may have to go get a lumpectomy next week"

"Oh." I'm not sure how to respond to her admission or if I should even care.

"Hmm........Nikki." She looks at me with eyes that are tearing up. "I'm scared."

This is getting awkward. Bren is as soft and cuddly as a porcupine. In the last year, she had three assistants come and go from under her. At some point, each of the girls ended up in my office crying, begging me to give them advice on how to handle their horrible situation. I didn't have much to say to them, but mostly, leant an ear. One of the girls wished Bren would get cancer and the other one wished that Bren would get hit by a truck. That is the intensely negative feelings Bren evokes in people by mistreating them. And yet, here she was in front of me, vulnerable and pouring out her guts about her fear of having cancer.

"Bren, I'm so sorry to hear that." I say.

I am such a sap.

"I don't like the person I've become in this job," she repeats.

I'm still confused as to why she's confessing this all to me, but begin to feel sorry for her.

"I can't believe Chester has acted in such an inappropriate way. I am so disappointed in him and in who he is. I used to have so much respect for him."

Oh my Lord! There are tears coming down her face.

"He is hurting this organization. How can we be the Center on Ethical Business, and have our CEO take advantage of his situation?"

I guess Bren has forgotten to lump herself in the unethical category. Sister, It is a little late for you to get a conscience.

"I mean have you seen how Consuela is milking us?" she continues with her soapbox lecture. "She comes and goes as she wants. She is traveling all around the world, and there is not even a job for her. He gave the temp a fancy title, Director of Global Affairs and gave her the big office. What kind of bullshit title is that anyway?" Her nostrils are flaring and her face is turned up in disgust. "Director of Global Affairs? I mean what the fuck does she do anyway?"

"I guess nothing is more flattering than a bosomy woman half his age admiring him," I chime in. Ugh…why did I just say that?

As she continues to talk and work herself up to a tizzy, she gets redder and redder from anger. I think she reaches a point where she can almost glow in the dark.

"He doesn't care about what we do. He is just here for the salary. All Chester cares about is traveling around the world with Consuela. They can't even be reached by phone or email when they travel together. I mean can you reach them?"

"I haven't really tried," I murmur.

Bren has got to be kidding me. She is acting like a jilted lover, and of all people, Bren has no right to be mad, considering that she has been having a love affair with Chas Chandler's right hand person, Patty Ray. In the nonprofit world, a romantic relationship with a funder, especially one associated with a corporation can be a big scandal.

Now she is flushed red, and she is jabbing the air with her index finger. "Consuela is a joke. She wears these super short dresses with her tits falling out all over the place." Bren gestures with her hands. "She thinks she is a player. A big fish like me. She is nobody. She is tasteless," she hisses.

"She does behave inappropriately," I add.

"I am forty five years old. I am too old for this shit. I wonder if I'm pretty enough to go out on interviews."

Pretty is not exactly the words I would use to describe Bren.

She continues, "I wonder if I need to lose weight?"

That would be an affirmative.

"Do I need to color the gray in my hair?" She yanks at the gray strands.

If she can get past the first two points, I don't think the gray would matter.

"I'm not young anymore, the thirty-year-olds are hot on my heels gunning for my job."

When did I become her therapist?

"I don't want to be here anymore. When I got into non-profit work, it was at the height of AIDS. Almost everyone I knew had it or died of it. I had passion and a cause. I don't feel that anymore. I've sold my soul to the corporate devil."

"It's definitely a different world now." I agree with her sentiment.

"All the corporations care about now is their public image and fulfilling their philanthropy requirements. They want their logos slapped on some worthy cause. Their money does not come out of passion and altruism, but because they want to sell more products and be more visible. It's free publicity. I feel like a prostitute."

I have to admit she's right on this one. Working on the Summit with the InCare people has made me see a side to this whole business that is ugly and messy.

"I want to do something that makes a difference. I want to get involved with helping women and empowering women, maybe a microfinance organization. Do you know of any organizations? I know you are involved with that stuff."

"Sure. You can try, End of Hunger Project; Women for Women; Peace Center."

"Great...what do you think I should do, Nikki?"

"Look Bren, you are the Vice President of Fundraising. You have a great skill set and you can venture out on your own. You can be a freelance grant writer, and work from anywhere in the world."

"Hmmmm.... wow, I never thought of that." She smiles at me. "It's definitely something to reflect on. Thank you."

I smile back at her, happy that we've finally made a connection.

"I spoke very frankly with Chester a few weeks ago about his womanizing behavior with Consuela, and I thought that would wake him up." She is speaking in a softer tone, a voice I've never heard come out of her mouth. "I thought it would be a hard cold reality check. I told him about his very seductive and suggestive love poem to Consuela, and how it's been circulated around the office. I thought that would jolt him."

I didn't know that she had read the poem also. I'm going to get mad at Weston later for this.

"With this whole Consuela situation, I'm realizing that Chester has completely checked out, and he's ready to retire. But, he has to work since he's lost a lot of money with the current economy," I say.

"Well, shame on him. That's not my problem. He needs this job to support his very expensive lifestyle – from his $300 ties to his gold cuff links, and God knows how many women. I mean have you seen his expense report? It's through the roof," she says.

I wonder how the hell she has seen his expense report? The only person that deals with the finances at the Center is Henry.

"Have you been witness to anything?" she asks.

Next thing I know, my mouth has a mind of its own and it starts rambling, "Morning…meeting…clichés…"

I can't stop myself. It's all spilling out.

"Condom…office…band-aid."

Bren is staring at me in disbelief, her jaw wide open. I've never seen her speechless. I want to shut up, but can't stop myself.

"Cleaning people… can you believe it?" and it's done. I've told her the whole long, dirty slimy disgusting story.

We both sit there in silence. She shakes her head in disbelief.

"Wow." Bren slaps her face to bring herself out of her stupor. "I can't believe he would do that."

"I know, but he did. He's not the person I thought he was," I respond.

"He would actually go so far as to throw a band aid on the floor and try to cover his ass?" Bren is still disturbed by my story.

I sit in silenced shock at myself. Even though I was disappointed with Chester, I shouldn't have told everything to Bren. I don't know what happened, it all just came pouring out.

"Nikki," she falls silent and turns towards her computer.

"Yes?"

Bren lets out a deep sigh and stares at me with her black beady eyes. "You should know that I have gone to the Board of Directors with a sexual harassment accusation against Chester," she says. Bren's eyes are no longer tear filled, but like big giant gumballs popping out of her face.

"What are you talking about?" I jump up. "Why would you do that? He hasn't done anything to you."

"I know, but it's the only way to go after him." She sits back at ease in her deceptive throne.

She continues, "I wasn't sure if I had a strong case, but now, especially now, with the condom story…"

She is giving me her infamous witch smile. Mouth pursed shut, right side curled up into a snicker, age lines above her top lip, eyes shiny from the thrill of revenge.

"I am sure they will want to speak with you." Now she gives me a full smile.

She has tasted blood. My blood. Chester's blood. My heart feels like a lump of lead in the middle of my chest.

"I'm gunning for Chester." She points her finger at me and makes a piston sign. "It's time for him to go anyway. He should have retired last year," she says, still smiling.

Slowly, like a festering volcano, the heat from my stomach rises to my chest. My breath becomes shallow as the heat reaches my head. My face feels like it's on fire. I must be the same magenta color as Bren.

"Chas Chandler has retained counsel and they are going to conduct a formal investigation. I was hoping they would simply not renew Chester's contract and keep it clean. You know, just tell him that it is time for him to retire," she says.

I stand there seething at myself for feeling weak and trusting her.

"Once Chester is gone, they will likely make Henry the CEO and then I will be the number two in charge."

I wonder if I can get away with strangling her?

"Chas will tell Chester next week that they will open an investigation. I think Chester will go ballistic and he will probably know that it is me that has gone to the Board."

My mind races to find a remedy and fix this situation. Maybe I can lie to the investigators or just completely deny that I ever said anything to Bren about the condom story. I could simply say that Bren made up the story.

Bren continues running her mouth, "But you especially are in a particularly vulnerable position because he is your immediate supervisor."

Surely she can't truly be concerned about me. She is so smug and sure of herself.

She lets out a laugh. "I don't know how you work with him so closely. Day in and day out." She holds up her hands. "I can't stand his grubby little hands."

I envision throwing myself across her desk. My arms reaching for her throat to strangle her. Shaking the shit out of her as her head bobbles in every direction. Oh, the pleasure that would give me. But, alas, I patiently and calmly, albeit outwardly, listen.

"Nikki, at this point, what we say and decide to divulge is up to each of us and our conscience."

I find it ironic that she is talking about a conscience. Granted Chester has behaved very poorly, but Bren is no angel. I feel like she is reading my mind and can see my thoughts running across my forehead. I've got to give it to her. She is good.

"When I heard that they were going to open an investigation, I felt sick to my stomach. I have been struggling on what to say. And, you know, I have to tell you that there is a part of me that wants to protect him. Chester is the one in the wrong, and it makes me sick that everyone else is walking around feeling as if they have done something wrong or they have to protect him. It is a weird victim mentality."

I can't imagine Bren as a victim of anyone.

"Nikki, you can trust me. Is there anything else I need to know?"

Hell no. Side effects of trusting Bren include dry mouth, dizziness, diarrhea, and spontaneous human combustion to end your misery.

"No. Nothing else."

***

CHAPTER 17

Chester suggested I travel to Washington, DC to scout out the venue and meet with Wish's staff to hammer out the final details of the Summit. Even though I am only taking the Amtrak Acela train, the thought of traveling for work for the first time is exciting. It feels grown up. Also, I am more than happy to get away from all the drama of work and at home. After I schedule the meeting with Wish's secretary, I receive a call from the main man himself.

"I can't wait to see you," says the Barry White-ish voice at the other end of the line.

"I didn't know you were going to be there," I say.

"I will be. I want to make sure everything goes smoothly."

"You are so busy. I thought I would be working with Sharon?"

Sharon Devereux is Wish's Chief of Staff.

"What? You don't want to see me? Or are you afraid of me?" I bet he's smiling.

"I'm not afraid of you," I blurt out in a high-pitch voice.

"I won't bite. I promise," he says.

I feel myself blushing and can't stop grinning. I suppose because of my sexless life, and the drama at home, I find myself thinking of Wish more and more. He is constantly on my mind, and what he doesn't know is that I've been having fantasies about him; fantasies of us walking hand in hand on the beach, me looking amazing in a white bikini; fantasies of us making out and making love; fantasies of us cooking together and having deep conversations.

Regardless of how busy I've been at work, I have turned into Wish's Internet stalker. I've Googled him, and read every article about him. I've visited his blog and Facebook profile. I've seen all and any of his pictures, his family and friends' pictures. I know that his wife looks like a real live version of Jessica Rabbit with a Ph.D. She is a leading business coach to CEOs and high-level diplomats. In all of her pictures she is dressed like a fashion model, wearing what appears to be designer dresses and suits. Her legs reach from the floor to ceiling and she has the perfect hourglass body, with perky boobs to match.

In one of my internet stalking searches, I came across an album cutely named, 'Wish and Carol Through The Years.' In every single picture, they are holding each other tightly like a life jacket on a sinking ship. There is a picture of them on the beach, she is wearing a long white dress and he is wearing a white t-shirt and shorts. He has her scooped up in his arms and twirling her around and around. The caption reads, 'Second best day of my life. She said yes.' There is another picture of them on their wedding day.

He is of course looking absolutely man-alicious sexy in his tuxedo and she looks amazing in a taffeta strapless mermaid dress with an embroidered top and shirred waist. The caption reads, 'The best day of my life. I'm a lucky man to have such an amazing woman choose me.' In yet another picture of them cycling together through the French Alps, he trailing behind her, the caption reads, 'Carol is my better half. She always beats me in everything.' She seems perfect. He seems perfect. It all seems so perfect. So I don't understand what the hell he is doing with me? What the hell is going on?

I play hardball, "If you continue talking to me like this, I am going to hang up and suggest to Chester that someone else handle this project."

"No, we don't want that now, do we? I'll stop. I apologize if I made you uncomfortable. Besides, Sharon will be there also."

I cover the mouthpiece on the phone and let out a deep sigh, "Ok, I appreciate that. I'll see you in a couple of weeks."

Truth be told, I am nervous about going to DC to meet Wish. I haven't seen him since our lunch meeting, and I find myself wanting to impress him with my business smarts and acumen. I feel the need to prove myself to him since he is such a success – he has written numerous books, is constantly interviewed as an expert in the news, he travels the world for speaking engagements and works closely with world leaders.

So even though I like him, admire him, and fantasize about him, I know that in reality I should not go there. Here I am working at the Center on Ethical Business and am all about being moral and ethical and making the world a better place. I mean how could I think about being with a married man? I would be no better than Chester and Bren or even Consuela. I can't let myself go there. It would be totally hypocritical. Besides, I'm sure I'm not the first or only woman he is hitting on, or so I keep telling myself.

He had texted me a few days before, making me even more nervous with anticipation.

It's close to noon as I knock on his hotel room door. I do my best to regulate my breath. I don't think I've ever had this much anxiety about anything. I tell myself that I shouldn't even feel any nervousness. Nothing is going to happen. This is work and that's it. It's all very simple.

I am clutching my rolling suitcase so hard that I can feel my hand throbbing. I hear footsteps approaching the door. I suck in my gut, straighten my shoulders, stand taller, and take a deep breath in through my nose, feel my diaphragm expand and then exhale through my mouth. As he opens the door, and looks at me, he takes my breath away. We both simply stand there staring at each other. There he is in front of me, all six feet and three inches of him, in a white shirt without a tie, and dark gray pants.

I finally manage to speak. "Can I come in?" Remembering to smile and look as friendly as I can muster under the circumstances.

He stands in front of me looking absolutely delicious, and blinks for a few seconds.

"Errr... yes...sorry," he opens the door wider and steps to the side to let me in.

He helps me take off my black Biya embroidered coat without taking his eyes off of me, and hangs it up in the closet. He turns around and almost lurches towards me. Next thing I feel are his arms, his body, his whole being around me. Hellooo...I think he is the only person on the planet who can give these abundant encompassing hugs. Peter has never hugged me like this. I wrap my arms around him, and pull myself to him. I slowly move my hands down his muscular back and rest them on the small of his back. He has one arm across the back of my shoulders and the other one around the back of my waist. My breath has gotten shallower, and I begin to feel his hard on through his pants.

Nikki, remember that this is business. Wish is a married man, and I am with Peter. Do not let yourself go there.

I pull away and step back to put a couple of feet between us, and cross my arms. "It's good to see you. How are you doing?"

"I'm great," he says with a twinkle in his eye. "And even better now that you are here." His gaze penetrates right through me. "I've really missed you."

I smile at him without saying anything. I feel my knees trembling in my knee high, three-inch black leather boots. I casually walk across his living room suite at the Intercontinental and over to the armchair, trying not to let my legs crumble from under me. Wish sits on the sofa and stares at me with a big smile on his face.

I don't hear anyone else in the suite. I begin speaking to break the tense silence. "Where is Sharon?"

"Sharon couldn't make it. Some emergency business came up that she had to handle."

"Oh. Ok. Is everything ok?"

"She's at the White House handling a briefing for me."

I'm not sure if I'm troubled by Sharon's absence or happy that she is not here.

"You've been quite busy in these past few months. You are all over the place," I say.

"This past year, I've flown over 700,000 miles. Can you believe that? I am passing myself in airports."

"You've done some good work."

"I don't want to talk about that," he says.

I rear back, "Oh...ok. What do you want to talk about?"

"You...Us."

"Ummm... Wish, I came here to discuss the Summit. There. Is. No. Us..," I say.

"Yes there is. And you know it. I've..."

He falls silent and looks down at his hands. I don't know what to say, so I keep quiet.

He continues, "I've...I've...um...I've never felt this way about anyone."

Everything that happens next happens in slow motion. He stands up and walks over to the armchair and kneels before me. He takes my damp limp noodle hands into his and looks me in the eyes.

"I can't stop thinking of you. You are constantly on my mind. I wonder what you're doing? Who you're with?" He smiles. "What dress you're wearing?"

He looks me up and down, "By the way, I love that red dress on you."

Oh, this little dress that I just happened to pick up at Bergdorf's yesterday especially for our meeting. For the past week, I'd been casually browsing the department stores after work, and had convinced myself that I was simply delaying going home to papa Peter. Yet I would repeatedly find myself in the dress department pondering what I would wear to my Wish meeting. I finally settled on a Marc Jacobs burgundy red dress with beautiful mini pleats in the front that gave the illusion of draping. It had a v neckline, three quarter sleeves, with a black patent leather belt for the cinched waistline, and it fell right above the knee. It actually goes well with the yellow and red color scheme in the suite. It is professional with a hint of sex appeal. I know it's totally tacky, but I am thinking of returning it when I get back to New York. The damn thing cost me one month's rent.

"Thanks, it's just an old dre--"

"I love you."

I pull my hands away and rear back, but am trapped in the chair. "What?"

"I'm in love with you."

Ok, this thing is getting complicated real fast. I push him out of my way to stand up. He falls back onto the floor and catches himself with his hands. I walk away as fast as I can.

My back still to him, I shake my head. "No you are not." I turn to face him as he picks himself off the floor. "You don't even know me."

"I know you. I see you, Nikki."

I'm sure he runs this line on other women. Besides, what about Jessica Rabbit?

"How can you love me? I could be some psycho ax murderer for all you know." I throw my hands up, "Trust me. You do not love me." I slash my hands through the air.

He is laughing out loud. "Trust me. I know you're not a psycho or an ax murderer."

My knees are wobbly and I drop myself on the sofa with a loud thud and place my head in my hands. He walks over to sit beside me, and gingerly puts his arm around my shoulders.

"And I know that we have a deep connection. I feel it...you feel it."

A maid knocks on a door across the hall and announces, "House cleaning."

I pull away from him. "What gives you the right to pop into my life and say that to me?"

I find myself annoyed with him and can hear my voice tremble as I snap at him. "You're a married man and you know that I'm in a relationship. Why are you creating this drama and putting me in this position?"

Wish sits upright. His jaw falls open, closes, and falls open again. He is silent. For a moment it is so quiet inside his hotel room that you could hear a cricket chirp.

He keeps looking me at and then at the floor with big droopy sad eyes, like a dog that's just pooped on the carpet. He is finally able to maintain eye contact for a few seconds.

"Look. I've never felt this way." Now the floor, shaking his head. "It's insane. I've got a lot of responsibilities....and the last thing I expect is to have--" Back at me, "my heart belong to you."

Jessica Rabbit or Nikki Johnson? Surely this can't be that difficult of a decision. I wonder what I have gotten myself into.

"What do you want from me Wish?"

"I want you to say that you've missed me too. I want you to say that you love me too."

I feel the tension in my forehead, and wonder if I am getting a stress headache, "Well, I'm not going to say that. I don't feel that way." My voice still trembling, I grab one of the decorative orange pillows and begin to twirl the fringe. "Have you forgotten that you are married?"

He lets out a snicker. "No. I haven't. I do love my wife. I've loved Carol for ten years. I provide her with all of her creature comforts." He crosses a foot over his knee. "I give her everything. I play a role with her, and most of the time I feel like I can't breathe."

My eyes wander to the cross and skull on the bottom of his shoes. "To her I am the same person I am in public. I can't be myself with my flaws, and I have to take care of everything. The whole thing feels like an act at times."

"I'm sorry, it sounds like it's a difficult situation."

"Carol is beautiful…I mean beautiful…everyone says how sweet she is, and she is one of the kindest people I have ever met." He stares off into space and gets a distant look in his eyes.

I look down at the red and yellow pillow and run my hands over the yellow middle-eastern motif embroidery.

"Two years ago, she started to turn the lights off when we…" he pauses and begins to chew on the corner of his bottom lip. "Well, I…err… don't want to put out all of our business, but, I have to say that she is perfect for what I do. I just wonder if she is the love of my life. I know I am hers, but I just don't know." He looks at me as I feel the embroidery under my palm.

"I was dating a woman who had two kids and I thought we could get married. You know, be a family and start our own family. But some of my closest friends and advisors reminded me that for my work, I needed to have a wife that could stand behind me and support me and my purpose. I needed someone who could deal with my twelve to sixteen hour days, my constant traveling and inconsistency, constant phone calls, and cell phone mania. So, I decided to marry Carol three years ago."

"I thought you've been married for ten years?"

"I've known her for ten, married for three. She was a good friend."

He clarifies with an expressionless face. "I'm not sure I did the right thing." He begins to gnaw on his bottom lip again and I wonder if it's going to start bleeding.

I return the pillow to its original corner and turn to face Wish. I throw my arm across the back of the couch.

He reaches over and strokes my face. "But with you it's different. I have never been so turned on in my life… have you ever met someone that you just wanted to put inside of yourself?"

Before I can answer, he says, "That's how I feel about you."

"Wish, I don't really know what to say." He leans towards me as if he's going to kiss me. I do my best to be smooth and not pull back too fast. "I am flattered, but I don't think I can give you what you are looking for…I'm sorry."

He stares at me in silence for what feels like slow painful eternal minutes. He finally gets up and walks over to the desk, and begins to flip something open, "Ok…are you hungry?" He says without turning around.

"What?"

"We can order some food, and get down to business." He shoots a quick glance my way.

"Errr…Ok."

He walks over the red Persian carpet and hands me the menu. "The food here is pretty good. Let me know what you want."

As I grab the menu from him, I try to make eye contact, but the knock on the door distracts him.

It's only the hotel maid. "House cleaning."

I follow Wish's polished black Barter Black dress shoes as he walks across the room and opens the door. I hear him thanking the maid and telling her that he doesn't need cleaning. He takes the privacy please sign and hangs it outside the door.

My eyes follow him as he silently walks to the desk and leans over his laptop. Through his white dress shirt I can see the broadness of his back as it tapers down to his waist. His buttocks seem like they are the perfect size, firm and round, but not too big. His legs are long and lean.

"Do you see anything you like," he says as he shoots me another sideways glance.

I quickly snatch my eyes away from studying his body and back towards the menu, and respond with the first thing that I see. "Some sort of fish would be nice. Maybe the trout."

He reaches for the phone and places our order, the sautéed rainbow trout, stuffed with crabmeat and served with grilled white asparagus and roasted red bell pepper sauce for me, and the braised beef short ribs with parsnip puree, roasted oyster mushrooms, and baby carrots with sauce bordelaise for him. He orders a bottle of Perrier for the both of us.

While we wait for the food he apologizes and tells me that he has to do a radio interview and that it will probably take no more than twenty minutes, and to make myself comfortable. I pull out my notepad and begin flipping through the pages to review my notes. But I find myself reading the same line over and over and over again. I can't seem to focus on anything, so I start doodling, pretending that I am busy working. I listen in on his interview and am impressed with the grace, poise, and smarts that he answers the reporters' questions with.

As we sit there eating and reviewing the Summit agenda and speakers, I feel awkward, a bit like a silly little school girl blabbering away. I know I am saying something about the speakers and the theme of the Summit, but there is a total disconnect between my mouth and ears. I just hear myself rambling on and on and not making any sense. I am speaking faster and faster, as my brain runs on autopilot trying to make sense of everything that just transpired. The harder I try to understand, the more exhausted and confused I feel. He just poured his heart out to me and told me that he's in love with me and now we are talking as if nothing happened. My stomach feels like there is a pack of wild animals running around in there and I start praying that I don't throw up in front of Wish and all over the dress that I plan to return for a full refund. I do my best to focus myself back on the conversation.

"Wish, what do you think about you being the M.C. of the Summit?" I can't seem to stop shaking my leg under the table.

"You want to know what I think?"

In my delirium I did not notice that he had fallen silent and was not eating his food. As I finish my words, I finally notice how he's looking at me with an amused look. His eyes are slightly twinkling and he has a sweet smile on his face. I must look like a dimwit. Or, he must see how nervous I am. Definitely nothing like the poise and grace of his Jessica Rabbit wife.

"What?" I stare dumbfounded and breathless as he gets up from his chair and walks over to me from his side of the table. My eyes follow him until he reaches me. He has a fiery intensity that scares me, thrills me, and turns my world inside out and upside down. He reaches down and takes the fork from my plate, and cuts off a piece of the trout.

"What are you doi--" He feeds me the trout and stands over me as I begin chewing and continues to hold my gaze.

His crotch is close to my face and I lean back in my chair to put some space between us. He leans down and is on his knees and face to face with me. I see him coming towards me as I continue to chew. Next thing I know, his full, luscious, juicy, soft lips are on mine. He presses lightly against my lips. In my shock I swallow my food whole and almost choke on the trout. Oh God, please don't let me have fish breath or worse, a free-floating piece of leftover trout. Although, I don't think trout is too fishy. I risk it, and open my mouth.

His tongue is in my mouth. It's soft and warm with a tinge of sweetness. He slowly searches for my tongue. I let him find it. I inhale a whiff of Jean Paul Gaultier, and my body automatically moves closer to his. His kisses make me feel like the hot chocolate from City Bakery, hot and bubbly, but times a hundred. He nibbles and tugs lightly on my bottom lip. I hear the fork landing with a loud clang on the plate as he wraps his arms around me. He presses his lips a little harder. Wish makes me feel like a woman, a grown, sexy, beautiful, bodacious woman.

He stands up and lifts me up with him, all the while still kissing me. He draws me closer, and I raise my head towards him. Feeling his body pressed against mine, I wrap my arms around his wide shoulders. I lower my shoulder blades so I can fit in below his armpits and press myself into him even more. He cusps my face with his hands and softly caresses and kisses my cheeks, eyes, nose, chin, even my eyebrows. The palms of his hands feel soft, definitely no calluses or rough patches on them. He pulls back and looks at me dreamily and whispers, "You are so beautiful," and I actually let myself believe him. He strokes my hair out of my face and runs the tip of his index finger over the arch of my eyebrows. He brushes his lips against mine and wraps his arms around my back. His hands grip my lower back and his fingertips squeeze the top of my butt. I don't dare budge. I want him to keep gripping. His lips glide down the side of my neck, kissing, caressing, and sucking.

I feel his hard on and it jolts me. This is moving way too fast for me. I'm not sure if I should be doing this. I push him off, but he is latched on, and lets out a soft moan. He tightens his grip on my back and continues to kiss me with all of his full force. Somehow, dinner be damned, we end up on the floor of the hotel room continuing our kissing, our hands begin to discover each other's body parts. He is on top of me as I stroke his hair, the curve of his neck, down his back, and across his shoulders, down his arms and into his fingertips. His hand runs down my neck and starts caressing my breasts. Our legs are intertwined.

Must. Stop. Now. No….yes…no…yes. Oh Lord, this feels good.

Finally, I push him off. He lies on his side with his arm across my body and burrowing his nose into the side of my neck.

He lets out a deep groan. "Hmm…you smell so good."

I pull away and face him. "I think we need to stop." I am flustered and out of breathe. My expensive dress is wrinkled.

Wish looks hurt. "Should I not have kissed you?" He stands up and walks over to the room service table cart and pours himself a glass of water.

"Well," I smile thinking of his kisses. "I didn't say that." I continue to lie there staring at his backside.

He throws his head back as he gulps his water, returns the glass to the table and walks over to his laptop. He plays some Ella Fitzgerald singing Let's Do It (Let's Fall in Love), and turns around to give me a naughty smile and moves his eyebrows up and down.

He is way too cute to resist. He walks over to me with an outstretched arm with the same wicked smile on his face. I return his smile and reach up to grab his hand as he pulls me up with force, into his arms and onto his lips to kiss me again and again. He scoops me up as he continues to kiss me. Next thing I know, he throws me away and I am flying through the air. I hear Ella singing, 'Birds do it, bees do it. Even educated fleas do it.' I let out a high pitch squeal as I land with a thud on the bed. Still smiling, he saunters towards me, gets down on bended knee and rests my right foot on his knee, unzips my boot and tosses it behind his shoulder. His eyes twinkle from his naughty smile and I notice the dimples cut into each side of his cheek. Next, he puts my left foot up on his knee. The sound of the zipper slowly gliding down my leg only builds the yearning for his touch. I feel his breathe against my face as he sits up and reaches behind me to unzip my dress.

I arch my back and suck my stomach in as much as I can to pull in my belly fat roll. I shimmy out of the dress as he pulls it up and over my shoulders. He kisses my right shoulder, nips around my neck, runs his finger in between my cleavage, caresses my breasts, kisses my belly and nuzzles my belly button, squeezes my hips and kisses the top of my panties. Next thing I know, my black lace panties land in the same pile as my boots.

Ella croons in the background, 'Romantic sponges, they say, do it.' Wish comes back up and presses his lips against mine. He begins to suck on my tongue, and I feel myself getting more and more turned on. His kisses are not the soft and tender kind. There is a hunger and voraciousness to him that I have never experienced before with anyone. In the good old days when Peter and I had sex, it was sweet and tender, yet never full of passion. In fact, compared to Wish, all of my past boyfriends seem like little boys.

Wish is a real man and with him it is so different. It is like he is trying to inhale me into him. He rips off my bra from my body and cups my breasts with both hands as he kisses and caresses them. My fingers fumble as I try to unbutton his shirt. I am only able to undo a few at the top, so I lift the shirt over his head. He has a few light tufts of curly brown hair on his chest, and I am so happy that he's not a hairy beast. To feel his bare skin against my chest is absolute heaven. I feel like someone just poured warm melted chocolate all over me. One would need the Jaws of Life to separate us.

Oh my God, he is sexy. His eyes pierce through me, his hands, strong and decisive on my body. He feels dangerous and wild below his polished surface, and I want to completely give myself to him.

Wish lets out a moan, "You are so beautiful. You have an amazing body."

And he doesn't think I'm fat! He thinks I have an amazing body. This is perfect.

I pull off his belt, and yank it off the way you see in the movies, to make that swooshing sound. His pants have three buttons on them and my hands are floundering as I try to open each one. He finally reaches down, and takes off his pants. He is wearing white Calvin Klein boxer briefs that snuggly hold his nice package in place. The white fitted briefs highlight his sienna colored skin and all the developed muscles in his thighs.

He wraps his arm around me pulling me closer to him, pressing my body, breasts, and legs against his body. I put my arms around him to draw him closer, and press my lips against his mouth. I want to taste his succulent lips. His tongue probes mine. I reach down to take off his briefs, and pull them down the rest of the way with my feet. I'm surprised by how limber I am. I can feel him throbbing against me.

Wish begins nibbling on my ears and neck. He cups and kisses my breasts oh just so right with the perfect amount of pressure. I do not have to show this man how to do anything. He is slow and deliberate with his hands and mouth, making sure every inch of me has received some sweet tender loving. I am so glad he's not rushing it and then I feel his hand slide down in between my legs.

"Hmmm…you are so hot," he groans.

He goes down to my belly and then even lower. I arch my back as I feel his lips on me. The pressure and intensity builds until I can no longer take it and let out a scream as he comes back up.

"You are amazing." He lays beside me and stares at me with affection.

I turn to face him. "I want you to make love to me," I moan back.

I throw one leg over his body. He grabs me with both of his arms and raises me on top of him and begins to kiss me with fervor. I feel him slide himself inside me. His hands are on my hips and we begin to glide and gyrate simultaneously. As we begin to move faster and faster, I feel the intensity building up in me again until we both explode together.

We lie there, conjoined completely, sweating, panting, and in complete bliss. His arms wrapped around my body. This is the best sex of my life.

"Nikki?"

"Hmmm?"

"Thank you for making my fantasy come true. I've wanted to make love to you from the moment we met."

I lie on top of Wish's Chest, soaking wet, feeling his heartbeat. I absorb him through my every pore and let myself feel an ecstasy I have never felt before.

***

CHAPTER 18

Law Offices of

Adken, Mung, Pars & Pero LLP & Affiliates

Dear Chester McMadden,

The Foundation for Moral Rights & Responsibilities would like to inform you that we will conduct an investigation into the $5 million grant the Foundation awarded to The Center for Ethical Business.

The grant was awarded under the aegis and good faith and reputation of the Center. However, the Foundation has come to believe that the grant was not allocated properly and according to the grant guidelines.

We hope that this investigation can be resolved judiciously and request your full participation in this matter.

Sincerely,

Gail Adken

Gail Adken J.D., LLM,ESQ.

cc: Chas Chandler V,

Center for Ethical Business, Board Chairman

Holy shit, is all I can think as I finish reading the letter. As Chester's right-hand person, I open all of his mail, and to start off my morning like this is not what I was hoping for. I wanted to work in nonprofit and do my small part in making a difference in the world. What I definitely did not sign up for is all this drama. A few days ago, Chas Chandler asked Chester to come to his office for a private meeting. Chester felt upbeat about the meeting and thought it was about his upcoming contract and raise. As if he already didn't make enough at $250,000 a year. He was asking for an additional $50,000. I simply went along with Chester's impression and didn't say anything. When he returned to the office, he had the most glum and distraught look on his face. I have never seen him like that. He asked me to not interrupt him and hold all of his calls. After about two hours of sitting in his office, he emerged out of his cave and left for the day. I knew that Chas had informed him about the sexual harassment investigation.

Now back at my desk, it is up to me to deliver this second blow. I wonder how I should tell him about this letter. He'll probably have a heart attack, and even though I'm angry with him, I don't want him hurt. He's an old dude. I slowly walk into Chester's office, both afraid of his reaction and worried about him. My stomach is knotted up.

He is sitting in his black leather chair and has his back turned to the door. He is deep in thought staring out of his large office windows towards the intersection of Sixth Avenue and Forty Second Street.

I straighten my jacket and clear my throat. He turns around to face me, looking despondent. Even though he is dressed immaculately in his Brooks Brothers dark navy suit, white shirt with a red tie, and Pink gold cufflinks, he gives off the feeling of a deeply disturbed man. His eyes are puffy with dark heavy bags under them. His skin looks sallow and pale. The little white hair that is left on the top his head is disheveled. He manages to fake a smile.

"Do you need something?" He asks.

I feel sorry for him, and am hit by a pang of guilt that I spilled my guts to Bren, and gave her so much ammunition.

Still standing at the door, I raise the letter. "There is something here that you should see right away."

He notices the worried look on my face and pushes himself wearily from his chair to stand up. He looks so feeble. I walk over to him hand him the letter. He practically snatches it out of my hand and quickly scans it. His eyes get bigger and bigger and bigger and he begins to breathe faster and faster as he reads the letter. I stand there, motionless, watching his reaction and wondering what he will do next. It feels like he is sucking out all of the oxygen out of the room. What if this Foundation investigation pushes him over the edge? All of a sudden he pushes his chair back so hard that it hits the wall with a loud thud. He comes running from around his desk with a gusto I have never seen. He is heading towards me like a bull towards a red flag. I jump out of his way to let him pass, and almost fall over his guest chair. I run to his office door, and watch him speed-waddle down the hall and into Henry's office. I hear the door slam shut.

I walk over to behind Chester's desk and stare down at the bustling intersection. It is almost the end of winter, but still one of the coldest times of the year in New York City. Everyone is wrapped up in dark colors. It's a sea of black down and wool coats, hats of all shapes and colors, scarves blowing like personal flags as they trot to their next destination. This is a town where people come to make it, to make their mark in the world and feed their ambitions. I was no different, and now I wonder what has happened to me. I have changed. At one point, I would have never even considered doing what I did with Wish. Working at the Center and this Summit is making me see a different side of the corporate and nonprofit worlds that I don't like.

I am jolted out of my thoughts by the sound of Chester's office door closing. I spin around and see Chester standing there in shock. He walks over to the guest chair and eases himself down.

I walk over to him and place my hand on his shoulder. "Are you ok?"

He looks up at me, still shell-shocked and shakes his head. "I think so."

I walk to the guest chair across from him and sit down.

Chester shakes himself out of his shocked stupor. "We have to clean this up."

"And how can we clean it up?" I say. Anytime I've heard those words uttered in a movie it usually involves some illegal activity and to hear him say it makes me worried.

Chester walks over to his leather chair and sits down. He is now back to his full authority mode, someone who has things under control and in complete solution mode.

He continues, "Nikki, please do your best to get me and Henry, and Justine to see the President of the Foundation."
Justine is one of the program directors here at the Center and is responsible for the program for The Foundation for Moral Rights & Responsibilities.

"It is very important we nip this in the bud. I need you to move the ball forward on this as soon as possible."

Oh no, he is starting to speak in his business clichés again.

"Ok. I'll get right on it."

Over the next few days I juggle the Summit work and coordinate schedules and make appointments for Chester and Henry to see the Center's accountants and lawyers, and then finally the Foundation executives.

A few days later, Justine whirls into my office like the Tasmanian Devil, hair frizzed out and face red. "Ahminah need to talk to you," she slams the door shut behind her and throws herself into the chair.

Justine Maxwell is from Minnesota and even though she has lived in New York City for a long time, every now and again, her Minnesota accent pops, usually when she is excited. She is a program director at the Center for Ethical Business who was hired two years ago when the Foundation awarded the Center the $5 million for a new program. Her responsibility was to use the money to establish a program for youth to learn about ethical business and practices. Justine was always frustrated and struggling to run her program. Not out of incompetence, but because at every turn, Henry and Bren would undermine her efforts.

"Lemme just tell you what happened at dese meeting with the President of the Foundation, Warren Peace." She is practically yelling as I strain to understand her. "Dat was da worst meeting I've ever been in. I am sitting dere listeninen to Warren charging us with fraud. Fraud." She is practically screaming.

"And of course I can't even say nothing since Henry intentionally excluded me from all dem meetings. Here I am running da program and I have no idea what da financials of my program are."

"Well, you of all people know how Henry micromanages," I say.

"Yeah. Fer sure I do." She leans towards the desk and slams her fist down. "Chester is just a buffoon who is only here for the money."

"I'm not so sure about that. I think he does believe in this work," I say.

My comment silences Justine for a few seconds, then she heaves out a heavy sigh. "Oh fer geez, maybe you are right. She hunches over, looking defeated, "His strength is being the front man and public face, but he lets Henry control everything behind the scenes." She looks like she is about to start crying. "You know what happened today at the meeting?"

"No, Chester didn't say anything to me," I respond. For the first time understanding the cliché saying of 'ignorance is bliss.'

She shakes her head in disbelief, "Chester calms Warren Peace down by apologizing, and saying that we will certainly cooperate and answer any of their questions." She throws her head back with a laugh. She is calmer and speaking normal English again. "And then, from nowhere, Henry jumps in." She throws her hands up for effect. "What an idiot that one is. He has no social skills. Do you know what he did?"

That must be a rhetorical question since she doesn't give me any time to answer.

"Henry gets angry and tells Warren that he is wrong and inappropriate for accusing the Center of fraud."

"Really? Please tell me that he didn't do that." I shouldn't be surprised. I don't know why I expected anything different from Henry.

"Oh you betcha! Here we are at the complete mercy of this guy, and Henry is being a belligerent brat. Warren ended up yelling at us and we had to walk out of there with our tail in between our legs."

"Really?"

"He basically kicked us out."

"Wow, and here I thought Henry was a total wimp," I say.

"And now, Warren is more adamant about the investigation. He is pissed off and out to nail Henry for his tricky accounting tricks."

"Shit. What do you mean tricky accounting tricks? What did Henry do?"

"I don't even know where to begin. The intent and purpose of the grant was to make the program self-sustaining. The Foundation gave the Center for Ethical Business $5 million, but we had to raise $3 million in matching funds. Henry was happy to get the money and spend it. There was money allocated for me to have an assistant, which Henry never allowed me to hire."

"Wow. I didn't know all this," I say.

"Oh yea. You betcha." She furrows her forehead with concern. "He billed other people's travel and expenses to the Foundation."

My jaw drops open.

"Chester's $20,000 American Express bill and his cavorting around the world with Consuela was billed to the foundation," she says.

"No way!" I cover my mouth in disbelief. "Justine, this is beyond unethical. I mean, how can this be going on behind the scenes? We are supposed to be the Center for Ethical Business…aren't we?"

She lets out a laugh that sounds like a witch cackle.

"Nikki, I'm sorry, but wake up! What's wrong with you? You don't really believe that, do you?"

"Well…yes…I think I do…I mean that's why I wanted to work here… and why I accepted the Communications role."

She stares at me with disgust, lips turned up, and forehead full of wrinkles.

"Don't you believe in it?" I am hesitant to hear her response.

She continues her combination venting and dumping on me, "That's an oxymoron. Ethical Business?" I lean back in my chair and let Justine's words sink in. "There is no such thing as long as the bottom line is the most important thing. They don't care about people."

My head feels like mush. There is some big event at the United Nations and in the background I hear protestors marching down Sixth Avenue, beating drums and chanting in unison, 'No blood for oil…no blood for oil…no blood for oil.' I close my eyes and let my head sink into the back of my chair. This is turning into a nightmare.

I hear Justine's voice, "Chester has been on lavish trips with Consuela to Paris, Buenos Aires, Rio de Janeiro, London…South Africa."

"All in the name of work," I say opening my eyes and looking at Justine. For the first time, I allow myself to really see the severity of Chester's behavior.

I swivel my chair as I watch Justine walk behind my desk and look out of my window at the protestors. "These people think they can change this screwed up system." She shakes her head and lets out a deep sigh as she stands there watching the protestors for a few more minutes.

She walks back to her chair. "And you know what else?" She is somber. "Bren, as the fundraiser for this organization, was supposed to raise the money. She had no interest in doing it. I repeatedly sat in on those management meetings, and she and Henry would gang up on me to constantly shoot me down and shut me up anytime I brought up the funding issue."

"Why didn't you ever bring up these issues before?" She faces me as she leans back on the window ledge.

"I did, a couple of times to both Henry and Chester. Chester didn't care. He was too busy screwing around, literally with his little Latin trollop lollipop. And Henry outright told me that my job was to run the program and to not get involved in funding and accounting issues. That it was not my business."

"I don't understand why they would purposely sabotage the program and funding?"

"I don't know, but when the Foundation asked for proof that the Center had attempted to raise the funds, Bren sent them a list of various random organizations and foundations. She wrote in her email that she could not find copies of the letters on her computer or the rejection letters from the various organizations."

"That is the lamest excuse. It's like saying the dog ate your homework," I say.

"She outright lied. Bren is the type of person who is always blaming other people. I pulled in some high profile people to support this program, and Henry shut me down. I was on a business trip and he had my credit card canceled. I was left in the middle of bum-fuckville without a company credit card. I used $6,000 of my own personal funds to run the trainings and workshops for two hundred people. I had to buy all the supplies. I had to feed them."

Henry's micro-management boggles a lot of people's work in the office. Since I work directly with Chester, I have mostly escaped his heavy handedness, and I think on some level, Henry resents that. After I got my promotion, Chester added my name to the senior management distribution list, much to the unhappiness of Henry and Bren.

Justine carries on, "Henry had his own fucking agenda. He and Bren sit back like peacocks, spreading their legs so you can see their cock size. They like to scratch each other's balls and let out hearty laughs…ha…ha…ha."

We both let out a laugh.

"You are right, but I always thought Bren was stronger than Henry."

"They painted the picture of the grand ship that they would sail. They sold the vision, and it turned out to be a cardboard cutout and behind it was just a dingy with no oars and big fat Henry with a big box of crayons busy coloring it in. At the end they said, 'Oops, we spent all the money and we didn't do our part.'"

"Well then, they deserve whatever the Foundation has planned for them," I say.

***

CHAPTER 19

"Nikki? Umm…do you have a sec?" Henry asks as he pokes his head into my office.

Not really, you wet noodle is what I would like to say, but respond with a big smile. "Sure."

"Umm…good…can you…umm…come into my office?"

My eyes still on his head, "Be there in a sec."

He disappears, leaving me wondering what he wants to talk to me about. Luckily I don't interact on a one-on-one basis with Henry too much, but usually more in larger group meetings.

I take my time to get myself ready, and finally meander down the hall into his office. He asks me to close the door. At one point, I used to watch some of the senior people at The Center go into closed-door meetings and be envious and wonder what they talked about. Now that I am on the other end of all of these closed-door meetings, I wonder if maybe I was better off in my old position in the cubicle.

Henry's office is expansive with a large desk, two guest chairs, and a six-person conference table that is littered with piles of folders and papers that never seem to move. Behind Henry's desk are two large piles of folders each about a foot high. On his desk are blue, red, and green manila folders with papers sticking out.

"Henry, how can you work in all of this mess?" I ask as I sit down.

He is surprised by my question and lets out an uncomfortable laugh as he looks around.

"Umm…well…there is some sort of order…ummm…that I only know about."

I give him a smile and scan the mess that is his office, and can't imagine what type of unique organizational system he may have.

"Umm... I wanted to talk to you about something, Nikki...Umm...I'm sure you know about this...you know...umm... sexual harassment investigation into Chester. This is very uncomfortable for the whole staff...ummm...and more so for you, I imagine."

"What are you talking about, the whole staff? Who else knows about this?" I snap at him. I push his turtle and his winter wonderland snow globe from the outer edge of his desk so I can have a place to rest my arms.

"Umm...well, the lawyers want to ...umm...question some of the staff...umm..."

I watch a bead of sweat running down his forehead, as he reaches over to get a Kleenex and wipe himself.

"So you're telling me that the whole office knows?"

"Only a few people."

"Look Henry, I don't like any of this," I respond.

What does he expect me to say, that I'm loving it. For Bren to have some of the financial information about Chester's expense reports means that Henry must be in cahoots with her. Henry thought that he would be CEO two years ago, but Chester decided to extend his stay and contract for another two years. Henry must be plotting away. He thinks with Chester gone, that the Board of Directors will automatically make him CEO.

"Umm...Chas Chandler has assured me that...umm...they will move very quickly on this investigation."

As he's talking, I notice the large round sweat stains under his armpits.

"Umm...and has asked me to be the point person for coordinating, you know, the...umm...staff interviews. The lawyers want to speak to you today at 5 o'clock."

"What?" I shout. In my panic, my hand slams against the snow globe hurling into the picture frame of his smiling wife and daughter decked head-to-toe in fishing gear. With a loud crack, both the globe and the frame are broken. His desk is splattered with white flickers. There is a soup of mini trees, mini people, and shards of glass floating on his desk. Most of the folders are soaked.

"Oh my God." I jump up and reach for the Kleenex. "I'm so sorry." Kleenex isn't doing the job, so I run to the kitchen and come back with napkins to clean up.

We are both silent as I dry off his desk, and Henry wipes the silver glitter from all of his folders and papers. I hear him wheezing as he walks back and forth between his desk and his conference table to lay out the papers to dry. This little mishap gives me time to think of a way to get out of this or at least delay it at its best.

After we finish cleaning up and Henry's breathing calms down a bit, we start on the subject of the investigation,

"Look Henry, this is a very uncomfortable position for me to be in. I've developed a relationship with Chester, as a friend and a mentor. I hate being dragged into the middle of Bren's plot for revenge." And your need for power, I want to say.

He shakes his head and pants out "Umm…I can understand how you feel. I've worked with him for fourteen years."

"I can't speak to them today. I have an appointment after work that I cannot miss," I say as I gulp and rub my nose. Of course I am lying.

Henry squints his eyes and gives me a deathly look that makes the hair on my arms stand up.

"Ok…ummm… I'll find out if they can see you at another time….ummm…they want to quickly be done with this. Do you understand that?"

I hear police sirens in the background and shake my head in silent bewilderment. I get out of his office as fast as I can. I run into my office, and put my head down on my desk with a loud thud. I wonder if I can just disappear. I want everyone to leave me alone.

Right now, I despise the world. I hate Chester for his stupid reckless behavior. I hate Bren for being such an angry, blame-game, bitter, lying wench. I hate Henry for having no balls and letting Bren run him. I hate Peter with his stupid kid. And I hate Wish too. I hate Wish the most right now, for turning my world upside down. Mostly, I am angry with myself. I wish I could handle all of these situations better. As great as my Wish moment was, I know that I have only complicated my life further.

I hear someone knocking on my open door. I raise my head to see Henry standing there. He gives me a-you're-so-pathetic smile.

"Nikki, umm... they want to see you on Friday."

I nod my head in silence.

Henry meanders off. Friday is two days from now, and I have no idea what to say or do.

I run down the hall and into the cubicle area to pull Weston out for a walk and get some fresh air. Once outside, we huddle into a quiet corner at the Prêt A Manger. Weston buys me an almond croissant and a chai soy latte to calm me down. There is nothing like emotional eating to temporarily make you feel better. In between wolfing down my croissant and taking swigs of my latte, I tell Weston about my conversation with Bren and Henry, and the investigation from the Foundation. He listens to me with a generous ear and tells me to email his brother, Eric, who is a corporate attorney. We head back to the office and I send an email to Eric asking for his help on what to say or do.

I leave the office that evening bundled up in my ankle-length black down coat, my brown Ugg boots, dark gray wool hat, black leather gloves lined with cashmere and a bright red wool scarf, which all add another ten pounds to the weight I'm already feeling. I decide to walk home in the freezing twenty-three, but feels like fifteen-degree weather, to clear my head and to prolong the inevitability of interacting with Peter and Zuni.

As I step out onto Sixth Avenue, the cold, sharp wind cuts across my face like razorblades. I can see my breath in the black, cold air. I take part of my scarf and wrap it around my nose and mouth, and tuck the loose end inside my coat collar. My face immediately warms up from my exhalations. I stop by a deli and pick up some green tea with honey to keep me warm on my trek home.

My mind wanders to Wish. For the first few days after our rendezvous I was in absolute ecstasy. Lying in bed at night staring at the ceiling dreaming of Wish, I would replay our lovemaking scene over and over again in my head. I even kept the dress for an extra week so I could have his smell near me. I would secretly run into my closet to scoop the dress in my arms and take a prolonged whiff, which luckily, I was able to return in mint condition. I was feeling like a sixteen-year-old girl in puppy love. Peter was, of course, too busy dealing with a rebellious teenager to notice my wanderlust.

But slowly the guilt started to creep in. How can I lose myself like that? What was I thinking? Here I have a good man at home who cooks, cleans, and is doing his best trying to do the right thing by being a responsible father. I always thought of myself as someone who had morals, and held myself firmly to those beliefs.

As I reach Herald Square, despite the wool socks and the fleece-lined shoes, my feet feel like two big cold loaves of brick. I wonder how so many people can shop in one small area? I decide to push forward, dodging the tourists and shoppers going into Macy's. Waiting for the walk signal to change, I watch all the young girls going into Victoria's Secrets to buy lingerie and undergarments that someone has defined as sexy. I realize that I too am one of those girls.

After I get out of the insanity of the shoppers, I slow down my pace to my usual saunter. My thoughts wander to the various situations at work. How can I blame Weston for his affair with Omar? Or even for that matter, Omar for being a closeted gay married man? How am I better than Chester and Consuela? Bren, even? Let's not forget about good old Bren, who is having an affair with a funder and is now drumming up false charges against Chester. I am no different than any of them. If anybody were to look at me right now, they would call me a slut, a cheater, and a home-wrecker. I have turned into someone I don't recognize, but I am not sure the old Nikki was so great either. She was too idealistic, clueless and naïve. I don't know what is going on with me, but feel myself sinking low.

Ever since I saw Wish over a week and half ago in Washington, DC, I have not heard from him. Not a phone call, an email, or a text. I wonder where he is. I wonder what he is doing. I wonder if he is with Jessica Rabbit or someone else. I wonder if he thinks of me the way I have been thinking of him every second of the day. I wonder if he misses me the way I miss him, so much so that it hurts in my gut.

But I'm sure if Wish did miss me, he would have called. Why didn't I trust myself? I knew better than to get involved with him. He probably just used me for sex, and all that fancy talk about feeling a connection, about loving me, about wanting to be one with me was just to get me to sleep with him. He probably saw it as a challenge, and he probably has a different woman in every city he travels to regularly.

I know how these hotshot, CEO business guys operate. They have a wife at home, someone who makes them feel safe and comfortable, plays mommy to them, and does the whole public wife shtick. But eventually, the routine of the comfort bores them, so they go out and have one or a few side chicks. Wish probably saw me as an easy target, and even described me as meek. Meek equals shy, tame, wishy-washy, and spineless.

That is what he thinks of me. Meek equals someone who can easily be taken advantage of. He thought he could use his handsome looks, his suave style, soft hands, earnest words and I'll-melt-you eyes to seduce me. I am now that gullible other woman, that side woman who has to wait around for him to come around. Somehow, I thought I was smarter than this.

Around Fourteenth Street I see a street vendor selling perfumes and colognes on a wobbly display table. As I walk past his table I spot a bottle of Jean Paul Gaultier's La Mer, its blue silhouette standing up arrogantly, sticking out from all the other bottles, trying so hard to be different. It stands there, mocking me. The African street vendor opens the cap so I can smell it. Not bad for an imitation. I sure can't tell the difference and for twenty-five dollars, a special just for me, I walk away with my very own bottle. I spray my scarf and smell Wish, that bastard, all the way home.

I pick up some orange tulips from the local deli as I get to our block. Our apartment is toasty and warm, and is filled with the smell of garlic and ginger. Peter must have made something Indian for dinner. As I take off my winter gear, I hear the sound of running water, clanging dishes, and Zuni and Peter talking and laughing. The hallway floor creaks with each footstep as I head towards the kitchen. I plug in my phone and practice my smile as I round the corner.

"Hi everyone," I announce myself.

Both Peter and Zuni stop speaking and stare at me in silence.

I glance from Peter to Zuni, than back to Peter, still smiling. "What? Why are you guys looking at me like that?" I wonder if I have a big hickey on my neck or something.

"What happened to you tonight?" Peter asks.

"What do you mean? What happened to me tonight? I worked late." I cut across our small kitchen, squeezing behind Peter and Zuni and over to the pantry to pull out a vase.

"We had a parent teacher conference," Zuni says as she returns to drying the plates.

I spin around without getting the vase. I completely forgot about the meeting Peter had scheduled weeks ago. "I'm sorry."

"Besides, I called your work and there was no answer and your cell went straight into voice mail," Peter says.

I start searching in the pantry for a vase. "Well I left about an hour ago and decided to walk home, and my cell phone died earlier today. Can you fill this up with water?" I hand over the vase to Peter as I begin rummaging with the plastic and paper wrapping of the tulips.

"You walked in this freezing weather?" Zuni retorts as Peter fills up the vase.

"Zuni, I'm sorry. I apologize. I completely forgot about the meeting. There's just been a lot going on at work and it slipped my mind," I say.

I genuinely feel bad. I do want to be there for Peter and help with Zuni in any way I can.

"It's ok," Zuni says. "I really didn't want you there anyway. It's a parent teacher conference, and you're not my parent." She challenges me by looking at me directly.

Zuni's words hits me like a bullet to the head, and I stand there paralyzed wondering if Peter will defend me. I look at him for some direction.

"Zuni, sweetheart, that's not a nice thing to say." He takes the plate from her hand, and pats her on the head. "Why don't you go to your room to finish up your homework and I'll clean up here."

Zuni turns around with flair and drama to run off to her room, but not before she shoots me a teenage death ray that burns a hole through my chest. In the meantime, Peter and I have locked eyes like two bulls. As soon as he hears Zuni's bedroom door close, he begins his sermon.

"You know how important this meeting was. I don't understand how you could have missed it." Peter is growling as he comes towards me with finger pointing.

In trying to establish me as an authority figure, Peter had insisted that I be present when he met with Zuni's teachers. Zuni had gotten caught in yet another fooling around in the bathroom incident and while she was a decent student, the principal had suspended her for a few days, and had requested a meeting with her parents.

"Like I said, I'm sorry. I'm just under a lot of stress right now," I say turning back to the flowers. "I got you some flowers." I feel guilty and want to appease him.

"I don't give a fuck about the flowers, Nikki."

I stand still as he swats the flowers away. A few stems fall to the floor.

"I need you....please look at me," he says. He is speaking to me like I am a child.

I cross my arms, take a step back and face him. Peter has never been this aggressive with me and I wonder if this will escalate into something more.

"I can't do this by myself. I need you to be a parent," he says. He keeps his voice low since he doesn't want Zuni to hear, but I can tell he wants to yell. Nevertheless, I can feel his anger and he might as well be screaming.

I don't want to be a parent I want to scream at the top of my lungs. I don't want to raise your fucking bratty spoiled rotten stinking kid. But instead I keep silent. The words don't seem to quite come out, and all I can do is stare at the ground.

"Nikki, I know this is hard for you. Zuni feels like you don't like her, and her feelings are important to me."

I pick up the tulips from the ground and put them in the vase. "Peter, she is resentful that you are with me. She is the one who doesn't like me."

"But you are the adult, not the teenager, and you need to make more of an effort." He walks out of the kitchen leaving the dishes unfinished.

Maybe he's right. Maybe I need to make more of an effort, and try to form some kind of friendship with Zuni. I should take her shopping or out to dinner soon. I can have an honest conversation with her on how she feels about me.

I am deep in thought when I hear my phone ring. I run to the hallway and by the time I rummage around my purse to find the phone, I've missed the call. When I see that it was Wish who called, all the heaviness and drama of the day and of Peter melts away. I listen to his voicemail.

"Hi gorgeous. I was calling to hear your voice."

It's nice to hear your voice too you sexy beast.

"I'm exhausted. This past week, I've traveled to Paris and Stockholm, and then to Los Angeles, Chicago, and New Orleans. Can you believe that? I don't even know where I am anymore. I'm sitting on the tarmac on my way to Washington now. I miss you. Call me when you can."

Hearing Wish's voice and message soothes my distressed soul. I hear Peter in the shower and decide to go chat up Zuni. I am going to make more of an effort.

I knock on her bedroom door. "Hey. It's Nikki. Can I come in?"

"I guess."

I open the door and walk in. On her wall are painted two by two squares of different colors of beige and gray. Zuni wants to redecorate her room, so her and Peter have been shopping for something more somber to match her teenage mood. Most of her floor is covered with black or gray T-shirts and skinny jeans. Her black wool coat, dark gray hat and gloves are thrown into a pile behind her door. Her bed is unmade and the sheets are hanging over her loft bed. Zuni has her back turned to me and I assume she is doing her homework.

"What do you want?" She doesn't look up or turn around.

"I was hoping you and I could have a little talk." I scratch my head and wonder if I should go more towards her or find a place to sit.

"About what?" Her back still faces me.

I see a pink pile of plastic peeking out from her half open closet. She must have thrown the beanbags in there. I grab both of the pink bags, which cause her to finally turn around.

"What are you doing?"

"I'm just getting something for us to sit on."

With my foot, I clear some of her mess from the floor and throw the bags down.

"Why don't you come here and sit for a few minutes. I need to talk to you about something."

She rolls her eyes. "Are you going to lecture me about something?"

I do my best authoritative, friendly mom impersonation by putting my hands on my hips, leaning to one side, and giving her a big I-mean-you-no-harm smile.

"No. I promise that's not why I'm here. Come, sit." I sit down on the beanbag.

She slams her pencil on her table and meanders over to plunk herself onto the beanbag. It lets out a big hiss as she lands.

She throws her hands up in the air, and her head back. "Ok, I'm here."

Still smiling, I lean forward. "Look, I know that this transition is hard for you."

She rolls her eyes again. And I secretly wish they would get stuck like that.

I continue, "I'm sorry about that, and I'm sorry if I've done or said anything that has made you feel uncomfortable."

Zuni remains silent and gazes at her feet. I can't take the tension in the house anymore. I've got to figure out a way to connect with this kid. I reach over and touch her arm.

"Sweetheart? Can you look at me?"

She raises her eyes sheepishly. For the first time, I genuinely feel bad for her. Before me is a scared little girl and not the spiteful rebellious teenager spewing hateful words. I push myself off the beanbag and sit on her floor to be closer to her.

"Look, I know that you want your parents to be together and you are not too crazy about me."

Her eyes start to well up with tears, and she takes her gaze back to her feet and pulls her arm away.

I guess a child of divorce never stops hoping that her parents get back together.

"I'm not trying to replace your mother. I don't even know how to be a mom. I just want us to get along somehow. We can have whatever kind of relationship you want. Ok?"

The poor kid is sobbing. I grab some toilet paper from her small bathroom and let her wipe her tears and blow her nose.

"Do you want a hug?"

She shakes her head 'no'. And I'm not really sure what to do. So, I just sit there and let her cry. After five minutes she finally stops, and tries to catch her breath.

"Zuni, why don't you tell me what's wrong?"

She looks up at me with puffy red eyes. She is twisting her tissue to the point of tearing it into pieces. "Well, I don't know how to say it."

"Sweetheart, whatever, it is. It's ok. Just say it." She looks at me in silence for a few long seconds.

"If it makes it easier, why don't you close your eyes."

She shakes her head in the affirmative and squeezes her eyes shut. "I'm dying," she finally blurts out.

I feel all of my blood rushing to my head trying to make sense of what this child is saying. Her eyes are still closed when I grab her arm in panic, "Zuni, what are you talking about?"

She opens her eyes, and repeats her words slowly, "I am dying."

"What do you mean you're dying?" I feel my hand squeezing her arm tighter. "I don't understand."

"I don't know how to tell Dad." She begins chewing her fingernails.

I take a deep breath and pull her arm away so she stops biting her nails. "Ok...tell me what's going on. Does your mom know about all this?"

She shakes her head 'no'. "My mom doesn't know."

I feel my heart pounding fast in my chest and listen to her every word. "What makes you think that you are dying?"

She sits upright. The tissue is in tatters on her beanbag. "Well, yesterday, when I went to the bathroom, I had blood down there." She points down towards her vagina.

I let out a sigh of relief.

She continues, "And it hasn't stopped bleeding, and my stomach has been hurting real bad. I've been putting toilet paper down there to soak up the blood, but I don't know what to do."

She begins to cry again and manages to say, "I'm scared."

She looks at me in shock as I let out a loud shriek of laughter and wrap both of my arms around her to hug her. She pushes herself free.

I can't help but smile when I speak to her. "You are not dying."

"I'm not? Then why am I bleeding nonstop?"

"You are having your first period. Congratulations!"

"What's a period?" She asks.

"Why don't you put on your coat and shoes and we'll go down to the drug store to get you some pads. I'll explain everything on the way there."

As we walk to the corner CVS drug store, I explain to Zuni what a period is and what it means for her and her body. Everything from the mood swings to the bloating and cramps to the food cravings to even how she can now get pregnant. Zuni is not thrilled that she will have a regular visitor each month, and go through all the physical changes. I guess at this age, it's difficult to see your cycle as something of a gift, a sign that you can bear life. On the way back, we stop by a deli and I buy her a hot chocolate. When we get home, I show her how to use the pad. Afterwards she gives me a big smile and hug.

I head over to our bedroom to tell Peter about my special bonding session with Zuni, but he is fast asleep. I go into the bathroom and decide to send Wish a text.

Hi there. Got your sweet message. Thank you. It was great to hear your voice. I miss you and hope to see you soon. Get some rest. Xoxo

***

CHAPTER 20

Back at the office the next morning, I receive a reply from Eric.

Nikki — you want to be careful of what you say. This is a deposition and if it goes into litigation, your words can be held against you. Your words can be twisted. I suggest you say the following and if they keep pressing you, give them my card (you can get one from Weston) and tell them to call me. They will try to intimidate you. Don't fall for it.

This is what you should say -- I hope you can understand the uncomfortable and awkward position I am in due to the reporting structure. My immediate supervisor is Chester. I certainly am willing to answer any and all questions, but there are two parties involved and I work for both of them. If this goes into litigation, I do not want my words to be taken out of context or misinterpreted. I've retained counsel and have been instructed by my lawyer to not speak informally, but on the record.
Let me know if you need anything else. Good luck — Eric.

I am edgy over the next couple of days, and even find myself yelling at Matilda, whom I usually can be patient with when she pulls one of her many office dictator routines. For the most part, I feel sorry for Matilda. The rumor around the office is that she is married to an Egyptian cab driver who married her for a green card, who apparently is never at home. So in order to compensate for her loneliness, Matilda has five cats to keep her warm and fuzzy. She is always covered in stringy white, gray, and yellow cat hairs.

Matilda is the first one in the office and the last one to leave. Her job is her life. Her life is her job, but unfortunately, the victims of her loneliness and control issues are her coworkers. One of her recent shenanigans is to ration out tea packets. She counts out three packets of the different kind of teas for an office of thirty-five people and locks up the remaining boxes.

So if anyone wants to have a cup of green, black, or any type of herb tea, and there is none left, they have to walk over to her cubicle at the far end of the office and ask her for a tea bag. She constantly tests people's boundaries and patience, and it seems that I was next on her list.

"Knock. Knock." I say through gritted teeth as I approach Matilda's cubicle.

Matilda's back is turned towards me while she works away at her computer. And as I get closer, I see that she is shopping for shoes on Zappos. She quickly closes her window browser and turns to face me.

"Yes? Can you not see that I am quite busy!" She contorts her eyes at me as if that's supposed to scare me.

I hold my smile back. "Can I get a packet of green tea?"

Why do I feel like an orphan begging for food.

"You would like tea? Again?"

"Yes." I reel at her.

"You drink a lot of green tea."

I am not sure how to respond to her.

She goes on. "Why do you like green tea so much?"

Why are you such a psycho? I want to ask.

I drolly reply, "I like the taste."

"I do not like green tea. I am not that a big fan of it." She must think we're having some type of negotiation. "How many cups of tea have you had today?" She asks.

I can't believe this is happening.

"Matilda, this is my first one." What the hell is wrong with her?

"Would you also like to know my blood type?"

She completely ignores my second comment. "Really? And there is none left on the counter?"

"Matilda, there are thirty-five people who work in this office. You leave out only three packets for the whole office."

"Still." She rolls her eyes, and makes absolutely no gesture to even get up. "These people are like vultures."

"There is a reason the office has coffee and tea for the staff. I don't understand why you hide it."

"Listen missy, I am not hiding it. It is called rationing. This is a nonprofit for God's sake."

Something in me goes dark. My stomach feels like it's on fire and the hot flames are quickly spreading all over my body and into my face. My hands and legs begin to tremble out of sheer anger. I want to make Matilda pay for all of my misery. I lean down to within an inch of her face.

My hands still shaking, I grab the arms of her chair, trapping her in place. "Matilda. Give. Me. A. Fucking. Tea. Bag." My voice is like a low animal growl. My eyes feel like they are about to pop out of their sockets.

Matilda pushes herself deeper into her chair. Her pale blue eyes turn big with fear, and she responds like a scared child. "Ok."

I straighten up and take one step back to let her get up, but keep a sharp, penetrating gaze on her to keep her cowering with fear. I follow her to the special supply closet that she keeps under lock and key. As she unlocks the door and pushes it open, I pounce in front of her and push her aside. I jump into the closet to grab a whole full box of green tea, and quickly run away as I feel her hand yank on the back of my shirt to stop me.

She yells after me, "Hey. Come back. You can't do that! Bring that back."

After making my cup of tea, I head towards my office and see Weston approaching me with a big, cheesy grin on his face. He follows me into my office and closes the door.

"Guess what I did?" He asks giddily as he covers his mouth.

"Do I want to know?" I slump in my chair.

He lets out a loud maniacal laugh.

"Oh no. I'm afraid to ask. What did you do?"

"I took all the tea packets from the kitchen, and when Matilda put out three more, I took those too, and when she puts out another three, I will return everything."

I don't know whether to laugh or cry. This place is insane.

"Well, I just flipped out on her because you took all the tea bags, Weston. I growled at the poor woman and even pushed her. Then I basically stole a whole full box of tea."

Weston is laughing hysterically.

"This isn't funny. It's pathetic! Look how low we've sunk. You're playing tricks on Matilda. I'm stealing tea and pushing the poor cat lady. I swear I'm going to lose my marbles soon. I have to talk to the lawyers tomorrow."

Weston has stopped laughing, "Oh, shit. Are you serious?"

I take a sip of my tea, close my eyes and lean my head back.

"You're under a lot of stress right now. When this is all over, take yourself a nice long vacation," he says.

"Maybe."

"I got to get back to work, but first, I need to check if the cat lady has put out more tea packets." He hops out of my office and towards the kitchen.

After all the drama I went through with Matilda, I decide to leave my green tea sitting on my desk to get out of the office for a few minutes. I need some fresh, exhaust filled New York City cold air to help me think. I head down to the corner Starbucks to treat myself to a soy caramel latte.

As I sit at the window sipping away, I watch people through the glass windows rushing through the cold New York weather. Despite the weather, the expensive housing costs, the competitiveness of everyone trying to make a name for themselves, and the various crazies loose on the streets, I love this city. It is definitely a one-of-a-kind place where the impossible and unimaginable can happen, both in the good and bad sense. Where else would I meet various titans of industry or for that matter, someone like Wish Michaels.

My mind slowly drifts to Wish. As mind shattering as the sex was, it was a mistake to go there with him. I think deep down I knew how wrong it was when I got off the train at Union Station in DC, but I didn't pay attention to the nagging voice. I had a rule for myself to never get involved with anyone who was married. Why should I? What was in it for me? Absolutely nothing. Yet, here I was with yet another broken rule. First Peter and now this. Thinking about Wish is taking too much of my energy, and I need to focus on my work and this impeding Summit. I take my latte and head back to the office.

***

CHAPTER 21

On Friday morning, I dress in a boring gray suit that is one size too big for me, and wear my glasses. I sure as hell can't look sexy or attractive while being interrogated by the attorneys. And by now, I have memorized the 'can't speak informally' schpeel. My stomach is in knots as I walk into the fancy office building on Park Avenue.

I take the elevator straight up to the thirty-fifth floor and am awed as I step out into a luxurious and modern office with lots of large windows, expensive tan leather furniture, and beautiful artwork on the walls. I introduce myself to the receptionist and am told to wait for Michelle Ramses. As I sit on the soft leather sofa, I take out my notes to myself and read it over once more.

"Hello. I'm Michelle Ramses."

Before me stands an attractive brunette lawyer with long hair, a short skirt, high heels with no stockings, and red lipstick.

It is definitely not warm enough outside to not wear stockings is all I can think.

I jam my notes into my purse and stand up to shake her hand. "Hello, I'm Nikki Johnson." She nearly crushes my bones with her man grip. "It's nice to meet you." I fake a smile.

I follow her to a large conference room where another attractive lawyer with blond hair and in a short skirt is waiting for me.

"This is Heather Smith. She will be helping me take notes," says Michelle.

Heather and I do the customary polite handshake and exchange a few nice empty words. She returns to her laptop ready to take my every word.

For some reason, I see these two as my enemies and am already nervous and on the defensive. And besides, I find it trés bizarre that there are two very attractive women asking me questions about sexual harassment charges against Chester.

Michelle begins, "Nikki, thank you for taking the time to come in today. I am not sure if you know what is going on."

I stare at her blankly as if I don't know. Silence is all she gets.

She continues, "There have been a few allegations brought up against Chester about an inappropriate sexual relationship with a subordinate and inappropriate comments made to some women in the office."

I am taken aback for her statement.

Michelle continues, "We have been hired by the Board of Directors to investigate."

I am surprised that Bren has made this bigger than her original allegation. From what this lawyer is saying, this investigation involves multiple women and not just Bren.

"We are an unbiased third party and I will ask you some questions that will be kept confidential to the extent that we can."

Confidential to the extent that we can. What twisted lawyer speak. "What does that mean?" I ask her.

"Well, we have a responsibility to our client, Chas Chandler and the Board of Directors for the Center for Ethical Business. We will report our findings to them. You have to understand that this is an investigation." She points her finger at me, and is speaking to me in a condescending way.

Well you have to understand that I don't have to answer your freaking questions, I want to say.

I take a deep breath in and am about to begin my monologue when I notice a small video camera in the far corner of the conference room ceiling that is covered by a black glass orb. I can see the red light shining through. Before coming here, I had done my research on this law firm and the fact that it is one of the best and biggest law firms in the country did not calm my nerves at all.

Michelle notices the direction of my gaze. "Oh, I'm sorry I forgot to tell you. We are recording this interview. It's company policy. I hope you don't mind."

I don't think my minding would matter much. I squeeze my hands together and say my lines. "I certainly am willing to answer any and all questions, but there are two parties involved and I work for both of them."

Michelle puts her pen down and glares at me.

I do a mental reminder to myself to breathe and talk slowly to not show them that I'm nervous. I continue, "If this goes into litigation, I do not want my words to be taken out of context or misinterpreted."

The sound of Heather's typing is like a jackhammer that stabs my thoughts. I try not to let it distract me and squeeze my hands harder to help me focus. "I've retained counsel and have been instructed by my lawyer to not speak informally, but on the record."

As I finish off, I see a big smile on her face. She cocks her head to the side, still keeping her glare on me. She glances at Heather and then back at me, throws her head back and lets out a thunderous chortle.

When she finally stops laughing, her face gets dead serious, jaw tight, nose flaring, eyes squinting.

"Well, let's not project that this will go into litigation. Right now, we are conducting an unbiased investigation. Do you understand that, Nikki?"

I feel like I am going to pee in my pants. "Yes," I manage to croak out.

"And I hope you will answer our questions to the best of your ability," she finishes off.

I take a heavy gulp of air. The bright light from the windows reflects off the white walls and it feels like my eyes are being seared in their sockets.

"Look." I let out a heavy sigh. "I am going to take the advice of my lawyer under consideration and not answer questions informally."

Michelle slams her palm down on her notepad and leans in towards me.

"Listen here Ms. Nikki Johnson." Chas Chandler is the Chairman of this organization and he has hired us to look into this matter. As an employee, we are asking you to answer our questions today."

I feel like my chest is in a vise that is being squeezed tighter and tighter. My throat feels dry and scratchy. And, I think I did just pee on myself. I am not sure how to do this. I don't want to lie, but I don't want to tell the truth either. Maybe I can disclose some half version of the truth. As Henry said, they have interviewed other staff people, and I'm sure they have been grilled on the actions of Chester and Consuela.

I cave in. "Ok."

God, I am such a wuss. Aggressive women intimidate me. Why can't I be more assertive? I'm tired of being such a weakling. I make a mental note to myself to resolve my mother issues. Maybe even look into therapy.

"How long have you worked at the Center and how did you start?" Michelle asks.

"I've been there about a year and half. I started as a temp, then worked as an Assistant to the CEO, and now I am the Director of Communications."

"Really? That's a fast advancement, wouldn't you say?"

"Well…I'm a hard worker, and I have ambition."

She squints at me and exchanges a look with Heather. "Hmmm…interesting."

No need to get any more nervous than I am already feeling. I'm not on trial.

"Are you aware of any activity that indicates inappropriate sexual behavior or conduct in the office?"

Since in my weak moment I had told Bren about the condom story, I tell them about that sordid mess, but not the band-aid part.

"Are you aware of any inappropriate behavior with a staff person or consultant?"

"Well, I've heard rumors about him and CROW…I mean Consuela."

"Would you like a cookie? They are really good"

They're probably poisoned with truth serum. "No, thank you. I'm trying to lose weight."

"No way." She gives my body a scan over and it feels like she can see through my drab gray suit that hangs loosely in all the right places.

"You have a nice figure." She smiles a friendly 'I am your friend' smile.

I return her smile.

"I think I will have one," she says. She reaches over to grab a cookie. Her hands are porcelain white, without any blemishes, protruding veins, or sunspots. Her fingers are long and thin, and of course her nail polish on her long oval nails is vixen red. I watch her pick up a chocolate chip cookie and take it to her mouth. She closes her eyes to show off her long lashes and smoky eye shadow. Her red lips close around the cookie.

"Hmmm…this is delicious." she finishes off the cookie.

I feel dirty. I think I've just witnessed something illicit.

She switches back to her lawyer mode. "Well, there have been allegations of an inappropriate relationship with a Consuela Roberta Olalla Wilfredo. Are you aware of anything that would indicate such a thing?"

"Well, he does give her preferential treatment in that she does not really have a schedule."

"What do you mean?"

"Well, she sort of comes and goes as she pleases. Everybody else is in the office from nine to five, and Consuela comes in late, takes long lunches, leaves early, and even works from home. Working from home is not office policy and no one else is given that privilege."

"And did anyone ever have a conversation with Chester about Consuela's hours?"

"I'm not sure, but I don't think so, at least, not that I am aware of. There is a sign-in- book in the front by the reception area for all staff to sign in and out and there was an incidence where people were writing something in Consuela's slot."

"What were they writing?"

"I don't know. I didn't see it."

"So how do you know people were writing things?"

"Because an email went out to the whole staff about treating a co-worker with respect and not questioning each other's time and when someone comes in or leaves."

"Who sent out the email?"

"Chester."

"And he mentioned Consuela by name?"

"No. But it didn't take a rocket scientist to figure out whom he was talking about. There is no one else who does that."

"Did he ever find out who was writing in the book?"

"He never said anything to me."

She pauses here and stares out towards the window to reflect on my answer. I'm hoping this is the end of it and am grateful for the break.

"Are we done?" Please let her say yes.

She snaps her head towards me, and lets out a snicker. "No. Far from it."

Yikes, that sounded sinister.

"And how did Consuela's lack of a schedule affect the staff?" She continues with her interrogation.

"It made everyone angry. They felt they were working hard and she was getting a free pass. It brought down morale that Consuela was being given preferential treatment and no one really knew what her job was."

"Are you aware of a poem that was written for Consuela?"

"Sort of."

"What do you mean sort of? Either you are or you aren't."

"I've heard about it."

"Have you seen or read the poem?"

I feel my chest getting hot. My underarms feel wet.

"I have never read it."

I just hope that the sweat stains don't leak through my suit.

"Hmmm…really? That's interesting."

I feel a sweat bead running down my chest and into my bellybutton.

"So was there anything else that suggested inappropriate behavior?"

"Consuela would continuously flirt with Chester."

"And how would she do that?"

"She would wear low cut shirts and short skirts, and then throw herself across his desk to reveal various body parts."

"Anything else?"

"She would always laugh at his corny and inappropriate jokes. I know that doesn't sound much now, but it's one of those things that you had to be there for. And she was always touching him in some way."

"Touching him? In what way?"

"I've seen her touch his back, almost like rubbing it. I've seen her straighten his tie, and in some meetings, she unnecessarily reaches over to touch his arm or some other body part."

"That's a bit unprofessional. Would he flirt back? And would he do anything to encourage her flirting?"

"I didn't see him flirt back, at least not in public. And I don't really know if he was doing anything to encourage her flirting except having a cheesy grin on his face."

"You could hear the laughing and giggling from his office?"

"Yes, when the door was open."

"And how often would the door be closed?"

"Quite often…well actually most of the time Consuela was in there. She would close the door with a loud noise when she went into his office, and I could hear the giggling and laughing"

"And how long would the door be closed?"

"Maybe ten to fifteen minutes."

"How do you think her flirting made him feel?"

How does a big-tittied young chick flirting with a seventy-year-old man make him feel, is how I'd like to respond.

"I can't really speculate on that," I say. All of a sudden I feel self-conscious and realize that I have divulged too much.

"When he travels, do you make his arrangements?"

"Yes."

"When he traveled with Consuela, did you make those arrangements?"

"No. Those were made by Consuela."

"And how did that happen and was that the norm?"

"I am not sure. It just happened that she started doing it, without me knowing. I was only told about it after the fact."

"And when he traveled with Consuela, was he reachable?"

"Yes, he was reachable on his cell, and he would check in with me."

"And what about any poems? Have you seen any of them?"

I try hard to remember everything that I am answering so she doesn't trip me up and my answers are consistent.

"Oh, yes, I usually type them up for him, since he does not type."

"And what type of poems are they?"

"I remember a poem to a friend who had cancer, his children, his grandchildren, his father…you know that type of sentimental stuff."

"Have you seen any sexual or inappropriate poems?"

"No."

"Inappropriate could be anything that makes you feel uncomfortable."

"No, I haven't seen anything inappropriate."

She starts to twirl her hair.

"Has he ever given you poems?"

"Well, I write poetry, and he is a former English professor. I've asked him to look at some of my poems. And he has let me read some of his poetry."

"And how long has this been going on?"

"I'm not sure exactly, but I would say probably from the beginning."

"Has he ever said anything or done anything to make you feel uncomfortable?"

I feel more sexually uncomfortable here with you then I've ever felt with Chester.

"No."

Still twirling her hair.

By now she is completely oozing sexuality out of every orifice. I get the feeling she is flirting with me.

"Has he ever given you gifts?"

"Yes."

"What has he given you?"

"A handkerchief, some household candles, a wallet, some flowers."

"And why did he give you these gifts?"

"It was for a birthday, Christmas, or if I did a great job with an event. But, he is very generous in that way. He's given other staff member gifts.

Things like books, cards, flowers."

"Has he given a male staff member a gift?"

"I think so. I think he gave a tie once that I am aware of. But most of our staff are women."

"What's the most memorable gift he's given you?"

She asks me this question with a smile as if we're just a couple of girlfriends hamming it up.

"Nothing that is too memorable."

Her ploys are not going to work on me. Besides, I thought she said she was unbiased, yet her questions are definitely trying to lead me to answer a certain way.

"Have you ever ordered any gifts for Consuela or written any messages or poems for her?"

"No."

"Do you ever order gifts or write notes for him for others?"

"Yes, I have ordered flowers and gifts to Board members and some colleagues in the field and have written the messages, but nothing for Consuela."

"Has he ever brought his romantic partner to work or does he ever talk to you about his romantic life?"

"No."

I find myself getting irritated. She keeps asking me the same question in a different way. I am so over this shit.

"Do you have any plans for this weekend?"

You've got to be joking me?

"Wha-a-a-t?"

"Any fun plans?"

"In fact, yes I do." I cross my arms and cock my head to the side. "I will be recovering from this deposition."

My comment and sharp tone takes her by surprise, and makes her reel back in her chair. She gives me an awkward smile and glances at her notes.

"Has he ever locked his office door?"

"Not that I'm aware of."

"Does he mostly leave his door open or closed?"

"It's mostly open. And for some meetings, he closes the door. But he generally has an open door policy. Anyone can walk in and talk to him."

"What time does he usually come in and leave?"

"He generally comes in around eight thirty in the morning. He sometimes leaves around five."

"Does he stay late?"

"It's about 50/50. There are times he stays late."

"Do you work late?"

Why do I get the feeling that she is implying something?

"There are times that I've worked late and there are times I've gone in on the weekend when I have a lot to do."

"Does the staff go out? Have you ever gone out with Chester?"

I take pause for a second to deliberate how I am going to answer this question. I feel like she is trying to trap me into some sort of a confession.

"The staff does go out for lunch, dinner, drinks. I've gone to lunch with Chester and even a few business dinners."

Damn it. I shouldn't have given up that bit of info.

"Has he gone out with other staff people to lunch or dinner?"

My stomach has been knotted up this whole time and I'm not sure how much longer I can take. Maybe I can fake a fainting spell or tell them I feel like I'm going to throw up.

"Yes, sometimes he goes out to lunch or dinner with other staff members."

"Have you ever witnessed any inappropriate behavior with other staff members?"

"No."

She gives a dirty look that makes me sit up straight. "Are you trying to avoid answering my questions?"

I didn't grab any boobies. Why is everybody picking on me?

"No." I stare at her innocently and blankly at the same time.

"Have you ever seen any condom wrappers or anything sexual in his office besides that one time?"

"No." I make a grossed out face. I have to stop being defensive and make her think I am on her side.

"Do you have anything else to say?"

"Look, for what it's worth, I think it's a bit of an internal witch hunt going on."

"Really? Why do you say that?"

"It's just my gut sense. I don't know what is really going on. But there is something else that is motivating this investigation."

"Ok. I am going to get my notes together and may call on you again if I think of anything further."

Please don't ever call me. I never want to go through this excruciatingly painful experience again.

"Ok. Sure."

At this point I don't want to say anything more. She latches on to every little syllable and finds a question to ask. I thank them, grab a cookie, and get the hell out of there as fast as I can.

***

CHAPTER 22

After my inquisition, I head home. I can't stand to even think about work and this whole situation anymore. As I sit down in the subway, I close my eyes and replay the questioning over and over again in my head.

Why did I let her intimidate me? Eric had warned me that they would try to bully me into cooperating. I knew what her tactic was and yet still caved in. Why did I answer so many questions? I wonder if they will question me again? Could I have been more forthcoming? I am mad as hell at Chester. He was supposed to be my hero; the person on my side who showed me how to maneuver the nonprofit world and help me succeed. He has clearly broken some rules and crossed some major ethical lines. So why do I feel the need to protect him? Do I have some sort of daddy issue, I wonder?

All of a sudden, I feel someone tapping me on the shoulder. I open my eyes and turn to my right. In the seat next to me, is my stalker guy. Lanky, wearing an old stained t-shirt, cargo pants ripped at the knees, beat up sketchers. Not as dirty as a homeless person, but definitely a close second. His face is taut and covered by a patchy and scraggily dark brown beard. In a city of eight million people, what are the chances of seeing the same crazy person twice?

"Hmmm….hmmm…..hmmm…. girl. You again."

I rear back.

"I been thinkin' o you ever since I saw you. Ha…ha….ha…." His cracked dry lips part to reveal a mouth full of missing teeth. "You know what I'm talkin' bout."

I look at him, frightened. How can I get out of this one?

He continues, "I mean. F. I. N. E. hmmmm."

He is practically in my face. I move over as much to the left of my seat as I can, but really there is nowhere to go. I jump up, but it is difficult to maneuver in the packed train. A few people shimmy out of the way to let me get away from stalker guy, but there is not much room for me to move away from him. He moves over to my old seat.

"You got a man?"

"Yes, I have a boyfriend."

Why am I even talking to him?

"Well, he ain't here now, is he?"

As the train slows to a stop, I eye the door. "This is my stop." I lie.

"Can I get your digits?"

"No."

The train doors open and I begin to move with the sea of people getting out at Fourteenth Street. I yell behind me as I step off the train, "I don't think my man would like that."

As I stand on the platform waiting for the next train, I wonder what the hell is wrong with me. I can't even tell a borderline homeless guy to leave me alone. I feel like I just got abused by the lawyer, and now I have been polluted with stalker guy's funk, and now I'm heading to a place that's not even my home anymore. Maybe Wish was right. I am a weak, and meek little girl.

The deposition and berating thoughts about myself run through my head all the way home. As I walk through the front door, I see Peter running around frantically. He gives me a quick glance over as he runs from the living room to the bedroom.

"Where have you been? I called you at work," he yells over his shoulder.

I follow him and stand watch as he grabs a small duffle bag.

"The lawyers. Remember?"

How could he forget?

"Oh yeah. Sorry, I forgot." He doesn't even look at me but instead runs over to the closet and begins to pull out some clothes.

"What are you doing?" I ask.

"This is why I've been calling you all day. I had submitted a proposal for a job, and they just called me today to fly out to Atlanta for a presentation tomorrow morning at their Board retreat. My flight is in a couple of hours, and I'll be back home tomorrow by noon."

"Oh ok." I'm still in shock over my interrogation.

He goes into the bathroom and grabs some of his toiletries, runs back to the bag sitting on our bed, and tosses them in there. Still wearing my coat and boots, I walk to the edge of the bed and gently sit down.

"So, it'll just be you and Zuni tonight," he says. He looks at me with a worried look.

I am too exhausted and drained to say anything or care.

Peter continues, "I know that things have been really hard for you at home and at work."

Buddy, you have no idea.

"And I have been overwhelmed with dealing with a teenager too. But, I promise." He cups my face in his hands and looks me in the eyes. "Things will get better soon."

"I hope so. Because I feel like I'm going to crack soon if something doesn't change."

I take off my boots and scratch the red bumps on my legs. "Have you been getting bit?"

"What?"

"This past week I've had some type of bug bites on my legs."

"It's probably all the stress you are under," he says.

"I'm going to take a bath."

"Well, Zuni hasn't done her chores this week."

"Why do I need to know that?"

"Part of her chores are to clean the bathroom. She hasn't cleaned the bathtub. It's dirty."

"I guess it'll be a shower then." I give him a smile and drop my clothes into a pile on the floor.

Peter comes into the bathroom to give me a kiss goodbye before he runs out to catch a cab to the airport. I guess it wouldn't be so bad to have a bonding night with Zuni. Besides, after our 'period' episode I feel closer to her and she hopefully to me.

I let the water run over me to wash off the stench of The Center for Unethical Business, the deposition, and stalker guy. Only after my fingertips turn pruny, do I get out. I hear Zuni playing some Justin Bieber song about needing somebody to love.

I put on my white terrycloth robe, wrap my hair with a white towel, and go out to find out what Zuni wants for dinner. I don't feel like cooking and will just order some dinner, maybe a pizza, and let Zuni watch one of her reality TV shows. I knock on her door, but she can't seem to hear me over the blare of her stereo. I slowly crack the door and poke my head through. On Zuni's bed sits a skinny, pale boy with shaggy brown hair. He is not wearing a shirt. As I stare at him in shock, Zuni steps out from behind the door shirtless, wearing only her skinny jeans. My mouth falls open.

"Don't you know how to knock?" She snaps at me as she covers her budding boobs and recovers her grunge t-shirt from the floor.

"I knocked." I yell through gritted teeth. I head over to her stereo and slam it off.

"Get out of my room!"

"Excuse me...you're telling me what to do in my own home?" I yell back.

"What are you doing home anyway? I didn't think anyone was here."

She must have let her teen lover boy in while I was in the shower. I decide not to respond to her, I'm the grown up here, right? And I will take charge. I shoot her a dirty look of utter annoyance and turn around to look at shirtless Casper, the friendly ghost boyfriend, sitting in front of me. He quickly pulls his white t-shirt over his head, which by the way is not a good look since it washes him out even more.

"I don't care who you are, but you need to get out now!" I say this with the most authoritative voice I can muster. Oh, and I make pointing gestures with my index finger, a little trick that I have learned from Bren, to intimidate ghost boy and Zuni.

Zuni jumps in front of me. "No." She pushes me. "You can't tell him what to do."

"Watch me," I say as I brush Zuni aside and stare at the boy, who is now standing up and shifting from foot to foot, and not quite sure what to do next.

"I think I better go." He pushes past me with his head hung low. I hear the front door close behind him. I turn around to face Zuni.

"Zuni, I thought we talked about the whole boys and sex thing," I say calmly.

"Fuck you." She slams her index finger towards me. "We didn't talk about shit." She reaches up and pulls the towel off my head.

I thought we were on good terms and am shocked by the turn of events. I'm wondering if this is going to get physical, and not sure about how to respond. I decide that if she touches me again, I'm going to retaliate.

"You are a bitch and I hate you. I don't know why my dad is with you." She is screaming and flinging the towel at me.

All I can think to myself is no this little brat did not just yank the towel off my head. I don't know how to handle this and quickly shift gears to calm her down.

"I'm sorry I got angry. It's just that I was caught off guard when I walked in here. You're not supposed to have boys over."

"Get the fuck out of my room." She throws the towel at me.

I stand there for a couple of minutes as we stare at each other.

I finally decide to walk out. I feel angry and defeated. I remember being that age and having raging hormones, but at the same time, I wasn't a spoiled, little, moody bitch. I get myself dried off and throw on my comfy worn out gray sweatshirt that makes me feel cozy and safe. It's perfect for times like these. I muster up the courage to approach Zuni again to simply ask her what she wants for dinner.

"I'm not hungry." She is terse. "I'm going to a movie with my friend Jenny. Is that ok with you.....Mom?" She emphasizes the word 'mom' for as much sarcasm as she can muster.

Not daring to fully step into her room, I stand at the threshold of her door, leaning against the frame and do my best not to take her anger personally act.

I ignore her snotty tone. "Ummm...sure. It's a Friday night. I don't see why not." I want to get on her good side again. "Just leave me her phone number, and be home by 10 pm." I give her $25 dollars for her night out. Getting her off my hands for the night is priceless.

I am happy she is out of the house for a few hours. I have never been in a position where I have to take care of her all by myself. Peter has always been around and served as a buffer and an authority figure. When she gets home at ten, it won't be so bad. We both will probably go to bed without too much more of an interaction.

I let myself settle in for the night and treat myself by ordering a cheese pizza from Two Boots. I burrow myself in the couch with my chick flick of choice, Bridget Jones's Diary, and enjoy my pizza.

I must have dozed off because when I wake up I realize the movie has stopped playing and it is 10:30 pm. I feel like such a sloth. I'm curled up on the corner of the couch, wearing a baggy sweatshirt and sweat pants. My hair is a wild and frizzy mess, and there's an open pizza box in front of me with a half-eaten large pizza. I get up, dust off the crumbs from the outside and inside of my sweat shirt, run my hands over my hair to smooth it out and decide to go check on Zuni. I find her room empty and decide to call her friend Jenny. 917-616-9845.

"The number you have dialed is no longer in service. Please check your number and try again," the automated voice says on the other end. I dial again 917-616-9845.

"The number you have dialed…" I slam the phone down.

I can't believe that little witch gave me the wrong number. What should I do? What should I do?

I pick up the phone and slam it back down. Ok, calm down. No need to call Peter. I can figure this out. Maybe she's heading home right now. I walk over to look out the window. Nope, I don't see her. I put on my fitflops and take the elevator down to the lobby. The doorman is snoozing behind his desk and about to fall out of his chair. I head over to the large glass doors and step outside. The cold night wind cuts through my loose sweatshirt and pants. I might as well be naked out here. I cross my arms to keep myself warm. I turn to the right. I don't see her. I turn to the left. I don't see her. I stand there pondering what I'm expecting to find out here.

Should I go back up and put on my coat and go look for her? Where am I even going to start? I don't know where she went or where her friend lives, and this is New York City, she could be anywhere. She could be having sex with ghost boy! She could be run over, lying bleeding on the street! She could be mugged! She could have fallen into the train tracks and electrocuted! Oh my God, she could be dead! Dead!

I turn around in a mad dash and run back in as fast as I can. My fitflops make loud thumping noises against the floor. Passing the now startled doorman, I trip and fall flat on my face. My body is spread eagled across the floor. My right fitflop lands behind me. I quickly jump back up, pick up the fitflop off the floor, take the other one off and go back up to the apartment. I'm too worried to be embarrassed.

No need to work myself into a tizzy. I'm sure she just lost sense of time. I can wait it out. I'm sure the brat will be home soon. She probably wants to punish me for ruining her I'm-about-to-lose-my-virginity moment. I have to distract myself.

I'm freezing to the bones. Peter would be happy to know that I don't have enough fat on my body to keep me warm. He's probably sleeping peacefully in some fancy hotel room. I make myself a cup of chamomile tea, plop myself on the couch, and cover myself with a flannel blanket. I flip through the TV for what feels like two hours, but when I check the time, it's only been thirty minutes. I get up and pace back and forth for a while then look out the window again. Back to the couch for some more station flipping. I finally stop on an episode of I Love Lucy. It's the Vitameatavagamin episode. Lucy would have known what to do. She would have sprung into action with some crazy plan instead of sitting here watching TV. I am inspired by watching Lucy and decide to call the police.

"How old is the child and how long has the child been missing?" The dry and unemotional woman on the other end asks me.

"She's thirteen, and well, she was supposed to be home at 10:30 and now it's 11:45 and she's not here. I don't know what to do."

"Do you have any reason to suspect something has happened?"

189

"Well, she's not here. She could have gotten raped or mugged or something."

"Ma'am, did you try calling her?"

"Helllooo...are you hearing me? If she had a phone, I would call her and would have no need to call you."

"I suggest you not yell at me Ma'am." Ok, I admit, I am yelling. The dry voice continues, "It sounds to me like the case of a typical teen ignoring curfew. She is thirteen years old. This is what they do. I am sorry but I cannot do anything under these circumstances."

"But I want to file a missing person report." I am still yelling.

"Ma'am, you can file a report if you have just cause to believe something has happened. I suggest you wait a reasonable amount of time."

"I think it's been a reasonable--"

"Ma'am, Ma'am," She tries to cut me off.

"--amount of time," I say raising my voice.

"As I stated before, it sounds like the case of a typical teen being rebellious. If she does not show up by tomorrow, then I suggest you call us."

"What do you expect me to do? Just sit around?" I ask annoyed.

"I don't care what you do Ma'am. All, I am saying is that we cannot do anything yet. It is too soon. I suggest you drink some warm milk and go to bed."

"But I hate milk."

"Goodbye." The heartless voice hangs up on me.

Maybe I should take her advice. I decide to take myself to bed and wait it all out. Maybe Zuni will show up in the middle of the night. Of course I can't fall asleep. I lie there flip flopping around the bed like a fish out of water. My mind races to all of the horrible things that can happen to a thirteen-year-old girl running around New York City in the middle of the night.

No point in lying here so I head back to the sofa to watch some more TV. I finish off the last half of the pizza. I find some chocolates, and even ponder the milk thing, but decide against it. Finally at about five in the morning, I fall asleep on the couch, angry, and not believing that I am going through this crap.

I wake up to Peter shaking me awake. I bolt upright out of shock and wipe off my eye boogers.

What time is it? Why is he home so soon? Did the police call him because Zuni is dead? What am I going to tell him?

"What's wrong with you?" Peter looks at me inquisitively. "And what happened to this place?" He looks around in disgust at the greasy pizza box, chocolate wrappers, and empty coke can thrown on the floor. Crumbs are strewn on the couch, on top of the blanket, and on the floor.

"There's something wrong," I blab out. "Zuni and I had an argument because she was about to have sex with a ghost boy in her room and then I let her go to a movie, and she didn't come back all night. I didn't know what to do. I called the police and they told me to wait. All I could do was eat."

He stares at me in disbelief, trying to make sense of it all. "What are you talking about? I just checked on Zuni, she's sleeping in her room. I think you were having a bad dream."

This whole thing is a bad dream. "What?" I run towards Zuni's room and throw open her door. There she is, lying fast asleep like an angel who can do no wrong.

From deep in my bowels rises a flame that takes over my whole body. The flame of anger propels me forward as I stomp towards her peaceful body, and begin to shake her.

"Wake up." I yell.

She doesn't budge. "Wake up." I scream and shake her even more vigorously. Her head bobs back and forth. Peter pulls me away as I struggle to let myself loose from his grip. Zuni slowly opens her eyes. Peter is holding both of my arms from behind me.

"Where the hell have you been, you little bitch," I yell, unable to shake myself loose. "Do you know that I was up all night frantic because of you?"

I am convulsing from anger and am unable to stop myself. "Do you know that I was running around like a crazy woman thinking you were lying dead on the street? I called the police!"

Peter yanks me back harder. I want to strangle the little bitch.

"Well, you are acting like a crazy woman," Zuni retorts as she sits up on her bed. She smiles at me. "Nikki, are you ok? Did you have a bad dream?"

"Oh, don't play dumb with me, you little brat."

"Nikki. You need to calm down and stop calling her names," Peter says.

"I'm not playing anything. Dad, I've been home all night."

"Nikki said that you had a boy in your room, that you got into a fight so she let you go to the movies with your friend Jenny," Peter debriefs Zuni.

"Dad, you have Jenny's number, you can call her and ask. I didn't have a boy in my room and I didn't go to the movies, and I've been in my room all night. Nikki even ordered Pizza for dinner." Zuni looks at me with a look of disdain.

"Ok, why don't you go back to sleep," Peter says as he continues to hold me. I feel so helpless and angry. I begin sobbing as Peter pulls me out of Zuni's room and guides me into our bedroom.

"Nikki, I don't know what's going on with you, but I believe her. Why would you do something like this?"

"That little bitch is lying," I scream in between tears.

He grabs my arms tightly, as if he were going to shake me, then quickly lets go and takes a step back. His eyes are like red flares and his breathing is heavy.

"Don't you ever refer to my child in that way ever again." Peter wags his finger at me. "I never want to see a repeat of today. Do you understand me?...Ever." He storms off and out of the apartment, yelling on his way out, "I need to go calm down."

As I stand there aghast at the turn of events, I hear Zuni's footsteps approaching our bedroom.

She opens the door. "See what happens when you fuck with me," she laughs.

***

CHAPTER 23

On Monday I am glad to be out of the house. After the situation with Zuni, my whole weekend was shot. Peter and I tiptoed around each other in polite icy conversation, while Zuni was unusually chipper and cheery.

I am happy to be in the office and have it all to myself. Chester has taken a personal day. Both the sexual harassment and the foundation investigation have thrown him and the senior management team for a loop. I am happy that Henry and Bren have been closing their office doors. It means they are leaving me alone. No emails, instant messages, or closed-door conversations with them. I am looking forward to taking a long lunch with Weston to fill him in on everything and have someone to vent to.

As soon as we get situated at lunch and order my beer, my cell phone starts to ring. Since it displays a number I do not recognize, I ignore the call. Whoever it is can leave a message, and besides, I don't want anything or anyone to interrupt my much-needed relaxation time.

"I'll check the message later," I announce. I continue to tell Weston about my weekend as I drink my beer.

Thirty minutes later, my phone rings again, with the same unrecognized number. I feel tipsy from my first beer, but since this is my work phone, I reluctantly decide to answer it this time.

"Is this Nikki Johnson?" The voice on the other end of the phone asks.

"Yes, it is. May I help you?" I slur out.

"Yes. I am Dr. Dung and Chester has given me your name as an emergency contact."

"What do you mean as an emergency contact? What's wrong?" I know what's wrong but it's nothing a simple hospital stay will relieve.

"He has had surgery."

What kind of surgery?" I ask.

Probably Itty-bitty brain surgery?

"I am sorry, but I cannot disclose that information due to doctor-patient confidentiality."

"So why are you calling me? Did something happen?" This piece of Dung is ruining my lunchtime.

"He's ok. He is just coming out from under anesthesia and we cannot let him out by himself. He needs to be released to someone. Since you are the emergency contact, we need you to pick him up."

Sigh. How does Chester always know the perfect time to totally screw up my few pleasurable minutes?

"Ok, I will be there in forty-five minutes." I decide to pass on my second beer.

As I walk into the sterile and antiseptic hospital, I am overpowered by the bland taupe-ness of everything. There is a strong odor of chemical cleaners floating in the air, and after walking around for what seems like forever, riding up and down in lifeless silver elevators, I find the surgery ward.

"Hi, I am here to pick up Chester McMadden."

The nurse behind the counter points down the long corridor. "That way, behind the first curtain on your left."

I walk down the barren corridor not knowing what to expect. As I draw open the curtain, there is Chester, lying in a gurney on his big fleshy mountain of a stomach like a baby, his butt up in the air.

He is wearing a white hospital gown with a blue ribbon print all over it with two ties in the back, one on top and one around the waist. The back of his gown from the waist down is open and I can see his flat wrinkled, aged buttocks. There is a large white gauze wrap coming out of his butt area and taped on one side. I expect to see him sucking his thumb next.

Why? Why does this man traumatize me so? And talk about making someone feel uncomfortable.

I slowly walk up to him and although Chester is still groggy, he recognizes me. There is a strong smell of iodine coming from him that violates my nostrils, and again I'm searching desperately for a barf bag.

Chester lifts his head towards me and mumbles something incomprehensible. I hold my breath and take a step closer and lean down towards him.

"This is so embarrassing, Nikki," he mutters.

I see some drool on the corner of his mouth.

"Now you really do know everything about me. Hemorrhoids and all," he whimpers like a sad, albeit disgusting, little puppy.

In an effort not to choke from the smell, all I can do is take short, staccato gasps of air and take a step back.

"It's ok, Chester." He looks so old and vulnerable. I can't believe he has no one he can call to pick him up from the hospital. No friends, none of his girlfriends, and certainly no Consuela. I let out a deep sigh of guilt. I shouldn't have outed him to Bren. I was just so angry and hurt.

"I've been in worst situations." I give him a pathetic, guilt-ridden smile. "Besides, I've always wanted to pick you up from the hospital. Let's get you dressed and take you home."

With the nurse's help, he somehow manages to stand up and shuffle off towards the dressing room.

He emerges a few minutes later in pressed, starched jeans, the kind with a line down the middle and a blue shirt. This is the first time I've seen him without a suit and tie. I take him by the arm and start to lead him out of the hospital.

As we get into the elevator, he turns to me, and throws both of his arms around my neck and between tiny gasps of breath, slurs out, "You are reeeaaally special. I love you soooo soooo much. Will you marry me?"

Could this possibly get any worse?

I attribute Chester's ramblings to the anesthesia and decide not to say anything to him about his inappropriate comments to me at the hospital.

Later that week, Wish is in town for a series of business meetings with various funders, and one morning before work, I rush off to see him in his hotel room. Every time I lay eyes on that man, he has the same effect on me. I can hardly feel myself breathe.

"I've missed you," he says in between kisses.

"I've missed you too."

"I've missed you more."

Ok, I know this is totally cheesy, but don't hate me. Sex with Wish is always the same; absolutely incredibly amazing. I think this is one of the perks of being with an older man. They know how to work it and please a woman, and Wish is certainly no exception. After our hot sex session, we order room service and eat breakfast in bed.

"What are these?" He asks as he points to the various welts on my legs.

"I don't really know. I think I'm having some type of allergic reaction or maybe it's stress."

"You should really have a doctor look at that."

I am nervous about bringing up a certain topic, but decide to take the risk.

"Can I ask you something?"

"You can ask me anything you want." He strokes my hair and looks lovingly at me.

"Do you feel guilty?"

He smiles at me like I am a naïve child. "No. Not at all."

"Really? You're totally fine with everything? With us?"

"Look. I give Carol everything she needs and wants. I provide her with all of her creature comforts. I am a great husband and at the end of the day, she's happy."

"So, if she were to find out about you and I she wouldn't be upset?"

"She told me that I could be with other women, as long as she didn't know about it."

"Are you serious?" I nearly choke on my toast. "She said that?"

He shakes his head and takes a bite of his bacon. "Yup."

I wonder to myself what type of woman would want that kind of relationship. Does she really love the man she's with or is she with him for his money? Do they have some kind of arrangement? She plays the Stepford wife and he the philandering husband? And besides, as a woman, I would think you have to shut off a part of yourself off to not feel jealous or insecure, or just plain hurt that he's sleeping around. She probably has never given herself fully to him. I know if I really loved someone, I wouldn't want to share my him.

"And if she's seeing other people, I don't want to know about it."

He picks the breakfast tray off the bed and puts it outside his hotel room. I watch his nicely rounded scrumptious buttocks as he moves around the room. He comes back and throws himself on the bed.

I wiggle myself into his arms, lie on my side to face him for maximum cleavage exposure. "But Wish. I don't understand how you can be in that type of marriage. I mean, is that love or is she with you because you have money and take care of her? And why are you with her?"

He looks me straight in my eyes, and with a tone that is not as sweet and loving as before, says, "Whatever it is, it works for us right now."

I decide not to pursue the conversation further. "I'm sorry, I didn't mean to upset you."

"No. It's ok. I'm sorry if I snapped at you." He kisses my forehead. "Look, like I said, I have a lot of responsibilities. I have a $500,000 payroll to meet every two weeks. There are people relying on me. I have to be very focused and disciplined. I can't be distracted and scattered with a demanding wife. I need her to support me in every way."

"Wow."

He smiles. "I don't have any distractions, except you of course." He leans in and gives me a kiss.

I smile, and feel flattered like a total schmuck.

He continues. "You are my only vice."

Vice? He sees me as a bad habit?

I jerk away from him, "I need to get to work. I have a meeting to get to."

I feel like crying as I yank my clothes from the floor and run off to the bathroom. I can't even bear to look at him after he said those words to me.

***

CHAPTER 24

Back in the office, I sit at my desk wondering why Wish would be so insensitive and compare me to a bad habit. I bet he does feel guilty and can't even admit it to himself. Hell, I feel guilty, and I'm not even married. Even though he and his wife have an arrangement, it doesn't make it ok for me to be with him. It's against my own moral beliefs. Although things are going down the drain with Peter, I should have the courage to be honest with him. I should have handled it better than to just run off on Wish. I am too involved with Wish and don't like the fact that he can hurt my feelings. I resolve that I have to end it with him. I can't see him again.

I can't keep thinking about my personal life considering I have so much work to get done, and decide to turn my attention to the Summit when I see an email from Matilda.

Please gather in the conference room at 3 pm to celebrate Samantha's pursuing of her dream to be a massage therapist.

I'm happy to get distracted. On certain merry and joyous occasions, such as someone's birthday, marriage, birth of a baby, or departure to a new job, the office dictator, Matilda, has a party with cupcakes to celebrate the occasion within the family of The Center for Ethical Business. When I first started working at the Center, we were having cupcake celebrations at least twice a month. Initially it was jovial, and viewed by most people here as a break from work. But there were a select few, like Bren, who made it obvious that she was not interested in taking part in the celebrations. Over time, Matilda upon Chester's instructions, made these parties mandatory to build esprit de corps. Poor Matilda takes this job to heart and if she sees someone's belly bulging out or knows of an upcoming birthday, than she's all over it like white on rice. After a while everybody began to feel like they were in homeroom having their attendance taken, and if someone didn't attend, Matilda would make a note of it in the personnel files. The mood quickly shifted.

Today is the last day for the Center's receptionist, Samantha, and on cue, the whole office receives the customary email invitation from Matilda. Since everyone now wants to avoid these awkwardly bizarre get togethers, at 2:55, Matilda perkily hops around the office and pulls everyone out from under their computers to join the festivities. Finally, all trudge into the conference room and either take seats around the small table or stand stiffly around. And as soon as Samantha walks in, Matilda shrieks out, "surprise!" with a big grin on her face, as everybody else whimpers a barely audible "surprise" of course all in unison. Samantha squirms, smiles, and sits in her designated chair.

"Well, Samantha, we are so sorry to see you go," Chester begins his spiel. "You have been a wonderful part of our organization. I personally will be very sad to see you go since I am still waiting for my massage." He chuckles to himself.

Oooh...an agonizingly long and piercing silence coupled with awkward glances around the table and the shuffling of feet. You can hear the cupcake frosting melting. I make eye contact with Weston and we both quickly look away as if not to appear guilty. Guilty of what, I am not sure.

"What is everyone waiting for? Dig in," trumpets Matilda. "I've picked out some really great flavors this time from a new bakery in the theater district."

"Those look delicious. I love cupcakes," mutters Henry, trying to make the awkward moment disappear. "When I was a kid, I wanted cupcakes for every birthday."

Cupcakes with vodka, I bet, you of the bulbous nose. Henry's drinking has caught up with him. His nose is enlarged and glowing red with all the broken capillaries. I stare at him wondering why he drinks so much.

I know that his wife doesn't work and he has two daughters, one a senior in high school and the other a freshman in college. Supporting an upper middle class lifestyle in Westchester, New York for four people can't be easy. And then there is the cost of college for one kid and the fast-approaching college costs for the second kid. That's enough pressure to drive anyone to drinking. On the one hand, I feel sorry for him as a human being, but on the other, as a control freak colleague, I struggle to have patience with him.

A big part of the problem here at the Center is Henry. Because of his control issues, he does his best to minimize communication between staff members by putting fear in them and dismissing ideas and suggestions as wasteful. He once sent out an email stating that everyone should focus on their own specific job and if anybody had any new ideas or suggestions for another department, they should talk to him first. And I'm not making this up, but he ended his email by stating that, "Most likely people won't have any reason to come to my office."

My eyes and mind wander back to the cupcakes. Hmmmm, I wonder what color frosting I should choose. Should it be glow-in-the-dark pink, shimmering yellow, or dung chocolate frosting?....I think it will be dung chocolate. As I reach for the cupcake, I look up and see Bren recklessly eyeballing the cupcakes, internally debating if she should have one.

"Bren, you are not having a cupcake?" a poor naïve soul pops the question.

"They sure look yummy, but I'm trying to lose weight," retorts Bren all thorny.

Bren has an affinity for foods not conducive to losing weight – pasta, wine, and burgers, among other stick-to-your-ribs food. I see her eating meatloaf and mashed potatoes for lunch at least once a week.

Like a sack of potatoes, Bren plops back in her chair, purses her lips and sends death rays to the people munching their cupcakes.

"Samantha, what are your plans?" asks another poor soul.

"I'm going to study Reiki and get licensed in Shiatsu," Samantha oh-so-naively replies. "I really want to help people."

"That is quite an exquisite thing to do," chimes in Chester. "You are such a noble person. Will you be visiting people in their homes and making them happy?"

"Wha-a-a-at?" Samantha is shocked.

"Will you be visiting people in their homes? You know…. Some massage therapists do that," retorts Chester, completely oblivious to the inappropriateness of his comment.

"No. I would not be comfortable doing that. I will not be that type of a massage person," she replies, perturbed.

By now, everyone has quickly wolfed down their imitation cupcakes and begun to slowly inch their way out of the conference room.

"I have to get back to work. Good luck with everything" says Bren, and lumbers out like a football player.

"Yea, good luck," a few people repeat in unison and jetty it out of the room.

"We'll miss you, Samantha," adds in Henry. "You have been quite the resourceful person."

Resourceful? She was the receptionist and I bet besides, "Hello," this was the first time Henry ever talked to her beyond giving instructions that part of her job as the receptionist is to send him an email when someone in the office wants to meet with him. No need for her to come to his office.

"Samantha, come here and give daddy a hug." Before Samantha realizes it, Chester is on her with his stubby arms wrapped around her. She gives him a pat on his back and pries herself away from his belly paunch.

"Thank you, everyone. I'll miss you guys," Samantha nervously says and rushes out of the conference room and back to her desk.

These parties are the most awkward moments in the office. To say that Chester, Henry, and Bren are not the most social creatures would be a gross understatement. As the senior management team, they set the tone for the office, and the mood here is excruciatingly frosty and murky, even more these days with the various investigations.

As people scamper away, I hear Chester expounding, "What a great way to build esprit de corps. Why don't we do these cupcake parties more often?"

I guess nothing says esprit de corps like brightly colored frosted cupcakes.

***

CHAPTER 25

Back at my desk, the phone rings as I trash my chocolate cupcake.

"I think I figured what your allergic reaction is," says Peter.

"Really? What?"

"I got a letter from Zuni's school today saying that they've discovered bed bugs at the school and some of the kids have bug bites. I think Zuni has them too. I saw a few bites on her legs."

"But how did she get our whole apartment infested with bed bugs?"

"I don't know. Bed bugs spread fast."

Just like my anger.

"I can't really talk for long now. I'm out running some errands, but we'll search our apartment tonight." He hangs up the phone before I can respond.

I Google bedbugs and this is what Wikipedia tells me.

Bedbugs are bloodsucking insects.

Sounds familiar.

They are normally out at night just before dawn, with a peak feeding period of about an hour before sunrise. Bedbugs may attempt to feed at other times if given the opportunity and have been observed feeding during all periods of the day. They reach their host by walking, or sometimes climb the walls to the ceiling and drop down after feeling a heat wave.

Bedbugs are attracted to their hosts by warmth and the presence of carbon dioxide. The bug pierces the skin of its host with two hollow feeding tubes. With one tube it injects its saliva, which contains anticoagulants and anesthetics, while with the other it withdraws the blood of its host. After feeding for about five minutes, the bug returns to its hiding place.

The bites cannot usually be felt until some minutes or hours later, as a dermatological reaction to the injected agents, and the first indication of a bite usually comes from the desire to scratch the bite site. Because of their natural aversion for sunlight, bedbugs come out at night.

I. Am. Going. To. Kill. Zuni. And Peter.

Later that evening at home, Peter and I start the hunt for bedbugs, and as soon as we turn over the mattress to inspect the seams, we see brown casings everywhere. Next, we go into Zuni's room, and repeat the same inspection, and sure enough, we find more casings. More bed bug crap on the couch. This is a disaster.

"You know what this means, don't you?" Peter asks me nonchalantly. How can he be so calm?

That we have to send your kid back to wherever the hell she came from.

"What?" My voice is shrill.

"We have to throw everything out. The mattress, the bed frame, sheets, couch, rugs, everything."

I hate my life. "I can't deal with this right now," I respond.

"Come on, sweetie. It's not that big of a deal."

"It's a big deal," I scream out at the top of my lungs. "It's a big, fucking, huge, ginormous deal, Peter."

His mouth is partially open and he's looking at me in bewilderment, but I don't care.

"We have to throw everything out. Exterminate our whole apartment. And what about my clothes? Huh? Huh? Huh? Tell me? I have to take everything to the drycleaners. Do you know how expensive this is going to be?"

"It's going to cost a few thousand dollars."

"Yea. It will. And I bet you'll want me to pay half of it."

"Well, this is our apartment." He crosses his arms and replies smugly.

I let out a loud shriek. "Yea. Well Zuni is your fucking kid."

"Is that what this is about?" he yells back.

"This is about everything. We have no life anymore. It's Zuni this and Zuni that. And besides, she absolutely hates me."

"Well she's a sensitive kid and she notices your discomfort. She thinks you don't like her either. I mean come on. Can you blame her? Especially after your last meltdown."

"Look, I don't want to deal with this, nor do I want to talk about Zuni," I respond.

"You never want to deal with anything."

"I'm leaving." I turn around with gusto and head into our bedroom.

"Leaving? Is that all you can do? Walk away?" He comes running behind me.

"Fuck you, Peter." I yell without turning towards him.

He grabs my arm and turns me to face him with force. "Stop coercing me into these situations," I shout as I try to wring my arm loose from his tight grip.

He grabs my other arm and holds me squarely, forcing me to listen to him. He brings his face close to mine.

"You need to grow the fuck up, Nikki." I feel the pressure of his fingers cutting the circulation off on my upper arms.

"You treat my poor little angel like shit, and you have the nerve to get mad?" He hisses an anger and venom that I'm becoming very familiar with.

"Let me go," I say with a deadly quiet calm.

With a slight push, Peter releases his grip from my arms.

"I'm going to leave now," I say.

"Where are you going?"

I would like to scream at him that it's not his fucking business, but that would take the drama to a whole other level.

"I'm going to stay with Weston for a few days. If I stick around here, I'm going to have a nervous breakdown."

Peter falls silent and walks out of the room, slamming the door after himself. I run to the closet and grab a duffel bag, hoping that it's not infested with bed bugs, and snatch some clothes from the hangers and stuff them into the bag. I walk out of the room like a steamroller and head towards the door. From the corner of my eye I see Peter sitting on the couch staring into space.

"Don't bother calling me." I slam the front door behind me. I call Weston as soon as I get to the lobby, hoping he can take me in.

Over the next few days as I crash on Weston's couch, I distract myself with thoughts of Wish. His birthday is coming up and he called me to let me know that he was going to be in New York City for the day for a morning meeting, but afterwards was free and wanted to spend the rest of his birthday with me. I put off my idea of ending my little romance with him and immediately started to hatch a plan.

After work I take myself to Fredrick's of Hollywood to shop for a super sexy, borderline or maybe not so borderline slutty piece of lingerie. There is so much to choose from, but I end up buying a naughty police officer outfit that comes equipped with a hat and handcuffs. There is nothing about this outfit that resembles a police officer's uniform. The top is a black lace low cut shelf bra with maximum cleavage exposure, and the bottom is a triple-strap thong panty. The hat is a sexy black vinyl mini cop hat, and the handcuffs are rhinestone. I plan to wear this with my four-inch thigh high black patent boots that I've never worn, but bought them because of a secret fantasy of how I would feel when I wore four-inch thigh high black patent boots.

Next, I head over to Babeland in Soho. Babeland is one of the best sex toy stores in the City and designed in a tasteful way so women can feel comfortable shopping. After an hour of browsing and letting my imagination wander, I pick up a pleasure feather, a lusciously colored plush red plume feather tickler, a tiny vibe fingertip vibrator, and the chocolate scented massage oil, along with some candles.

As I am at the cash register checking out, I hear a familiar voice, the voice of one, Bren Dabraccio. I turn around and see her standing there inspecting some colorful things on a display table. She is with Patty Ray. My jaw drops as Patty and I make eye contact. Patty's eyes look like two big green balloons, and she looks like prey that's been caught. Meanwhile, Bren is holding a strap on purple rubber dildo.

"I think I like th--" Bren says, as she looks up to see Patty's shocked face. She slowly follows Patty's horrified look.

"Hi, there. Having fun?" I say with a smile on my face.

Bren's scared and shocked face is priceless. She knows she's busted. This whole time she's thought that no one in the office knew about her affair with Patty.

Bren's scared look quickly turns into an angry scowl, "Hi," she responds curtly.

"Aaawkwaaard," I say in a high-pitched voice, still smiling.

Bren turns around and tosses the dildo haphazardly on the table, knocking down a long slim dildo, and a nude colored dildo that's as thick as a coke can. She grabs Patty's arm and pulls her out of the store as I finish paying.

***

CHAPTER 26

The big day of Wish's birthday is here. I grab my bag of sexual goodies that I had locked in one of my desk drawers, sneak out of work at noon by telling Chester that I have a doctor's appointment, and rush off to the Four Seasons to see Wish. Along the way and a slight detour later, I pick up a small red velvet cake from Buttercups, one of the best bakeries in the City.

Once I get to the Hotel, I find the lobby's bathroom and change into my police officer's uniform. I cover myself up with my trench coat, and leave the patent leather hat in the bag since I don't want to look like a prostitute. I am bursting at the lace seams with anticipation. Wish has rocked my sexual world, and I can't wait for him to make my other wishes come true.

As I knock on his hotel door, I light up the candle on the cake. He opens the door, and even though I can't sing worth a damn, I do my best breathy Marilyn Monroe impersonation, and belt out his birthday song.

"Happy Birthday to you.
Happy Birthday to you.
Happy birthday Mr. Michaels.
Happy birthday to you.

Thanks, Mr. Michaels.
For all the things you've done
The body parts you've conquered
The way you move your tongue
And our orgasms by the ton

I thank you so much."

He has the biggest smile on his face. And, I'm happy that he's happy.

"Baby, make a wish and blow it out," I coyly whisper to him as I raise the cake closer to his mouth.

He blows out the candle. "I think my wish already has come true." He takes the cake with one hand and wraps the other around me. With one swoop I am inside his hotel room and pressed against his masculine body. His lips are on me and I can feel his hard on through my coat. And to think he still hasn't seen my frisky police uniform.

I pry myself off of him, "I have another surprise for you."

"Really? I don't know how you are going to top your first surprise."

I take a step back. "Watch and learn, my friend."

I take my hat out of my bag and put it on, than I slowly begin to unbutton my coat and let it drop on the floor.

Wish is speechless as he begins to salivate. I can feel him making love to me with his eyes.

I pick up my baton. "There is a report that you are carrying something illegal on you." I swing the baton at him and smack it on the palm of my hand. "I have been sent over to frisk you."

His eyes wide, and still grinning. "Ok," is his only response.

I walk over to him, and begin to kiss him as I unbutton and take off his shirt, his pants, and finally his briefs. I push him to the bed and handcuff both of his hands. I begin to give him a slow tantric massage, a little somethin' somethin' I learned from a one-hour DVD purchased at Babeland. I use the toys to tease and arouse him for over an hour. Then we make slow and passionate love.

"Getting frisked by a cop has never been so much fun."

"Maybe you should be bad more often," is my salacious response.

We lie together in bed for a few hours, talking, laughing, and making love two more times until finally, we are both ravenous.

"I am so happy that we're spending your birthday together." I feed him a bite of the cake. "Happy Birthday."

As he nibbles away at his cake, he says, "There's only two people in the whole world I want to spend my birthday with."

I take a bite. "Who?"

"You and my …." then he catches himself and stares at me in silence.

I smile to hide my hurt feelings. "You mean your wife?"

"Yes. I'm sorry. I didn't mean to let that slip out."

"It's ok. You're a married man of course." The cake feels like a lump of brick going down my throat. "I can't ever forget that."

He smiles for what I interpret as meaning, 'thanks for not making demands.'

"Nikki, I'm very picky about the women I date."

"So what? I should feel honored?"

He lets out a laugh. "Yes. You are very special to me."

I'm not sure what to make of his comment. For someone who is so accomplished and smart, he always says the most asinine thing at the most inappropriate moment. His words always catch me by surprise and leave me feeling hurt.

I change the topic and we spend the rest of the afternoon talking about his work, travels and upcoming projects. After I leave, I stop by at work to drop off my bag, than head over to Weston's.

The next day at work I receive the rss feed for his latest blog entry and it reads:

Yesterday I spent an almost perfect birthday in New York City. Thank you to all my friends who made it a special day. What would have made it perfect would have been to have the love of my life, my wonderful wife, Carol, there. I missed you darling.

"Hey," hisses Weston as he sticks his head into my office.

"Hi, what's up?" I ask.

"Did you hear about what happened when you were out at your doctor's appointment yesterday?" He asks me with a smile.

"No-o-o." I am paranoid about his smile and wonder if he knows that I wasn't at the doctor's.

"There was pink cupcake frosting smeared all over the women's bathroom."

"What do you mean?"

"I mean some loony tune smeared frosting all over the bathroom."

"No way! You're kidding me. Are you serious?"

"Yea, and guess who found it? ......CROW!"

"Consuela?"

"She 'discovered' it." He does the air quotes. "And she said it was 'ritualistic' in nature."

"What the hell does that mean?"

"And then all day she walked around looking all traumatized. Like a wounded puppy, 'ohhh...ohhh...nobody likes me here, and I discovered the ritualistic cupcake schmear'." Weston throws his hands up and waves them like a scared child. "She was so annoying."

Through howls of laughter I manage to spit out, "Wow. You can't make this stuff up. That's insane. Do you think she did it herself?"

"You betcha she did. I mean, come on. Our office takes up the whole floor, you need a key to get into the bathroom, and people from the other floors don't use our bathroom. Besides, 'ritualistic in nature.' Hello! CROW is into that voodoo hoodoo stuff."

"How do you know what she's into?"

"I followed her," Weston replies.

"What do you mean you followed her?" I am shocked that he could

213

keep something like that a secret from me.

"Well, you know how she comes in late, disappears for half a day, and leaves early?"

I shake my head in affirmation.

"Well for three days last week, when she left in the middle of the day I followed her. Me and a few other people concocted a plan to find out what she was up to, and everyone had their eye out. So when it was time for her to leave, I trailed her."

He has my full attention. "And where did she go?"

"You would never believe it! She has a little shop set up in the lower east side as Madame Jaffar."

"What do you mean set up a shop?" I squint. "As a call girl?"

"Call girl, please. I don't know who besides Chester would sleep with her." He lets out a hoot. "I mean she poses as a psychic, as a fortune teller."

"I'm confused."

Weston is exasperated as he continues to draw the picture for me. "I mean that she puts on a blond wig with a blue turban, and she wears a long black velvet dress with her boobs hanging out everywhere and she wears rings on all her fingers."

"And she goes by the name of Madame Jaffar?"

"Yup. So, out of curiosity, I asked one of my friends to go see her."

"No, you didn't."

"Yes, I did." He's laughing. "Madame Jaffar/CROW read my friend's palm and told her future by reading tarot cards."

"Madame Jaffar told her that she was going to have a long life. And that she was a good person that aimed to be good. She told her that her love life was blocked, and that she shouldn't be ruled by fear. She should open her heart."

We both are laughing hysterically. "That's so generic. Everybody is afraid to open up their heart. How much did she charge?"

"$125. Can you believe that?"

"That's $125 down the drain, but that's pretty damn smart of Consuela," I respond.

"Wait, you haven't heard the best part yet. Madame Jaffar told my friend that there were people out there who were blocking her happiness, and holding her back by sending her negative vibrations. And that for an extra $250, Madame Jaffar would give her special crystals and candles to meditate upon."

"Weston, you can't make this stuff up. I mean this place is the twilight zone."

***

CHAPTER 27

I'm tired of feeling bad over arming Bren with incriminating evidence regarding the sexual harassment investigation into Chester. If the sexual harassment charges came up organically from someone he had actually hit on, then it would be one thing. But to have Bren going around trumpeting charges against him is a different thing.

Despite his behavior and unlike Bren, Chester is not malicious and hateful, and everyone is conspiring against him, even people he has trusted for years, like Henry. Even though he has behaved beyond inappropriately with Consuela, I feel like I've betrayed him. All these stresses in my life are making my right eye twitch. I look maniacal.

After my interrogation, I received a call from the attorneys strongly requesting that I help them in getting all of Chester's emails and calendar items for the last year. This whole thing is dirty and grimy, and all because Chester couldn't keep his pecker in his pants and Bren's need for power. If I had a choice, I would rather throw Bren under the bus than Chester any day. At least he has treated me decently.

"Good morning, Chester." I walk into his office, cheery.

I close the door and sit down.

"What's wrong with your eye?" He asks as my eye twitches.

"Last night I lay awake at two in the morning thinking about everything that is going on."

"Oh, Nikki." He looks at me with a worried look. "It's not worth it."

The pathetic soul has no idea what is going on. My eye twitches. "Listen Chester, the work environment here is very adversarial and aggressive." I wring my hands together. "And it does not foster a team environment."

I take in a deep breath and let it all out. "Bren is into the blame game and because you, as the CEO, did not handle Bren's anger in the beginning, when she had so many assistants come and go from under her, when she physically got aggressive with me and put her hands on me, now it has turned against you."

He shakes his head and remains silent to let the sirens of an ambulance pass. He finally lets out a heavy sigh and says, "You are right. I don't like conflict." He lowers his eyes and stares at his lap. The poor guy looks defeated.

"Well, as a CEO, you cannot be conflict averse. Part of your job is to deal with conflict." I hear myself say with a sharp frustrated tone. Wishing he would man up!

"I know. And now it is too late. There are a couple of people that have it in for me."

My eye twitches. I wonder if I should enlighten the poor man about what's really going on here.

"Chester, there are more than a couple of people." I grimace.

"Re-e-e-a-a-l-l-l-y?" His eyes bug out and his mouth falls open. He stares at me in utter shocked silence.

"Yes," I whisper to his still shocked face. "You are being watched very carefully."

Chester leans back and sinks into his leather chair. This news is a surprise to him and I can see his brain working as, I think for the first time, the magnitude of the investigation begins to sink in.

"Don't trust anybody," I point my thumb in the direction of Henry's office.

"What? No...you mean." His face is contorted in pain. "Even Henry?" Chester's head hangs low in disappointment. "That breaks my heart," he manages to mumble. "I never thought Henry was that kind of a person."

His eyes are tearing up and I can only imagine the betrayal he must feel.

Chester and Henry have worked together closely at the Center for over fourteen years. Chester has always relied on Henry as his second-in-command and trusted him with every little organizational secret, and I think even the Consuela affair. Chester had even attended a few private parties with Henry's family.

"We never had this conversation, ok?" I say.

"Of course."

"I know you are hurt, but Henry is that kind of a person. Especially with Bren whispering in his ear about being the next CEO."

There is an unspoken understanding around the Center that when Chester retires, Henry will automatically be the next CEO, regardless of how the Board of Directors or the staff feels about it.

"I guess he's ready for me to go then." He curls his lip with disgust.

I watch him as he pushes himself off and up from his chair. He walks over to the window and stares down Sixth Avenue. He finally turns around with a pained expression on his face. "Nikki, have I ever done anything to make you feel uncomfortable?"

Wow. Is he that clueless?

I push my hair back and scratch my head. "No. I don't think so." I cringe inside.

I should mention the whole hospital fiasco, but for some reason can't seem to bring it up. I blame it on the anesthesia.

Chester walks over and leans back on his desk to face me. He looks me straight into my eyes, "Nikki, I want you to know that I have never, ever had a relationship with any staff member or have ever wanted to."

I cannot believe he is still lying to me. Is he that delusional?

"I have never had any relationship with anyone associated with this organization," he says with emphasis.

Could it be that he is telling the truth and nothing ever happened between him and Consuela?

"It's important for me to have you believe me," he finishes off.

But what about the poem and her running around like she owns the place? Could everyone be wrong? Maybe it was simply inappropriate flirting.

He continues, shaking his head, "I may have sent the occasional joking emails saying let's run off to Paris or Venice together."

"Well…you can't send those types of emails, Chester. As a CEO, you simply cannot put yourself in that position with women who work for you or are affiliated with this organization."

In other words fool…don't poke the payroll.

"It would break my heart to know I've ever made you uncomfortable. You know everything about me." He smirks. "At times, I think too much. But I consider you a good friend."

All this talk about being friends with him makes me feel nervous and a bit uncomfortable, especially with this investigation. I change the subject.

"I've talked to the lawyers," I blurt out.

He stands upright. "You have?"

His eyes bulge out and his face turns red out of fear.

"Yes, they grilled me for several hours last week about everything."

"What do you mean 'everything'?" He begins to pace.

"Well, I can't get into the specifics." I follow him with my eyes as he walks back and forth. "But under the circumstances, even a benign question could be insinuatory."

"Like what?"

"Umm…well…for example, they asked me if you've ever given me gifts."

He walks back to his chair and throws himself down. "Of course I have," he yells and catches himself as he sees my distraught face. He gives me a half smile. "You once said something to me that I really cherish to this day. You said to me that I taught you how to really give. That touched my heart."

I shake my head thinking of that comment. Chester has been very generous with me. Anytime I've handled a big project well, he gives me a thank you card acknowledging my great work. He gave me a beautiful silver bracelet for my birthday, and a gift certificate to the Elizabeth Arden Spa for Christmas. Sometimes, when he comes back from his travels, he brings me a gift from the area. I never thought it weird or felt uncomfortable with his gift giving. He by nature is a generous person, and has also given gifts to other staff members.

"What are your plans with the investigation?" I ask.

"I am not sure what to do about this whole sexual harassment investigation," he sighs. "I simply need to wait it out. I want to finish this year and then retire. Unfortunately, I need the money."

Dude, everybody needs money! How could he be complaining about money when he rakes in so much?

"Well, Bren found out that you are trying to renew your contract for another two years, and that is part of the reason she is going after you."

"How did she find out? Is she watching my emails?"

"I don't know. But it could be a possibility. I think Henry is having the tech guys do some type of dirty work."

I see him tearing up again at the betrayal from Henry. He covers his face with his hands.

"Listen, Chester, you have made the situation worse with Consuela. You have only added fuel to the fire."

Still covering his face, "what do you mean?"

"When people were writing things in the sign in book by her name, you should not have sent an email to the whole office. It didn't take a rocket scientist to know that the email was about her. You had a staff meeting and talked about how we should all work together as a team. Everybody knew you were referring to her. You sent an email to Bren and cc'd the management team telling her that she could not talk about Consuela in such a negative way."

He doesn't like what I just said to him and gives me a look of disappointment. "Yes I did," he says with force. "Bren was just mean and nasty, and I should have been stronger with her."

Yea, but you grew your balls too late is what I'm thinking.

"No, you should have been stronger with her a long time ago. It was too late for you to send an email defending Consuela. You made it worse… So, don't send any more emails or do anything further. Just let it play out."

"Ok."

"And I don't know if you've retained an attorney," I say.

"No. I didn't even think of it. Since this whole thing is so ridiculous."

"You may want to speak to someone as soon as possible and consult an attorney on this."

"I think you are right." He shakes his head.

All of a sudden I feel empowered, and continue with my unsolicited advice giving. "I think you should send an email to Chas letting him know that you want to retire at the end of this year. You have only five more months to go."

"Hmmmm..," he ponders for a minute. "It would diffuse the situation."

"Yes. The Summit will be a big success. And I know that you want to leave with your legacy intact and with dignity. You don't want to be fired or leave under the weight of an investigation."

"You know, when I came here this place was in shambles. The Chief Operating Officer at that time came to me and asked me to go to our funders and ask for extra money because he didn't think that we could meet the next month's payroll. Now that is bad. I have built this organization from the negative to $20 million a year organization. I have worked very hard to do that."

"Well, you should remind people of the great work you have done. Bren wants to make you the fall guy. She wants to be the big person in charge. She knows that she can run Henry."

"Well, I am not going to let her do that."

For the first time in a long time, I feel slightly proud of Chester.

"I should have fired Bren a long time ago," he mutters to himself. "And now I am paying for shying away from that decision. I'm mad. I am going to fight this.

I find it odd that he's getting angry and belligerent now.

"This is going to get messy." He slams his palm down on his desk. "I have worked hard for this organization and I will not let Bren take me down."

My stomach is churning.

"Look, it's not the time for you to be combative. You can't fight this in the traditional sense. Get a lawyer and your fight is to protect yourself, your name and reputation at this point."

"Ok. I am going to take your advice."

"Chester, we've never had this conversation. Ok?" I stand up to leave.

"We've never had this conversation. Not even under torture." He smiles.

***

CHAPTER 28

The next morning I have a conference call scheduled with the InCare Public Relations and Marketing team to go over the Center's plans to get media coverage for both the Summit and InCare. I've come up with a detailed plan that I think they will be happy with.

"Good morning, everyone," I announce into the speakerphone.

"Good morning," is a unison reply from the InCare executives on the other end. "Nikki, there's four people on this end, two from the PR department, and two from Marketing. The CEO may join us, but we are not sure. It depends on his schedule."

Yikes. I was not expecting the big cheese to be on the call, otherwise, I would have had Chester attend the meeting. I cross my fingers and pray that the InCare CEO does not show up.

"Ok. That'll be great if he does."

The voices on the other end of the line introduce themselves, and we exchange hellos.

"Let's begin, then shall we?" I ask.

"Go for it," a few people respond.

"I emailed everyone my communications plan for the Summit. Does everyone have that in front of them?"

"Yes, we do. One quick point though. Going forward, anytime you refer to the Summit, please use the full and official name, 'The InCare Global Summit on Corporate Social Responsibility. We want the whole world to know that we are behind this," dictates the command from the other end of the line.

"Ok. Not a problem. As I was saying, I have a detailed plan for the Summit, and I thi---"

"Nikki? Uhhh…uhhh…uhhh…the full name please."

"I have a detailed plan for the InCare Global Summit on Corporate Social Responsibility, and I think you will be happy with it." I repeat through clenched teeth.

I feel like a circus monkey.

"Well, we looked through this plan of yours, and we have some concerns."

"Oh…uhh…You do?" I ask.

"Yes. I don't think you are doing enough to get us coverage. We want all the biggest and major news outlets there and to do interviews with our CEO. How can you guarantee that?"

"Well, as I'm sure you know, with the press, nothing is guaranteed. A lot depends on breaking news of the day, and usually they don't confirm their attendance until the day of the event or a few days before."

Silence from the other end.

I continue, "My angle on the InCare Global Summit on Corporate Social Responsibility (I feel like a monkey again) is to sell it as a first-ever event that will have a major positive impact on business and the nonprofits that are doing wonderful work. Nothing like this has ever been done before. But, it's a fine line. Reporters don't like to feel that they are being sold a story as advertising for a corporation."

"What are you implying, Nikki?" One hostile voice asks.

"I'm not implying anything. Simply, stating that we have to tread lightly. We can't push this as an InCare event, but more of a Center event. Otherwise, the media will be turned off and not be interested."

"We are giving the Center $1 million dollars to help launch InCare as a loving and caring business. You need you to work hard to achieve that."

I feel a flame flicker in my stomach. "Ok. I can try my best," responds the monkey.

"We would also like to have our new logo on all the printed materials, all PowerPoint presentations, and several banners throughout the event, including a large one on the stage."

Big gulp.

"I'm sorry. Can I put you on hold for one second? I'll try to get Chester on this call also. I think his feedback will be important."

I can't deal with these people and their unreasonable demands all by myself. I run into Chester's office, but he is not there, and the receptionist informs me that he has stepped out. As I go back into my office and sit at my desk, Weston pops his head in.

"Whoa. Why do you look so frazzled?"

"I have the stupid InCare people on a conference call. Talk about a pain in the ass to deal with. All they care about is their image and getting free advertising."

He stares at me as I continue my tirade, aware that I have them on hold and I have to get back to the call soon.

"These people are totally insane. The Center is their whore now because of their freaking $1 million dollars. They want their logo on everything. I mean have you seen their logo? It's a logo of a tree, all green and nature looking. Their new tag line is 'we have deep roots in our communities.'"

"Yea, sure they have deep roots. Roots of toxic chemicals that result in cancer and birth defects," responds Weston.

I let out a laugh, "Yeah, that should be their new tag line. I'm jumping through hoops to get them free advertising so they can continue polluting and killing people. Anyway, I have to get back to the call. Can you close the door?"

I hit the speaker button on the phone. "I'm sorry for putting you on hold for so long. I was not able to find Chester."

Silence.

"Hello? Are you guys there?"

A stoic voice responds, "Nikki, we've been here the whole time. We heard everything you said about us."

Oh my God! Oh my God! Oh my God!

"If that is the feeling of the Center, then we will have to rethink our sponsorship."

"No. No...No...wait. I am so sorry. Please wait," I scream into the phone. "I'm very sorry about what you just heard. It's no excuse, but it has been a very stressful day. I do hope you'll accept my apology. I apologize. I'm sorry."

"Goodbye."

"Wait. I said I'm sorry." I scream. "Don't go. Wait."

The line goes dead.

I'm not sure what to do at this point. I call Wish on his cell phone, but he's travelling overseas and I can't reach him. He's going to think I'm a complete loser, but I leave him a frantic rambling message.

I run to Weston and tell him the horrible news, and his only response to me is, "Girlfriend, you are royally screwed."

"You're not helping," I scream.

As I skulk back into my office, I see Chester walking down the hall, "I need to talk to you. It's an emergency."

"Nikki. I already know what happened." He frowns and doesn't make eye contact with me as he walks into his office.

I follow him in. "You do? How?"

"The CEO of InCare called me on my cell phone."

"Oh...uhh...he did?"

"Get Henry and Bren in the conference room now."

I run out of his office and tell Henry and Bren to meet Chester and I in the conference room. This is going to be a nightmare, and I'm dreading my encounter with Bren. As we all settle in the conference room, Chester asks me to tell everyone what happened. A flurry of indecipherable words leaves my lips to the horrified faces of Henry and Bren, and the only thing that I am aware of is the high pitch of my voice. I don't think I have ever been so mortified in my life. When I am done speaking, I stand in silence, teary eyed, staring at everyone.

"I always knew you were incompetent," yells Bren as she throws her pen at me. I sidestep out of the way before it hits my head. "I knew you couldn't handle your new responsibilities. What the hell is wrong with you?"

I don't have anything to say. She is right. I am incompetent. How can I screw up so royally?

Chester jumps in to save me from Bren's wrath. "Look everyone, the damage has been done. The CEO of InCare wants to pull out of their sponsorship. Pointing fingers will get us nowhere at this point. We have to fix this somehow."

"Ummpppf," sighs Henry. "What did he say when you spoke to him on the phone?"

"He was quite upset and refused to accept any of my apologies. I don't know what we can do at this point."

"Henry and I told you from the beginning that we didn't like the idea of the Summit. Can that snake oil salesman, Wish Michaels, help?" snorts Bren, looking like an angry Bull.

"Umm…, I already called him?" I contort my face in pain.

"What?" Chester jumps out of his chair. "Why didn't you tell me?" he asks.

"I'm sorry." A tear runs down my face right there in front of everyone. I know that I'm being totally unprofessional, but can't stop myself. "I panicked after the call, and called him." I wipe my eyes.

Wondering if my tears will get some sympathy.. "He didn't pick up, but I left him a message."

"Oh Nikki, I wish you hadn't done that." He looks at me like I am a pathetic little child.

I feel about two years old and two inches tall. I look over and see Bren sitting back in her chair staring at me with glee in her eyes and a smirk on her lips. That witch is enjoying seeing me suffer.

"I'm sorry. I panicked." I mumble as I sink into a chair.

"Ok. Nikki, come with me. I'm going to call Wish," says Chester.

I follow Chester into his office and we call Wish again. He doesn't pick up and Chester leaves him a message, and suggests I leave for the day so I can think about what I've done and its ramifications.

It's probably better that I leave the office. I am in no shape mentally or emotionally to get anything accomplished. Now that InCare has pulled their support for the Summit, I am probably going to be out of a job, despite the fact that I've helped Chester out with his stupid investigation. I thought that the nonprofit world would be saner and filled with people with a just an itsy bitsy teeny weeny bit more heart and soul. That it wouldn't be as cutthroat or competitive as the corporate world.

Boy, was I ever wrong. It is no different. Yes, sure there are the occasional squirrely people like Matilda, but those at the top of the food chain are no joke. The Center for Ethical Business may be a nonprofit, but everything that is currently happening here is characteristic of a great corporate espionage novel. But this is no novel. This is my freaking life.

When I get home, there is nobody there, and the whole apartment is almost empty. While I stayed at Weston's, Peter trashed anything that was bed bug infested, which means, all furniture, pillows, rugs, paintings, and anything wooden. He took every piece of our clothing to the cleaners to either be washed in super-hot water or dry cleaned. I can't even imagine that bill. The landlord brought in an exterminator and had the whole apartment sprayed while Peter and Zuni stayed at his parents' house.

The landlord then hired a bed bug sniffing dog to come sniff out the other ten apartments on our floor and the apartments above us and below us. Apparently a bed bug infested apartment is not just one person's problem, but in New York City, it becomes the whole building's problem since bed bugs can go in between bricks and drywall and across wires and pipes. Luckily they were all clean.

The only piece of significant furniture is a full size air mattress in our bedroom. I walk around the blank canvas that was once our home and take it all in. There are no more photos of smiling happy pretty people in shiny silver frames. No more, books on health, nutrition, and cooking. No more plants and vases filled with flowers. No more pretty throw rugs, and no more cherry blossom gardens. There are greasy and crumpled bags of Thai and Indian take out in the kitchen. The containers full of leftovers left haphazardly open.

I lean on the wall and let myself slide to the floor. I know that I have so much to be grateful for. There are people that are far worse than I am, but I can't help feeling depressed. This empty and hollow apartment with its blank white walls signifies what my relationship with Peter has come to. How could my life be heading in a happy direction and in the course of such a short time, be the exact opposite?

My feelings about Peter are all a mish mash of confusion. Of love, care, and tenderness and of resentment, anger, and betrayal. Peter doesn't move me the way Wish does. But then am I just living in lala fantasy world regarding Wish. If by a long shot Wish left his wife for me, could I even be with a man who I couldn't trust, considering how we got our start? Maybe neither one of these men are for me.

Peter called me over the past couple of weeks and left me numerous messages, but I haven't returned any of his calls. I don't even know what to say to him. I don't even know what I want anymore. I do need some time away from him to think for myself. I'm not sure I can take his positivity right now, and want to take time to find my own voice. I did send him an email asking him to give me some time to think and clear my head. I decide to leave and go back to Weston's before Peter gets home. Besides, I have to try to get some semblance of rest to prepare myself for what will happen with this whole InCare debacle.

The next day at the office, Chester asks me into his office to call Wish on his cell phone. I hold my breath as we hear Wish's phone ring.

"Wish Michaels speaking," he answers.

I shoot a nervous glance at Chester.

"Wish, Good morning. I am so sorry to be calling you on your cell phone, but this is an emergency," says Chester.

"No problem, my friend. What can I do for you?"

"Wish, I sincerely appreciate you saying that. I have you on speaker phone and have Nikki Johnson sitting here on the call."

"Aaah, yes. The infamous Ms. Johnson." Wish lets out a laugh.

From the deep bowels of my gut, I feel the flicker of a hot flame. I'm not sure if I'm embarrassed at my mistake or I'm angry that he did not return my call.

"Hi." I manage to squeak out in a shaky voice. I can't believe he finds this whole thing so amusing.

"I want you to know that I just got off the phone with the CEO of InCare," Wish continues.

Chester runs his hand through the little hair he has left on his head and shoots me a fearful look.

"He's extremely pissed off, excuse my language."

"Yes, I can understand his sentiments," says Chester.

"Nikki, what you did was extremely unprofessional," Wish continues.

I feel my face getting hot. Does he think I don't know that?

"I don't understand why you would say those horrible things about a company that is giving you guys money to sponsor this momentous event?"

There is silence in the room as Chester looks at me for an answer. I return his look and hope to get some help, but he continues with his silent disapproval.

"I'm sorry," I manage to mutter. I take a deep breath, and admit to myself that I shouldn't be defensive. "It was a mistake and a stupid accident on my part. I thought they were on hold, and umm…well it doesn't matter. It was just plain stupid on my part."

"Well, I spoke to him at length and was able to get him to calm down," Wish says.

Chester nearly jumps out of his chair and yells with glee into the phone, "Oh, you are a savior. Thank you so much. How did you manage to do that?"

"I told him that Nikki was young and wet behind the years. He has a daughter so I appealed to his fatherly side."

I can hardly breathe out of sheer humiliation.

Wish's voice is softer and almost conciliatory. "Nikki, please don't be upset. I had to say whatever I could so he wouldn't pull out InCare's support."

"Nikki understands clearly," says Chester with force.

"Good. Everything will be ok, and they will continue with their sponsorship of the Summit."

"Thank you so much for saving us," responds Chester.

"It's my pleasure. Besides, I am also invested in this Summit."

"Well now, I, and the Center owe you a big favor."

"Nikki. You have to do everything you can to get them some good press coverage." Wish says.

"Ok. I will." My voice is barely audible.

"And next time, be sure to end the call before you say you are a corporate whore." He lets out a laugh.

"Everything is fixed." Let's all get back to work and make this a great event. Talk to you later."

***

CHAPTER 29

I see Wish a week later at the Four Seasons. The suite at the hotel has become our little cocoon. It's where I forget about Peter, Zuni, Bren, and work. It's a place for just Wish and I and whatever fantasy we have about each other.

"When I'm with you time stands still," he says as he kisses me and dreamily looks into my eyes.

"Aaah, baby, that's so sweet." I give him a kiss. I love kissing him.

"I love spending time with you. I usually am so busy that I don't spend more than two hours anywhere or with any one person, but I could be with you for days."

"I cherish our time together. I hate it when we go so long without seeing each other."

Still holding me in his arms, he says, "Hey. I'm sorry about that phone call. I hope you didn't take it personally, but I had to say whatever I could to save the Summit, and I couldn't let you off so easy with Chester there."

"It's ok. I understand," I say.

"Good." He kisses me and pulls me to the couch. He lays down and pulls me on top of him.

"Tell me about your relationship with Peter?"

"What? Why?"

"Because I want to know you more."

"Umm..ok. Well, I've been with Peter for about a year and half now and we used to have a great relationship until he made the executive decision to have his teenage daughter move in with us. And now everything about him and this situation is frustrating me."

"He has a child? Wow, I didn't know that."

"From his first marriage. Ever since his daughter, Zuni, moved in with us, it's just killed our relationship. Peter is in constant dad mode, and our lives changed overnight. He used to be my best friend and now I constantly want to avoid him."

Wish strokes my hair and listens.

"I've been feeling similar to what you described in your marriage. That feeling of suffocation."

"I don't think Carol is interested in seeing the real me. Just some hero figure."

"But I don't understand how you can be in a relationship like that."

"Well there is a difference between a want and a need."

"And you need her?"

"In some ways, yes I do. Even though I am a private person, I lead a public life. We have certain core beliefs in common, and she plays the role of a public wife very well. "

"But it's fake." I am getting irritated and try hard to control my tone and voice.

"Not really. It's very real. It's real for a big part of my life."

"But you said you feel suffocated with her."

What the hell am I trying to do? Convince him of the folly of his ways and that he should leave his wife?

"Many times I do. There are a lot of people who depend on me. Nikki, You are the only one in my life who doesn't want anything from me. Everyone has an agenda, including Carol."

I want you.

"I have to admit though that I feel like a sinner when I am with you," he finishes off.

The next day over lunch, I tell Weston everything. All the dirty sordid details of my life with Peter, affair with Wish, and the various investigations.

234

"You? Ms. Goody Two Shoes? You?" He shakes his head. "I would have never guessed."

I sit in silence taking in his reaction and feeling the relief of confession.

"I can't believe you've been going through all this. You, who secretly judges me for sleeping with Omar?"

I wish he would stop shaking his head at me.

"Yea, I'm sorry for that. It was wrong of me."

Weston stares at me in silence for a few seconds and finally says, "So, he actually used the word 'sinner'?"

"Yup. We were having such a nice and sweet moment, and then he goes and says something so messed up. What the hell is he thinking saying that to me?"

"It's pretty damn insensitive if you ask me. Did you say anything to him?"

"No."

"Why not?"

I shrug my shoulders and shake my head. "I don't know. I didn't want to upset him."

"Upset him? Fuck him. He obviously doesn't care if he upsets you or hurts your feelings."

I pout and prop my face in my hands.

"Nikki, you have to stop repressing your feelings."

"I did what I do best. Act cool and calm, like it didn't hurt my feelings. But inside I was really hurt."

"That makes sense. I mean to me, the word sin and vice implies, bad, guilt, and shame. I mean, why the hell would he use those words? Dude is obviously royally screwed up."

"I am pissed. He has pursued me and now that he is with me, he considers me a vice and himself a sinner."

"That's a little bit twisted."

"I hate this."

"I know how you feel. Look at me and Omar."

"I've become such a walking talking cliché. I never thought I would actually fall in love with him."

"That's love for you. Love without reason is the best thing." Weston imparts his wisdom.

"We have the most amazing sex."

"I'm sure that has a lot to do with it."

"What do you mean?"

"At the end of the day, it all comes down to sex. I mean think about it. You meet a random stranger. You have sex, and then you try to find and fit all that other stuff around the sex."

"You may have a point."

"You're damn right I have a point. We're just a bunch of chemicals and we attribute it all to this feeling or that feeling. It's total bullshit. You feel all this because you are having great sex with the guy. If the sex was bad, we wouldn't even be having this conversation."

"The sex is pretty damn awesome," I admit. "But, it's not just sex. We have a strong connection."

"Anyway, continue with your story."

"I don't understand why in his blog he's always writing about his wife – the love of my life this and the love of my life that, and how lucky he is to be with the love of his life."

"I have a few theories. Either he is a really good bullshitter or he is just one of those men that can't keep his pecker in his pants, or he is in an unfulfilling marriage and is just playing some weird rationalizing mind game with himself."

"I wonder if he's seeing other women?"

"He's a man." Weston reminds me dramatically, as he rolls his eyes and shakes his head. "He's a man who travels all over the world. You bet your ass he sees other women. In fact I wouldn't be surprised if he has different women, like you, at his most traveled destinations."

"Do you have to be so brutal?"

"Yes I do. Someone needs to wake you up."

"Wake me up? What about you and Omar?" I yell at him.

A few people in the restaurant look in our direction.

"Well, that's different. I'm single. You are not. And besides, I like Peter."

"You do? Why? Please remind me."

"Well aside from the Zuni thing, he's been good to you. And I'm sure he is stressed out too and trying to do his best."

I am tearing up now. "What's happened to me? I thought I knew myself." I push my plate of pasta back and start full blown crying.

"I'm a horrible person." I sob out. "Here I am letting myself be bullied at work. I am protecting a dirty old man, other people have taken over my home, and I've totally become a walking, talking cliché." I slam my head down on the table. "I'm in love with a married man, who has no intentions of leaving his wife, and I have bed bugs," I holler.

"Don't be so hard on yourself."

"I've broken every rule I've had for myself. I'm pathetic."

I put my head in my hands and begin weeping.

"I hate my life," I say in between sobs. "I haaaate myself."

Weston rubs my head and shoulders as I sit there balling my eyes out.

"Don't be so hard on yourself." He moves my hair to one side. "This is life. It's messy."

"This is too messy. I can't handle it."

Weston sits there with me as I cry and let out all of my pent up hurts, frustrations and disappointments. I'm grateful I have him as a friend, and I don't feel so alone.

When I finally stop sobbing, my face feels bloated. My eyes are puffy and my nose is congested.

"Let's go. I can't talk about this anymore. It'll only depress me."

***

CHAPTER 30

Since I've been under so much duress, and to show his gratitude for giving him advice about the investigation, Chester offers to take me to dinner after work one day, so we can relax a bit and talk about the Summit. Chester has quite the swanky taste, and knows all the posh restaurants in the city. He takes me to Petrossy, a ritzy and excessively expensive Russian restaurant on the Upper West Side. I guess this is part of why he says he needs the job for the money since social security won't cover his fancy dinners.

The restaurant is decorated in a cross of art deco style, ostentatious Russian, and something out of an Ann Rice novel. There are walls of ornate and carved glass between huge black gold gilded columns. Posh black leather chairs with gold stud detail, and red velvet sofas in the waiting area. On the ceiling, there's even a mural of a scantily clad woman, with long flowing hair blowing in the wind that reminds me of Chester's Venus poem.

As we follow the Maître D to our table in a quiet corner of the restaurant, I notice the table setting. There are gold-rimmed wine glasses on the marble tables, along with gold dinnerware; the plates are off white china with gold rim.

I don't think I've ever been to such a tacky, roll-my-eyes kind of place. All of a sudden I feel intimidated for some reason. I quickly scan my memory for the distinction between the salad and dinner fork; which goes where and for what are they used for? I remind myself to not put my hands or arms on the table; to sit up straight; to refrain from flapping my hands when I speak; and to act like a lady, whatever that means.

Chester orders a martini, shaken not stirred. But Chester is certainly no James Bond.

I order a glass of Italian Merlot.

"To you Nikki, and all the great work that you do, despite the InCare phone blunder," he toasts, beaming. He practically guzzles his drink down and orders a second round of shaken, not stirred martini. I've taken three sips.

"Let's not talk about our troubled work circumstances tonight," he declares.

I sit upright, aware of my posture more so than ever before since the stiff chair allows little room for movement. I put my elbow on the table and rest my face in my hand, as I listen to Chester talk about himself.

"You know that I am a member of the Metropolitan Opera. Ahh, I love opera, Nikki. It is so passionate and exquisite. I just saw La Donna Del Lago by Rossini at the Met. An Italian opera. It means the Lady of the Lake. I've been going to quite a few operas lately to help me forget about all this mess. Do you like opera?"

"Sure, I do...but have only seen a couple. The tickets are a little bit out of my budget."

"Well, if you were to let me, I am going to take you to one soon."

He finishes his third martini before the appetizers even arrive.

"You know what, Nikki?" He slurs a bit.

"No, what?"

"If people were to look at us now, sitting here in this restaurant. You, a young, beautiful woman with your long black wavy hair in that black wrap dress. By the way, you look beautiful, if I can have permission to say that."

"Thank you, Chester, that's very sweet of you to say."

"And me an older man, you know what they would think?"

They would think that you were a short, balding, old man, with a body like porky pig and a face like Dick Cheney.

"No, what?" Trying not to show my boredom.

"They would think I am your sugar daddy...well, you know Nikki,...I can be."

In my mind's eye I suddenly see his grubby little hands with their perfectly square nails stroking my bare tender flesh, his eyes bugging out from excitement, his face flushed red like fire, and him salivating like a Pavlovian dog. I didn't...I couldn't...think of anything further.

I have to quickly do something to switch the conversation. Maybe I can do my best airhead impression.

I laugh. "That's funny." Saved by the waiter bringing our food.

We talk more about Chester – his love of romantic poetry, his love of Brooks Brothers and Manhattan, his love of Italy.

Why do I feel like I am on a really awful date? How can he be hitting on me while a sexual harassment investigation is going on? Didn't we just have a conversation about his behavior? Is this not the very same uncomfortable place the lawyers were asking me about? This guy is completely out of touch and delusional. One minute a father figure and the next a sugar daddy?

By now he is on his fifth martini and I begin to wonder if he will ever stop drinking. He sure seems happy. We finally finish our dinner, and bid each other good night. Thank God.

The next morning as soon as I get in, Chester calls me into his office. He closes the door after me, which I have come to believe is always a bad sign.

"Nikki, I just want you to know that I trust you...completely." He puts an extra emphasis on the word completely.

"I trust you too, Chester." I continue my airhead impression from last night, pretending to not know what he is talking about.

***

CHAPTER 31

I've made up my mind that I am going to talk to Wish about his sinner comment to me the next time I see him. It just happens that the next time I'm supposed to see him is at the Summit in Washington, DC. On the train ride down to Washington, instead of reviewing the details and run of show and program for the Summit, I think about my conversation with Wish and how I am going to calmly tell him that he hurt my feelings. I will be the perfect example of an emotionally mature grown up woman who expresses herself with ease and poise.

The morning of the Summit I get up early and go over to the auditorium to do a test run of the day. To my surprise, I see Wish walking down the hall.

"Hey, I need to talk to you," I say as I run up to him a little bit out of breath.

"What's wrong?" He looks worried. "Did something happen with one of the speakers?"

"What? No…No." I respond. "I need to talk to you about us."

"I don't think this is a good time."

"Wish, I really need to talk to you. It can't wait."

"You're not pregnant are you?" He asks in a hushed tone.

I give him a weird look, "No. Why would you think that?"

"Because you're acting weird."

"Let's go in the green room for a few minutes," I say.

He follows me to the little side room beside the auditorium.

I close the door behind us.

"Nikki, what's going on? There's a lot happening today. This better be important."

"It is important. I wanted to talk to you about what you said to me about you being a sinner because you are with me."

"What? Are you serious? You want to talk about this now?"

"Yes….ummm…I do. That was really insensitive and it hurt my feelings."

Wish walks over to me and strokes my face with his hand. "When I'm with you I feel like I can breathe. That's what I meant by sinner." His voice is soft.

"That word just hurt my feelings. To me sinner implies a lot of bad things, like guilt and shame. You are the one that said that I am a vice for you."

He pulls back. "I've found out that people perceive things depending on where they are with their own emotional maturity." His voice is stern.

I look at him in silence and feel myself getting hot.

He continues. "You see yourself as bad, and that's why you interpreted what I said to you that way."

The heat is now in my face. What an arrogant prick.

"Now we are done with this conversation." He puts his hand up to stop me from talking further. "This day is too important for this nonsense."

He turns around and walks to the door, but stops short and turns around to face me. "Oh by the way, Carol will be here today, and I'd like her to sit in the front row. So if you could reserve a seat for her, that would be great."

The steam is coming out of my head and ears. "Go fuck yourself." I scream.

I've never talked to him like this, and he is shocked. He takes a step back and gives me a worried look.

I can't stop myself. All of my hurt feelings gush out. "You are an insensitive jerk, a liar, and a phony. You hear me? A big fat phony!" My arms are flailing in every direction.

"That's enough." He says to me in a stern parent voice. He turns around to open the door.

I quickly run over and throw my whole body against the door and slam it shut.

"Oh no. I will tell you when it's enough." I yell in a trembling high-pitch scream.

He stands back.

"What you don't realize is that if you are not with me, you would be with someone else. You are living a lie my friend, an illusion of a marriage. I would bet money that I am not your first affair nor your last."

I'm on a roll now and let it all come out.

"You've chased me and now you have the nerve to call me your vice, and yourself a sinner. And on top of all that, you bring your wife to this Summit. An event that I've worked so hard on?"

"You are not in your right mind," he says to me as he crosses his arms in defiance.

"Oh, I don't think so, buddy." I jab my finger in the air. "I've never been more in my right mind than in this moment you creep." I get closer to him and raise myself up to his face. "You know what?" I hiss. "Since the love of your life and I will be in the same room today, maybe I should introduce myself to her. I'm sure she would love to know the type of man she really is married to."

Oh my God. I've turned into Glenn Close from Fatal Attraction.

He tries to grab me by my shoulders, but I pull back and quickly turn around and run to open the door.

"This conversation is now over." I say as I gallop down the hall.

"Nikki? Nikki? Come back here."

I continue running.

"You better keep quiet," he yells behind me. "Please."

Good. Mission accomplished. All I wanted to do was scare him.

As the Summit commences, I stand guard and watch the speakers and audience arrive and get situated. Everything is going smoothly so far. Through sheer hard work and desperation, I've made InCare happy. The auditorium is packed and there are eight major press outlets there to conduct interviews and record parts of the Summit for their news coverage. The Center for Ethical Business and the news media will help redeem InCare and fool the public into thinking this is a great ethical and caring company that truly gives a shit about people and the environment.

Chester begins the Summit with a brief call to order so people can sit and be quiet, he then asks Wish to welcome everyone. As Wish approaches the podium, I eyeball his wife sitting so proudly in the front row, looking at him with admiration and hero worship.

"I would like to welcome everyone to The InCare Global Summit on Corporate Social Responsibility. Thank you all for making the time for this important event."

He has such a presence on the stage that I find myself mesmerized by him despite the fact that he is an arrogant, phony jerk.

He continues, "First and foremost, this event is made possible by the generous support of InCare. InCare is a corporation with a heart. They truly are a company whose mission is aligned with the greater good. Can we get a round of applause for InCare?"

And on cue, everyone claps like monkeys, including me.

"This event would not have been possible without the hard work of the folks at the Center for Ethical Business, and without the support of my lovely wife, Carol, the love of my life. Carol will you stand up so everyone can see you?"

Carol stands up and waves to the crowd as if she's Miss America.

She's wearing a dark pinstripe pantsuit that looks like it's tailor-made for her. Her long red hair has loose waves and frames her perfect face. I'm sure she is wearing makeup, but it sure looks like she isn't. She looks flawless and like she rolled out of bed looking beautiful. Wish continues to reveal the virtues of his wife.

"Without her support I could not be doing what I am doing. She is the one who puts up with my crazy life."

He continues to address the audience, but by then I don't hear him. It's like my ears have shut down to protect me. Ugh, what the hell was I thinking getting involved with this douche bag? Wish couldn't be more clear about who he is, what he is doing, and how he operates. It is me who is clueless and confused. Well, no more.

The rest of the day goes smoothly, with one bigwig speaker after another spewing the virtues of the unholy marriage between corporations and nonprofits. As I listen to them regurgitate the same bullshit, I find myself getting upset.

This is supposed to be my day to shine. I've pulled off an incredible feat, mostly all by myself, and under immense pressure from home and work. Yet, I'm only not enjoying it, but am getting angrier and angrier at the hypocrisy of it all. This whole thing is a ruse and I feel like a big charlatan for being a part of it all.

Nonprofits are at the mercy of these corporations. Since corporations have all the money, they dictate and even tell the nonprofits what to do and how to do it. Most nonprofits are clamoring about frantically to find money to pay the bills and keep the lights on, while a corporation will throw money at the nonprofit for their own evil agenda of selling a loving and caring image to the poor, gullible consumer, so we could buy more of their products as they continue to poison us and destroy the planet. What a croc of shit!

As the Summit draws to a close, Chester takes the stage to sum up the day and declare a call to action and next steps. Towards the end of his speech he asks me to come up to the stage.

"Esteemed guests, before you leave, I would like to thank the new Vice President of Communications at the Center for Ethical Business." He turns towards me and shoots me a wink and a big smile.

He continues, "for putting our event together singlehandedly. Nikki? Why don't you say a few words?" Chester's eyes look glazed over.

As I walk towards the podium, my heart starts to beat faster and faster. Chester takes a seat behind me in one of the chairs set up for guests. Everyone begins to clap as I reach the podium. I stand in silence behind the podium, grateful for its presence between me and the audience. I must have been holding a piece of paper in my hand because I begin to twirl it and pick at it behind the podium. I survey the people sitting before me. It is a sea of gray, black, and navy blue suits. It's been a long day and some people are fidgeting in their seats, probably ready to leave. Some are scrolling through their blackberries, while others are talking to the people beside them. I've never been in front of such a large group of people and am at a complete loss on what to say.

"Hello," I manage to squeak out. I had no idea that Chester was going to ask me to speak in front of people. What am I going to say to a room full of people who are used to public speaking? I'm sure they're not interested in the nice pleasantries I have to say.

Then all of a sudden something comes over me as I realize that this is my moment. This is my one and only chance to make things right with myself. To stop repressing all of my feelings and thoughts for the sake of looking bad or to make other people happy. I have to be true to myself and express myself fully, no matter what. I drop the mangled piece of paper to the ground and hear it land with an amplified thud. I take a step closer to the podium. I pull the microphone closer to my mouth and I clinch each side of the podium with my hands.

"Umm…thank you for coming…" I take a deep sigh in. "These companies don't really care," I scream at the top of my lungs into the microphone.

The room goes silent. I see people looking up from their blackberries, and people have stopped speaking mid-sentence. The people that have gotten up to walk out turn around and stand glaring at me looking frightened on the stage, their mouths open, looking around for someone to explain whether this is part of the program. The press cameras are rolling. I hear the cameras snapping away. Now I have everyone's attention.

I continue screaming, "These companies have invested heavily in marketing and public relations and they give money to nonprofits only to have the appearances of doing something good, so more people continue buying their shit."

I feel someone yanking my left arm to pull me away from the podium.

"Nikki, that's enough." Chester hisses at me, red in the face.

I jerk my arm loose from his grip and push him away with both hands. "Get away from me you dirty old pervert."

I turn around and grip the podium for support and yell into the microphone, "These companies show you blue skies, clean oceans, green fields and pastures, and happy people. Don't believe it. It is all a big fat dirty lie."

I now feel someone's arm around my waist lifting me to carry me away. I wrap my legs around the podium and clench the microphone with both hands and continue screaming, "They give you fancy tag lines, 'to do well by you,' 'saving our planet,' 'looking for better solutions,' 'caring about communities.' 'protecting you from storms.'"

I can smell Wish's cologne behind me. He's now trying to yank me away, along with the podium, but my legs are wrapped around the podium harder than they ever were wrapped around him. How dare he betray me like this?

"You're making a fool of yourself, Nikki. Stop," he yells into my ear.

I continue, "But no matter how much these companies try to fool you, you should know their basic strategy is to make as much money as possible by exploiting our planet and you. Do you hear me? YOU! US! They leave us with the pollution behind their profits."

Now as Wish is holding me, Chester and Henry are on each side of me trying to untangle my legs. I feel their strong hands prying my legs loose. I talk faster and faster, my words running into each other.

"Corporationsareoutofcontrol…theyrunwashington…andthesupremec ourt…theywanttoshow youthesausagebutnothowit'smade….theyjeopardizecommunitiesand……..T hey're EVILLLL an…"

My legs are free now and both Wish and I tumble down on the stage. I can feel his body on me.

"Get the fuck off of me," I scream at Wish, trying to unwrap his arms. "How dare you?"

"You're making an ass of yourself."

I manage to wiggle myself free and roll over to the side to get up.

"I don't care. I should tell everyone about you."

He grabs my arm and pulls me back down. "You better not, or you'll be sorry." I can feel his vise-like grip.

"What? You don't want me to tell the whole world you are a sinner, you freak?"

With one smooth swish move, he pins me to the ground and rolls on top of me. With one hand he holds my hands above my head, and with his other hand, covers my mouth. By now Chester and Henry have come over and are standing guard on each side.

Wish's eyes are bulging as he presses down on my mouth with his hand. In a cold steely stern voice, he says, "Nikki. You better calm down."

"hmmm…hmmehmmeme," I say as I try to wiggle myself free. But, it's no use. I try to bite the inside of his hand, but can't catch enough flesh. My teeth graze the palm of his hand.

"Calm down. You've said enough already to kill your career for good."

He brings his face down to whisper in my ear, "Nikki, please. Please calm down. You've said enough. Please calm down. I'm sorry if I hurt you." He looks at me with scared puppy eyes.

I fall silent and look into his eyes, and for a nanosecond I see the Wish I fell in love with. A feeling of peace spreads over my body as I let myself melt into the stage, feeling all of his weight on top of me. He slowly lifts his hand from over my mouth.

"I'm calm," I grunt as I roll my eyes. "I won't say anything else. Please get off me," I mumble.

He pushes himself off of me to stand up, and looks down at me laying on the floor looking like a big pile of mess. All of a sudden I feel self-conscious. I push myself up with my hands to sit as he extends his hand to me. With a quick powerful yank he pulls me to my feet. I'm completely disheveled. My hair has come out of its neat bun and is mad and wild all over the place. The top two buttons on my conservative navy blue shirt are ripped off and my black lace cleavage-enhancing bra reveals my enhanced fleshy cleavage. Half my shirt is pulled out of my pants revealing my stomach pooch. I run my hands through my hair and raise my head high. I refuse to feel embarrassed. As I tuck my shirt into my pants, someone jerks my arm and turns me around.

"What the hell is wrong with you?" Chester screams. All eyes continue to be glued to the drama being played out on stage. He leans closer to my face, and I can smell his bad breath. "How dare you embarrass us all like this?"

I grab my shirt with my hand to hide my cleavage. I don't have to listen to this old pervert. I tear myself away from his grip, and begin to walk off the stage.

"Don't you dare walk away from me!" He yells behind me.

I continue walking.

"Don't bother coming into the office tomorrow. You are fired." He is screaming at the top of his lungs.

I turn around and let out a loud crazy laugh. "Oh, is that right, you dirty old deviant?" Still holding my shirt closed with one hand, I rush towards Chester. "You." I tap his forehead with my index finger. "Can't fire me."

"Watch me." He looks like a stuck pig, his face red and rosy from anger and humiliation.

"You know why you can't fire me? Don't you, Chester?" I smile at him.

All eyes are on him now, as he searches his pea-sized brain for a comeback.

"I will see you tomorrow at the office to talk about everything," I finish off and storm off the stage. All eyes follow me as I walk out of the room.

Outside in the hallway, the reporters come chasing after me. They want to know my feelings and opinions on what corporate social responsibility really means and if it's just another empty buzz word. I answer a few questions and then from the corner of my eye I see Nancy Pattison, the board member who was so disgusted with the Center's outsourcing book, standing in the corner watching me with a half-smile on her face.

I smile and wave at her. I announce to the press, "Guys. You will want to talk to Nancy Pattison. She attended one of The Center's board meetings, and has a lot of insight to offer you about some of the Center's new publications."

Everybody's head and cameras turn towards Nancy, and they all surround her like paparazzi.

"Nancy? Can you say a few words to the press?" I say.

"I would be happy to," she responds.

"Ok, great. It's a bit noisy here. Why don't we go into the green room? Follow me."

I lead Nancy, the reporters, cameramen and photographers towards the green room. As I push open the door, the sight before my eyes nearly gives me a heart attack. Everyone else gasps and I hear the click, click of cameras.

Someone says with a laugh, "This is going to make great news."

In front of all the major press outlets, Nancy, and myself, stands Consuela, breasts exposed, tangled up in the arms and lips of Wish Michaels. If we had come in five minutes later, who knows what we would have walked into. Wish darts back and quickly pushes Consuela off of him. The cameras continue to click away. There is a loud thump as Consuela lands on the floor with her legs up in the air. Wish turns his back to the camera and tries to straighten his tie and hair. Meanwhile, Consuela looks like a hurt and frightened child as she crawls on the floor and scampers to put on her shirt. She sees everyone staring, taking pictures, and shooting their videos. With a pained expression on her face she lets out a loud yelp and crawls to hide behind the sofa. Unfortunately for them, there is really nowhere to go. There is only one way in and one way out, the door that everyone is blocking.

I, at this point, don't want to see any more of this debacle and hastily turn around to squirm my way out of the crowd of reporters. I can't imagine how Wish is going to charm his way out of this one, but I don't care. He's not my problem anymore.

***

CHAPTER 32

As I head back to New York City that evening, I hatch my action plan to take my life back. Enough is enough.

The next day as I go into the office, Bren jumps in the elevator before the doors close.

"Good morning."

She is smiling at me, a smile so big, that it looks like the sides of her lips are going to crack. Her cheeks are all puffy and her eyes are gleaming. I've never seen her like this.

"What do you want, you witch?" I ask.

"Don't be so defensive Nikki." She is looking sheepish. Her eyes on her feet now, "Look, I'm sorry."

"What? You actually know how to say you're sorry?"

"I've been out of control. I know. I've played with you on so many levels."

"You've done more than play with me. You have gone out of your way to make my life hell."

She stares at me in silence.

"You put your hands on me. You pushed me, you nut job!"

"Yea. I was just so frustrated. That was way out of line."

"Bren, you are a sorry excuse for a human being."

"Again, I'm sorry. I just wanted to tell you that you were awesome yesterday. I mean, the way you got up on stage and told the truth about all these companies."

"Well, I'm sure I will pay the price for that today."

"All this time I thought you were this weak little girl. But I've got to give it to you. You've got some serious balls, girl."

"Here's a life lesson for you. Being nice isn't a sign of weakness. You can be nice and strong," I respond curtly.

"I've come to a realization about something, and I need to make a confession to you."

"Look, Bren, It's ok." I put both of my hands up to stop her. "I don't need you to confide anything to me. Go find a friend, a priest or therapist, but leave me alone."

Damn this slow elevator.

"No, I really have to do this." She takes a deep breath and lets out a sigh. "I've realized that the reason why I've been giving you such a hard time is because I have a crush on you," she rambles out.

"What?" I make a disgusted face.

"I have feelings for you and I sort of handled them wrong. The way a little boy bullies the little girl that he likes."

"I...I...ummm..." I am at a complete loss for words or even thoughts.

"You don't have to say anything," Bren quickly says, as she takes a step towards me and plants a big wet hard kiss on my lips. Her snake tongue tries to encroach into my mouth.

I automatically push her off me. "What the hell is wrong with you?"

As she rears back, she says, "I've been wanting to use that strap on dildo on you ever since we saw each other at Babeland. We had a moment, didn't we?"

The elevator reaches our floor.

"You are delusional and completely insane." I step out of the elevator. "Don't you ever put your hands or any strap-on body parts of yours on me."

I run down the hall to my office and lock the door behind me. I can't make this stuff up even if I tried. After my speech at the Summit yesterday, I knew I didn't have a future The Center anymore nor with any of those companies that were present, or any nonprofits. For the first time in my life, I had to take care of myself first. I stayed up all night concocting my plan for today.

I stare in the mirror mustering up all of my courage and begin to give myself a pep talk.

"It's time for you now. No more suppressing yourself to be nice to other people. No more swallowing your feelings to make people like you. No more caring about what other people think of you. Enough is enough Nikki. Time for you to live your life for you and on your terms. Not Chester. Not Peter. Not Zuni. Not Wish. It's Nikki's time to live."

I take a deep breath and walk to Chester's office. "Good morning boyfriend." I close his office door.

Chester looks up from his computer, shocked that I am in the office, and probably even more shocked that I called him boyfriend.

"Don't be so surprised. I told you that I was coming in today so we could talk."

"There's nothing to say. I am so disappointed in you. I expected better from you."

"Really?...Are you serious? You of all people feel the compulsion to tell me that you're disappointed in me for speaking the truth? Give me a break."

"Every single one of our supporters are talking about pulling their funding. Do you understand what that would mean?"

"Yes I do. It means getting a backbone and getting your dignity back. But, I'm not here to talk about yesterday, nor do I care what happens to you or The Center anymore."

"Then why are you here?"

"I want out, and you will pay me to leave." I declare.

"You have absolutely lost your mind now."

"Oh no my old, dirty, perverted friend. For the first time in my life, I have all my senses."

I hear him gulp as he stares at me with big bulging eyes that look like orbs.

"That's right. I know where all the bodies are buried. I've seen inappropriate emails between you and your concubine Consuela. I know that you've spent company money to travel on 'fact finding' trips with her. You have made a pass at me, offering to be my sugar daddy. I'm sure that would not go over well considering your little sexual harassment investigation. And on top of all that, your little office bulldog Bren just kissed me in the elevator."

"What? I don't believe you," he responds.

"Are you calling my bluff?" I retort completely poker-faced. I lean across his desk, "I dare you to call my bluff."

He looks at me with an intent penetrating gaze. "Sit down," he finally says.

I head over to the guest chair and am amazed at how cool and calm I am during this time.

"Chester, not only can I sue The Center for sexual harassment for your sugar daddy offer, your anesthetic marriage proposal moment, and Bren's kiss, but also for harassment for the time Bren pushed me and threw a pen at me. At this point, it is in your best interest to make me go away. You get my point?"

He covers his mouth with his hand and stares at the ceiling.

"I don't believe Bren kissed you."

"That's all you have to say after everything?" I say.

"She hates you."

"Why don't you have the balls to finally confront her on something."

"I'm going to call her in here. You'll see--"

"Go ahead."

He picks up the phone, "Hi Bren. Can you come to my office? I need to chat with you about something."

When Bren walks in, she is surprised to find me sitting there. She looks at Chester, then at me, then back at Chester.

"Come in. Take a seat," Chester says.

"Bren, you know that the past few months have been quite stressful for Nikki, and well, yesterday was a catastrophe of the biggest proportion for us."

Bren looks at me for some type of sign of where this conversation is headed, but I remain stoic and keep my gaze on Chester.

"Yes, we've all been under a lot of stress." Bren is mechanical in her response.

"Well, now there is something else."

"What else can happen?" Bren laughs out.

"Nikki has just informed me that you made a sexual pass at her and kissed her this morning."

"What?" Bren yells out, as she slams her fists on Chester's desk. She looks at me with big eyes and a red face. "What? Nikki, why would you do that? You have really lost your mind."

"So, you're saying that it's not true?" Chester asks.

"You bet your ass that's what I'm saying. Can't you see that she's gone over the deep end? I mean come on, yesterday, and now this."

"Why are you lying?" I ask Bren.

"You're fucking crazy," she snaps back.

"You kissed me in the elevator earlier this morning, and you know it. I don't understand why you are trying to cover your ass." My voice is now at a higher pitch, the pitch of desperation. This could mess up my plans.

She sits back and gives me her infamous Bren smirk. The one that says, I got you.

"You clearly are insane. Actually what you are doing right now is sexual harassment." She's got the jagged lines on her upper lip showing as she points at me with her man hands. "You assume that because I am a lesbian that people would believe that I hit on you. How predictable of you," she says to me as she looks at me with disgust, lips curled, and nose scrunched, as if she's smelling sewage.

"You are a fucking liar Bren." I am losing my cool.

She scoots to the edge of her chair and faces Chester. "You moron. Can't you see what's going on?"

Chester the coward slinks back in his chair.

"She knows she's out of a job, and after yesterday's fiasco, no one will hire her."

She looks at me now. "You know that don't you? You've committed career suicide."

She should have been a lawyer. She continues with her cross-examination as she returns her icy gaze towards Chester.

"She wants to accuse me of coming on to her so she can get paid. The dumb little girl probably has no savings."

I listen intently to her tirade, wondering if Chester will believe her?

"It's your word against mine. Who are they going to believe? You, after your meltdown or me?"

I'm silent as I search my brain for answers.

"I mean how are you ever going to prove that I kissed you this morning? You can't! Because it didn't happen." She is smug and full of herself.

And then something goes off in my head. Bren kissed me in the elevator. All of the building elevators have hidden cameras installed in them that the building security monitors and records.

"I can prove it," I scream out as I jump out of my chair. "I can prove that you came on to me."

"And how would you do that?"

"You forgot one thing, you wench. There are hidden cameras in all of the elevators."

Her smile drops from her face and Bren turns white with fear.

"Everything that happens in those elevators is recorded. I know you've seen the little black bubbles on the back corner of the elevator that hides the cameras."

Chester turns his bewildered look towards Bren.

"Is this true?"

Bren doesn't respond and stares off into space.

"Bren?" Chester says.

"Bren. Look at me." Chester is now speaking in an authoritative tone.

Bren's jaw has dropped open and she slowly turns her head towards Chester.

"Is Nikki telling the truth? Did you hit on her and kiss her this morning?"

"Ummm...I....Ummm."

"You can um ah all you want, and keep lying, but all we have to do is go downstairs and look at the footage."

She looks over at me with a desperate look in her eyes. I have to admit that it feels good to see her squirm. God knows she's caused me enough grief.

"Will you please answer my question? Is it all true?" Chester asks again.

"Answer his question Bren and spare yourself the embarrassment of everyone seeing the video footage."

"Yes," she finally responds letting her eyes drop to the floor.

Chester is even grimmer than before. "Thank you Bren. That'll be all."

"What are you going to do?" She asks him.

"That's not for you to worry about. Please close the door behind you."

Bren looks over at me. I debate about whether to return her stupid smirk, but decide against it. There's no reason for me to be a total bitch.

Since I've found my new voice, I just can't help myself. I want to be a total bitch. "You are mean-spirited, cruel, and a downright gutter bully."

Bren's face is sullen. Her gaze falls to the floor as she slowly lifts herself out of the chair. She skulk towards the door.

"I hope to never see you again in my lifetime," I say as she closes the door behind her.

I turn around and face Chester, emboldened more than ever. "Now you have your answer."

He swivels his chair and stares out of the window.

"Chester. I don't want to be here anymore."

Without looking at me, he says, "You don't say."

"And Bren is right. After yesterday, no one will hire me."

He turns around to face me and with a face that is pink with anger, he says, "Well, Nikki, that's not my problem is it now? You should have thought about this before you made a fool of yourself and a mockery of this organization."

Oh no he isn't getting brazen with me. This is no time for me to show my fear and vulnerabilities to him.

"I could really blow you and this place up after everything that's happened, and to be honest with you I'd rather not go down that path. I would prefer I turn in my resignation and you pay me a severance. Clear?" I say trying my best to control the quiver in my voice.

"Oh, you are very clear."

"Great, and I'll go away." I give him a sly smile.

He tilts his head to the side and stares at me with a vacant look in his eyes. I find it a bit unsettling since I can't read him. He's usually so transparent with his expressions.

"I can offer you $5,000." His expression is fixed and still unreadable.

I can sense the little scared girl inside of me trying to take over and remain silent. I cross my arms and refuse to let myself be intimidated by him. I can't believe he has the nerve to get balls now. I am surprised at the paltry amount he's offered me.

"Are you kidding me?" I match his fixed expression. "I think you can do better than that."

"Ha," he practically screams out. "Is that right? What do you want?"

The previous evening I had estimated what it would cost me to live somewhere overseas comfortably for a year.

"I want $5,000 for ten months."

Chester's jaws drop open. "$50,000?"

A new sensation of power and strength comes over me. All of a sudden I feel like I am one hundred feet tall. I am fearless.
"Think of it as severance," I respond unfazed by his shock.

He snaps back as he stands up and leans over his desk to intimidate me. "You are crazy. We don't have that kind of money." He looks at me indignantly trying to intimidate me.

"This will be easier if you didn't think I was stupid. I know you have the money and if I took this to court, I will get a lot more money."

And then I pull out my ultimate bluff. "I've already consulted with an attorney."

He's taken aback by my fake revelation. He sinks into his chair. "You've talked to a lawyer?"

262

"You better believe I have." I am dogmatic.

"Nikki? Please? Where do you expect me to get that money from my dear?" His pained face and eyes plead with me.

A wry smile reveals the laughter I am doing my best to hold in. "Maybe…just maybe." I wave my index finger at him. "You can get it from your sugar daddy fund."

He looks at me slack-jawed and big-eyed.

I give him a big wry smile. "You know the same fund you use to travel the world first class with Consuela." I pause to build up drama. "Does that ring a bell?"

"I've got to give it to you." He shakes his head in disbelief. "I underestimated you."

I may be wrong, but I get the feeling that he is proud of me. "Yes, well, I'd rather be underestimated and surprise people than be overestimated and turn out to be a disappointment."

"I don't know how to justify giving you $50,000." He shakes his head. "Especially after yesterday and that you will no longer be working here."

"Must I tell you how to do everything?" I ask. "You can take it from your remaining paychecks."

"I can't do that." He is belligerent.

"Chester. I don't give a crap. It's not my problem. Figure it out." I shout.

He looks down for what feels like long painful minutes. "You leave me no choice. I'll pay you your severance."

Just the words I was hoping to hear. Although it was a little touch and go for a minute there.

"Great. I knew you would see things my way."

"Stay here. I'll be right back," he says. He comes back in after a few minutes and extends a piece of paper to me. It can't be.

I grab the paper and look at it. It reads, "pay to the order of Nikki Johnson." In the amount section, it reads, "$50,000."

"You had a great ride here Chester. Have fun cleaning up this mess."

I feel the weight of the paper in my hands as I walk towards the door. I've never had this much money in my hands and it feels both liberating and scary. But as I reach the door I am somehow overcome by a feeling of guilt. Damn this nice girl issue that I have. I turn to face Chester who looks old, fragile, and small in his big black leather chair.

"Look Chester. For what it's worth, I am appreciative of how kind you were to me."

He looks at me with a sad look.

"You did support me in many ways, and I'm sorry that things turned so sour."

"I'm sorry too." He shakes his head. "I never meant for things to be like this. I'm a weak man."

"I'm going to clean out my desk." I close his door and head to my office. I stand at the doorway and look around. I walk over to my desk and open the drawers. There are some crackers, some jasmine green tea packets, a bottle of unopened diet pills, and a t-shirt. Basically nothing I really care about. I put on my coat. I grab my bag and walk out.

***

CHAPTER 33

I leave the Center to meet with Peter at our empty apartment and talk about his plans for the apartment and what he wants for our relationship. As I ride the elevator down to the lobby, I think to myself that what I want for myself is a lot more important than what Peter wants for himself or our relationship. He is used to the meek Nikki that he can intimidate and dominate with his strong will, albeit without meaning to. He has not seen the new and improved I'm-gonna-take-charge-of-my-life Nikki.

On the ride home, I stand and clutch tightly to my purse, paranoid about losing my $50,000 check. Just two stops before mine, my stalker guy gets on the train. I do my best not to make eye contact, and quickly make a mad dash to hide behind a man that is taller and bigger in size than me. Too late. Stalker guy sees me.

"Well there you are my sexxxy girl." He hisses as he takes strides towards me and squeezes himself around people to get closer to me.

I keep looking away, pretending that I don't know he's talking to me.

"Hey, why don't you look at me?" He says as he gets closer. "What? You think you too good for me?"

Now people are looking at him and at the direction he's heading. Mine.

I look up and make eye contact with him as I clutch my purse ever tighter. "I don't know you." I say in a stern voice.

"Aaah, now the princess is talkin' to me?" He says, as he stands before me.

I look at him in defiant silence.

He continues, "Donch-ya know, I been thinkin' o you."

My voice gets louder. "Leave me alone. I don't care what you've been thinking of. Leave me alone." I scream.

"Naaaw…I ain't gonna leave you alone." He grabs my arm and yanks me towards him as the train jerks to a stop.

I shake my arm loose. This is my chance. The doors open and a few people get out as a few get in.

I scream at him from the top of my lungs, "Fuck you. Leave me alone."

With my right hand glued to my purse, I grab on to a pole for support with my left. I take a step back with my right foot and bring my knee up as fast and hard as I can into his crotch, all the while hoping that I hit my target. My knee lands on his upper right thigh. Not quite the target I was hoping for.

"Haahaahaa," he laughs. "You gonna get tough on me now."

Still holding the pole, I kick up my knee again. Stalker guy lets out a loud deep scream as both of his hands reach for his crotch. I jump back, and shout, "If you ever speak to me or lay a hand on me again, I will get the police to take care of you or I'll use my gun instead of my knee. Get my point, stinky?"

The automatic train announcement says, "Please step away from the closing doors." There's no way I can let myself get stuck on this train with him. Stalker guy begins to keel over towards me, as he looks me dead in the eye with an anger that even surpasses Bren's. I see the train doors beginning to close. My heart skips a beat, as I take a step back to avoid him from falling on me. I quickly make a mad dash and jump towards the doors, as if I'm sliding into third base. I land with a loud thud on my hands and knees on the filthy platform. The pain vibrates throughout my body. My palms feel like they're on fire, and my purse has fallen out of my hand. I hear the train doors close as I frantically look around. I see my purse on the platform. Lip-gloss, eyeliner, wallet, keys, and the check, all scattered on the platform. I look behind me to see Stalker guy slam his fist into the glass of the closed door. I shoot him the middle finger and a smile.

After dodging Stalker guy I decide to walk the next ten blocks home to gather my thoughts for Peter. By the time I walk into our apartment, I am clear on what I need to do.

"Hi there," I say as I walk through the front door.

Peter is in the empty apartment looking out the window.

"Hey." He comes over to give me a hug and a kiss.

"This place looks so large without any furniture." I say as I hug him and pull away.

While Peter and I finally talked on the phone, I had not seen him in the past few weeks.

"It does, doesn't it?" He looks at me with a quizzical look, a half smile and eyebrows scrunched together.

I wonder if I have the courage.

He runs his hand through his hair as he looks around the empty apartment. "I don't want to fill it up with so much stuff again. I've been looking at some modern simple furniture that will fit in here nicely. And we can get the lower style Japanese style beds."

"Ok." I'm not sure I can go through with my hatched plan.

"And baby, things will be a lot better I promise, now that the Summit is over. Oh, by the way, how did it go?" He grabs me with excitement.

I step back. "It was perfect. It went exactly the way it needed to."

"Really? Wow. I'm so proud of you." He is gleaming with pride as he looks at me dreamy eyed. "I knew you would pull it off."

There is no need to go into the detailed drama of it all. I don't want or need anyone else's opinion on what I did. I handled everything the way I needed to.

"Well now that the Summit is over, I know that things will change. You were under so much stress with work."

"Peter, can you please stop talking?" I blurt out as my arms flail in the air.

He is taken aback. "What....?" He stammers out. "What's going on?"

"I have something to say."

"Well, we can talk about everything over dinner. Let's go somewhere. My treat?" He smiles at me.

"No," is all I can manage to respond.

"I need to say something. Like right now."

"Uhhh...ok."

"You are right. I was under stress at work, but there has been a lot of stress here at home."

"I know, but I promise things will get better."

"I'm not so sure about that."

"Having Zuni here is a big change. I think we've all made some adjustments."

"I haven't made the adjustment Peter, and I'm not sure I want to. Zuni is thirteen years old. She will be living with us until she's eighteen. That's five more years. Five years. That's a long time. And it's something I never agreed to. You forced it on me!"

"She's my child. I don't have a choice in the matter. I am responsible for her until she is eighteen."

There's a part of me that feels like a bad person because I don't want to stick around for five more years of teenage drama and angst.

"I respect you for wanting to be a good dad. Really, I do." Is it selfish to want to live a life that I choose for myself? I continue, "But, it's not just about the five years. I am hurt and angry. You've undermined me, you've sided with Zuni and have made me feel like I am the bad person, and you've made major life decisions about my life without me."

"What are you saying?" He looks hurt and betrayed.

"It's not for me Peter…I'm sorry."

"I'm sorry." I take a step closer to him and touch his arm. "I don't want to hurt you, but having Zuni here has totally killed our relationship. I can count on one hand the number of times we've had sex since Zuni moved in. You're too stressed and worried about dealing with a teenager. I don't feel that you care about what I say or think or feel."

"Don't put this all on me. You've been under stress too, and you haven't exactly been a loving and patient person with Zuni. She has feelings too, you know. "

"You're right. I haven't been very mature about the whole thing. But Zuni has completely changed our life. My life. I can't do this for another five years until she's eighteen."

"So now what?" He looks at me bitterly.

"Look, I think we take a break for a while. I care about you, but this isn't working for me and I don't feel like playing house anymore. We're both just playing and going through the motions."

"This isn't what I want." His eyes are tearing up.

"I gave it a try for your sake because I loved you. But I'm discovering a lot of things about myself, especially how I let other people dictate my life."

"I never tried to tell you what to do," he yells at me. "Don't blame things on me."

"I'm not blaming anything on you. But I loved you and I felt bad and guilty if I didn't want to do something that made you happy. Even if it meant repressing my own feelings or going against what I wanted."

"Loved me?" He sits cross-legged on the floor. "You don't love me anymore?"

"I love you as a human being." I sit down to face him. "I care about you. I think you are a wonderful man. But I'm…," I can't finish my sentence.

"But you are not in love with me anymore, are you?" He looks so sad.

"I'm sorry, Peter. I don't want to hurt you."

"Well, you are." He jolts upright and storms off towards the front door.

I run after him. "Please wait. Don't go." I grab his arm.

He wipes his eyes and turns around to face me.

"I wanted to do the right thing with Zuni. I stayed because you needed me, but I see now that it's the wrong thing to stay with someone because they need you or out of guilt."

"Is there anything I can say to change your mind?" Peter says solemnly.

I shake my head no. "I can't change how I feel."

"I still love you," he says as he looks to the ground.

I reach over to him and give him a hug. He hugs me back.

After a few minutes we finally let go.

"What are you going to do?" he asks me.

Since this is his apartment, I am the one that has got to go.

"Oh, I don't know." I smile as I look around. "Considering, I have almost no possessions, I'm going to go on an adventure."

"What do you mean?"

"I have a little money and I think I am going to go travel for a few months."

"Really? Where?"

"I'm not sure. I'll have to see what spirit moves me."

He looks at me inquisitively, not recognizing my words. Yup, this is the new me. The Nikki Johnson who sees life as an adventure and will live it to its fullest. The Nikki Johnson who will be present in everything that she does. The Nikki Johnson that will not live from a place of fear.

"Well, I wish you the best." He smiles at me and gives me one last hug goodbye.

"Thanks. Good luck with Zuni."

"You know we will always be friends, don't you?"

"Yes, I do."

I step out into the cold air feeling a freedom I've never experienced before. I for the first time in my life will take care of myself. I'm not sure how or even what's next, but what I know is that everything will work out the way it needs to. The next day, I take my one suitcase of clothes and catch a cab.

"Where to?" The Sikh cabbie asks with a heavy accent.

"JFK airport."

"Where you headed to?"

"I'm not sure. I'll decide when I get to the airport."

"Really? That's crazy. I tell my children to never do crazy things."

"Never say never my friend. Life is not about the rules, but about the flow."

***

ABOUT THE AUTHOR

Naheed Elyasi is a globe-trotting marketing executive and author. Southern bred and Afghan born, Naheed fled Afghanistan in 1982.

Naheed was a contributing writer for Zeba Magazine, the first lifestyle Magazine for the over 300,000 Afghan Diaspora in the United States. Her writings are published in One Story, Thirty Stories: An Anthology of Contemporary Afghan American Literature, and Love Inshallah: The Secret Love Lives of Muslim Women blog.

She has also been featured in the Daily Beast and Moral Courage TV. To find out more about Naheed, visit www.naheedelyasi.com.

Made in the USA
Lexington, KY
03 November 2017